DISCARD

Murder After the Fact

Murder After the Fact

By ALBERT ASHFORTH

St. Martin's Press
New York

MURDER AFTER THE FACT. Copyright © 1984 by Albert
Ashforth. All rights reserved. Printed in the United States
of America. No part of this book may be used or
reproduced in any manner whatsoever without written
permission except in the case of brief quotations embodied
in critical articles or reviews. For information, address St.
Martin's Press, 175 Fifth Avenue, New York, N.Y. 10010.

Library of Congress Cataloging in Publication Data

Ashforth, Albert.
  Murder after the fact.

  I. Title.
PS3551.S376M8 1984   813'.54   83-21113
ISBN 0-312-55278-5

First Edition

10 9 8 7 6 5 4 3 2 1

For Erika, Claudia and Elisabeth

Murder After the Fact

1

The funeral for my Aunt Phyllis turned out to be just the kind of memorial service you would expect for a sixty-eight-year-old spinster who had lived her entire life in the same medium-sized city: a brief recital of the last rites in the presence of a small group of mourners, most of them the same age as the deceased. The bleakness of the circumstances wasn't improved any by the mid-March weather. The wind from the mountains west of Murcer carried a wintry chill that penetrated the bones of the elderly onlookers and I wished I'd worn a topcoat. The cemetery was atop a small hill that gave you a view of the rocky country in the immediate vicinity and, farther on, a view of the industrial city of Murcer itself. From time to time during the service I found myself glancing out at the smoky city and marveling at the extent it had grown in the fifteen years since I had last lived there.

The short service over, I shook hands with the acquaintances of my aunt who had taken the trouble to attend. Some I recalled from my childhood, but most had to identify themselves. At the head of the line was my aunt's neighbor, Gerald Hoffman.

"You remember me, son?"

"I certainly do, Mr. Hoffman. Thanks very much for coming."

"We were neighbors for almost thirty years. I'll miss her. She was a wonderful woman."

"She certainly was."

"Come by for a cup of coffee some time, young fella. I'm nearly always home now. Retired, you know."

"Thanks, Mr. Hoffman. I will."

The farewells were brief, without much emotion. My aunt had not been a person to encourage close friendships. Only one of the guests failed to say good-bye—a woman in her early fifties, a handsome woman whom I had seen during my childhood years in Murcer but whom I could no longer place. She attracted my attention for two reasons: the fact that she seemed to be unusually upset by my aunt's funeral, and the speed at which she drove her Mercedes sports coupe out of the cemetery parking lot. When she took the curve leading from the lot onto the highway, she nearly succeeded in turning the car over.

If it hadn't been for the weather, I would have preferred to walk back to the green and white wooden frame house on Weatherly Street that had been my Aunt Phyllis's home and in which I had spent my life until I was eighteen years old. Nevertheless, I let the chauffeur take me back in the warm comfort of the hired limousine. We made it back just before the arrival of the storm that had been threatening all morning.

Once back in the house, I made myself a cup of tea—Aunt Phyllis never drank coffee, so there wasn't any in the house—and sat down at the kitchen table to reread the letter I had found waiting for me at the house when I had arrived four days before. Aunt Phyllis had written it just a week ago, two days before slipping into the coma from which she would never again awake. She was clearly aware when she wrote it that she would not leave the hospital alive.

I concentrated my attention on the second paragraph of the letter, written in an unsteady, slanted scrawl.

> *After I'm gone, Clinton, I want you to know something that I was never able to tell you or anyone else all these years. You know I was never too strong for churches so maybe this is like a confession. I don't know. But I feel better just being able to write these words to you. When you find out, I know that you'll decide on what the right thing is to do. In a hollow place in the floor of the attic, just to the left of the south window and beneath the old lamp, you'll find a box, and you should be able to figure out from the contents what it is I want you to know. Maybe I should have destroyed these things years ago and shouldn't be burdening you now with something that happened so long ago. It was a horrible deed, and the guilt I felt weighed down my mind so many*

*years, and if I seemed to you to be a melancholy old
woman, this, I suppose, was the reason.*

*But always remember, Clinton, what I did I did for
your sake. Whether it was right or wrong, I don't know,
but I hope you'll be able to forgive me for it. . . .*

There was more to the letter, mostly reminiscences of the years
between my fifth and eighteenth birthdays when she'd been my
guardian and a note to the effect that she'd left a will in the care
of her lawyer, Max Wegman. But it was to the contents of the
second paragraph that I kept returning. I finally put down the
letter and lit a cigarette. For some reason, in the four days since
I'd been back in Murcer I had deliberately postponed following
my aunt's instructions, and I still wasn't anxious to find out what
it was she had wanted to keep hidden for all these years. Secrets
can be grotesque, unsettling things. But the voice from beyond
the grave was insistent. I stamped out the cigarette, drained the
last of the cold tea from the cup, and wearily hauled out the
stepladder I needed to gain access to Aunt Phyllis's dusty attic.

Without precise instructions I never would have found it. What
Aunt Phyllis had done was fashion a small, neatly hinged door in
the floor of the attic, and she had cut and replaced the two-by-
fours with such precision that the hollowed-out portion only became apparent after I had shone the flashlight over the area for
some minutes. I couldn't help but admire Aunt Phyllis's skill as a
woodworker. Inside the hollowed-out space was a small metal
container, a container that at some remote time had contained
cookies, probably the ingredients of an afternoon snack for a
hungry schoolboy. I fished the thing out, blew off the dust, and,
without opening it, climbed back downstairs to the kitchen. Once
again seated at the kitchen table, I spread the contents of the
container out before me, and after studying them for a while, I
could see why Aunt Phyllis's secret might have preyed on her
mind for almost a lifetime—and why she took such precautions
to keep the box from being found by anyone else.

The contents offered strong proof that, some twenty-eight
years before, my aunt had committed a murder. There seemed to
be no other way to interpret the meaning of the letter and the
varied articles I found in the small box.

What I had before me was a small-caliber revolver, some ammunition, two yellowed newspaper clippings, and a letter to my aunt written by an anonymous person I assumed was a woman.

The "horrible deed" that Aunt Phyllis had referred to in her letter seemed to have been the murder of a small-time racketeer. The story was told in the accompanying clippings from the Murcer *Telegram* of twenty-eight years before.

MURCER MAN SLAIN IN HOME

The body of Joseph (Joey Boy) Hauck was found yesterday morning in his apartment at 236 West Baker Road. The deceased had been shot twice, once in the back and once in the heart. According to police, the murder took place approximately 48 hours before the body was found.

Police theorize that Hauck, who had served two prison terms and who was alleged to have underworld connections, was shot as the result of a criminal dispute. According to Detective Sergeant Karl Breyer, who is in charge of the investigation, Hauck had recently told friends of having an income "that would set him up for life."

"Since Hauck is unemployed," Breyer said, "we would like to know the source of this income. It could turn up a clue to his murderer."

There was a second clipping, shorter than the first, and dated two weeks later.

HAUCK CASE CLOSE TO SOLUTION?

Murcer police may be close to solving the two-week-old murder investigation involving Joseph (Joey Boy) Hauck, the underworld figure who was found shot in his home.

"We're on to something," Detective Sergeant Karl Breyer told reporters yesterday. "If things pan out, we may have the murderer before the week is out."

Breyer would not elaborate on this statement but added that he was optimistic about chances of solving the murder.

The letter, which was undated, was still in its original envelope. Its connection with the other objects in the box was not clear. It read:

> *Dear Whore,*
>   *Keep your goddamn filthy hands off of my man if you know what's good for you. I swear I'll make you sorry if you don't leave him alone. Get your own man. If you can.*

There was no signature.

Although Aunt Phyllis never drank coffee, she was not against a glass of gin now and then. I found the bottle where she always kept it, behind the cereal box in the kitchen closet. I poured a generous shot, lit another cigareette, and gave the matter some thought.

The one unescapable fact seemed to be that Aunt Phyllis some twenty-eight years before, had been the person responsible for the murder of one of Murcer's small-time criminals.

Such a thing seemed hardly credible. Aunt Phyllis had been stern, old-fashioned, and straitlaced. What connection, I asked myself, could she possibly have had with someone whom the newspapers described as an underworld figure? No one knew better than I, who had lived in the same house with her for thirteen years, that Aunt Phyllis had led a life of blameless respectability.

I poured myself another glass of gin and lit another cigarette. Even as I watched the tobacco smoke curl lazily toward the ceiling, I felt a small pang of remorse. I had never been able to light a cigarette in my aunt's home without her making some kind of derisive comment. She had always regarded my cigarette smoking, a habit I had acquired at college, as a sure indication of my moral decline.

I had come to live with Aunt Phyllis, my mother's older sister, when I was five years old, immediately after the death of my father. I never had any recollection of my mother, who died after being struck by a car when I was two. My father I remember as a burly, loud man with a great shock of black, curly hair and piercing dark eyes. He was a man given to sudden bursts of laughter and equally sudden fits of anger; a random, unpredictable man whose sudden changes in mood were a source of puzzlement to me as a child. Aunt Phyllis always maintained that I took after my mother, an observation that she always punctuated by rolling her eyes toward heaven and exclaiming, "Thank God!"

If the memories of my father are vague and disconnected, it is partially because Aunt Phyllis so completely disliked him and never spoke of him after his death. "A horrible man," I remember her saying of him when I was eight years old. And I never attempted to speak of him after that.

I suppose that growing up without parents in an industrial city like Murcer can hardly be described as an idyllic childhood. Although she was a capable guardian, Aunt Phyllis was also a stern disciplinarian and the relationship between us was always strained. On a few occasions, in moments of anger, Aunt Phyllis had accused me of "complicating" her life, references to the fact that the responsibility of taking care of me had fallen to her. For my part, I had always felt a compulsion to defy my aunt, a need perhaps born of the resentment I felt toward her and life in general. As a result, while the old frame house she acquired after my father's death was more than adequate for both of us, it was never a place in which I felt really at home. The structure had a melancholy, unsettling quality about it, and the rooms, even by day, were dark and faintly depressing. I was happy when, at eighteen, I went off to college and no longer had to live there. As time went on, I saw less and less of my aunt and of Murcer.

And then there was the dream. For as long as I can remember, I've been haunted by the same dream, a nightmare of violence that would always begin in the same way—with the appearance of a shadowy figure whose face I could never make out. In the course of the dream I would incur the anger of this mysterious person who would then begin raining blows upon me as I tried in vain to defend myself or run away. The dream would always end in the same way, with the sensation of falling. . . .

I remember lying in bed as a child, terrified of closing my eyes, as I valiantly attempted to avoid that awful nightmare. Only after I had moved away from Murcer did the dream lose its terror for me. But even in later years I could never visit my aunt without the nightmare recurring, and I often wondered whether the dream wasn't in some way responsible for the fact that over the years my visits to my aunt became less and less frequent.

Just how Aunt Phyllis was able to get by financially, I never really understood. Although she never worked, she kept us both supplied with food and clothing, and I still remember the day when she told me she intended to see that I get a university education. I was fifteen and had already shown an interest in subjects like physics and mathematics.

"You keep up your grades, Clinton," she said at the time, "and I'll see to it that you go away to college."

Aunt Phyllis kept that promise. My tuition bills were always paid on time, and the engineering degree provided me with the opportunity to escape from the stifling atmosphere of Murcer and the Murcer mills, a fate that had claimed so many of my contemporaries. I knew I never could have been satisfied living out my life in Murcer. Just the thought of it made me shudder.

I walked out of the kitchen into the dining room, a chamber that had not been brightened any by the ponderous oak furniture with which Aunt Phyllis had furnished it. The living room was dominated by a brick fireplace, a long sofa along the adjacent wall, a coffee table, and an ancient rolltop desk in the corner. On the far side of the room stood two straight-backed chairs, one Morris chair, and, on the table in front of the window, a black-and-white television set. My task now was to sell the house and dispose of the furnishings and clutter, but it was not a job I felt like beginning right at that moment.

I decided to get out of the house for a while. The rain had diminished, but a heavy bank of clouds still hung over the city. I had my topcoat on and was headed for the door when the telephone rang.

The voice on the other end belonged to a woman who identified herself as Sylvia Cole, a member of the editorial staff of the Murcer *Telegram.* I said I was Clinton Ball, Phyllis Hailley's nephew.

"Oh, Clinton Ball," she said.

"You sound surprised."

"Well, it's only that . . . I mean, I think we know each other. I used to be Sylvia Benda."

"Of course. You were the girl with the pigtails who lived in the yellow house around the corner. The girl who rode the red bike."

"You *do* remember."

"How could I forget? It hasn't been that long. What can I do for you, Syl—I mean Mrs. Cole?"

"Sylvia is fine, Clint. What I'm working on actually is an obit . . ."

"Obit?"

"Obituary. For tomorrow's edition. On your aunt. I was wondering if you could fill me in on some facts."

"I'll tell you what I might be able to do, Sylvia. I'm on my way out of the house at the moment, but I'd be happy to meet you in the city and talk to you personally about my aunt."

"Fine. There's a luncheonette called the Mayfair a block down from the *Telegram* building. Is half an hour all right?"

"Half an hour is fine."

"I'll be in one of the booths."

"I'll recognize you."

"I'll be insulted if you don't."

I decided to leave the rental car, a Chevette I'd picked up at the airport, at the house and take the bus into downtown Murcer. The rain was just heavy enough to insure that I was fairly well soaked by the time the bus arrived. Of course Murcer weather had always been harsh. Perhaps it accounted for some of the attitudes of the citizenry.

On the bus ride downtown I was able to observe some of the changes that had taken place in the city in the past fifteen years. The numerous shopping centers that now ringed the city had caused the old downtown section to suffer commercially. On Stockton Street, Murcer's main thoroughfare, FOR SALE and FOR RENT signs were plentiful. The businesses that were there seemed just a bit tackier and more run-down than I remembered. In this respect, Murcer, I supposed, was no different from the other cities of its size around the country. In other ways, though, the city seemed to have prospered. The suburbs, consisting of ranch-style homes and garden apartments, stretched out into areas that had been woods and fields when I was small. The population of Murcer, I estimated, was nearly twice the size it had been during the years that I grew up there.

At the bottom of Murcer society there had always been a substantial level of poverty, people whose households didn't know the luxury of a regular paycheck. Most of these people lived in a section of the city called Oldtown, an area west of the mills on the far side of the freight yards. Aunt Phyllis had always been able to keep us out of Oldtown. As a child it never occurred to me to ask how she did it.

"What I did I did for your sake." My aunt's words kept turning themselves over in my mind. I asked myself questions, and I now wondered why it had never occurred to me to ask these questions while my aunt was still alive. Where had the money come from for food, clothing, and to buy the house? How was Aunt Phyllis able to afford my tuition at an expensive private college?

After weaving its way through the downtown traffic, the bus disgorged its passengers at the final stop. The *Telegram* building was one long block from the bus stop, and by the time I reached the luncheonette I was wet all over again.

A woman seated in the rear booth waved as I entered. Sylvia had changed. In her smile and in her movements I could see that the old perkiness was still there, but these qualities were now blended with the promises and unspoken challenges that inevitably seem to emanate from a mature woman.

"Welcome to Murcer, Clint."

"Thank you, Sylvia. It's good to see you again."

After the pleasantries, we just stared at each other.

Sylvia had medium-length jet black hair, gray eyes, and a delicate nose that was perhaps a shade too long. Her lips were thin with the hint of a smile at the edges, a facial feature that combined with a sparkle in her eyes to convey the impression that she found life just a trifle amusing. She wore a light blue blouse, the top button of which was unbuttoned.

I ordered two coffees, then asked her how I could help her with the obituary.

"Your aunt was one of Murcer's longtime residents, Clint. The paper tries to give good coverage to people like that when they die."

So I told Sylvia what I knew of my aunt, leaving out the one detail that was truly worthy of newspaper coverage—that she had once murdered someone. I ordered two more coffees and watched as Sylvia scribbled rapidly in a small stenographer's pad.

"So you've become a journalist," I said after she had finished writing and had closed her notebook.

"You might say that, Clint, although newspaperwoman would be a more accurate description of my work. I've been on the *Telegram* for almost two years. Most of the time I was doing women's page stuff and I hated it. A few weeks ago they gave me a chance on general assignment. Now I have to prove myself." Sylvia took a swallow of coffee, then toyed briefly with a thin gold chain around her neck. "What do you do?"

"I'm a production manager for a computer software firm located just north of New York City."

"I'm impressed. Do you enjoy it?"

"Very much, and I got into computers at just the right time. I've been lucky."

"And living close to New York City must be exciting. I've always wanted to live there. It's a lot better than living in Murcer, I'll bet."

"Murcer has changed."

"I'll say it has. It's not the same place it was when you were living here. There's crime, municipal corruption, congestion—all the problems of a big city with none of the advantages. When did we see one another last, Clint?"

"I graduated from Fairview High fifteen years ago. Except for occasional visits to my aunt, I haven't spent any time in Murcer since then."

"You're four years older than I am. Fifteen years ago I was just entering Fairview. Is there anything else I should know about you, Clint?"

"Like what, Sylvia?"

"Don't start playing dumb on me, Clinton Ball. It's hard for a girl not to believe that a handsome guy like you doesn't have a wife and four kids waiting for him at home."

"No wife, no kids, never married."

Sylvia looked thoughtful. "You're still a loner then."

"What do you mean, Sylvia?"

"I remember how . . . you were different from the other kids around the block. Far away in your own little world. You preferred being by yourself."

"You noticed that?"

"Everyone did, Clint. I even remember my parents commenting on it. I think it was one of the things that attracted me to you. I had a tremendous crush on you when I was thirteen. I guess that was the year before you went to college."

"I never knew I had an admirer."

"I got over it. In fact I got married when I was twenty-one. But it didn't take. We kept it going for two years before calling it quits."

"Children?"

"None. Thank the Lord."

desire to return. My years spent in this old wooden building seemed remote and formless, almost as if they were part of another existence. I decided I wanted to sell the place and leave Murcer. Once and for all.

Inside the house, I took off my raincoat, jacket, shirt, shoes, and socks in the outer foyer. I dried myself with some paper towels in the kitchen and was padding across the dining room on my way to the staircase when I noticed something unusual, something that caused me to pause, then squat down and look very closely at the dining room carpet. The carpet was damp. Not completely damp, only damp in spots as though someone had recently walked across it in wet shoes.

I wouldn't have noticed if I had not been walking barefoot myself. In fact, I was able to see traces of wetness after turning on the chandelier. There was no doubt that someone had entered the house and walked through it during the time I was gone. The likeliest place of entry was one of the side windows. A bench along the side of the house provided a perch for anyone wanting to climb through the window, and a large hedge at the front of the house obscured a view of this area from the street.

I looked around. Nothing seemed to have been disturbed. I had left the revolver and newspaper clippings on the kitchen table, but the letter I had replaced in its envelope and taken with me. The objects were still there, just as I had left them. I did notice, however, two drops of water on the table. The intruder, whoever it was, seemed to have stopped to read the clippings and look at the revolver, but hadn't disturbed them.

I lit a cigarette and sat down to think. I decided that I could do one of three things: I could wind up my aunt's affairs as rapidly as possible and leave Murcer forever; I could call the police and tell them someone had broken into the house; or I could do my level best to discover why my aunt had murdered a small-time Murcer mobster twenty-eight years ago.

By the time I had showered and changed into some dry clothes, I had made my decision. I took down a copy of the Murcer telephone directory and looked for the number of Karl Breyer. He was listed as living on West Bridge Street.

The phone was answered by a man. I gave my name and asked to speak to Detective Breyer.

"Well, I'm not a detective any more, not since I retired two years ago."

I asked him if I could come by and speak with him some time that evening.

"I'll be home all evening. What did you say your name was?"

"Ball. Clinton Ball."

"I'll see you later, Mr. Ball."

What impressed me most about Karl Breyer's home was the excellent condition it seemed to be in. Although the house was roughly the same vintage as Aunt Phyllis's, there was no comparison between the two. Breyer's place looked out on a well-tended lawn and was shielded from the street by a thick, high hedge. The building itself had been freshly painted, and the rotting wood had been systematically replaced. Someone had lavished a good deal of love and care on the house, with the result that it had a comfortable, friendly feeling about it.

I ascended the steps to the unlit porch and gave the buzzer a hard push. I could have saved myself the trouble.

"Evenin'."

The voice came from a corner of the darkened porch, and I gave an involuntary jump. A figure moved toward me from out of the shadows.

"Nothing to be afraid of. I was just checking out the window boxes there. Want to plant some begonias this year." He stuck out his hand. "I'm Karl Breyer."

We moved into the house, and once inside, I could see that Karl Breyer was a good looking, well-preserved man in his mid-fifties. The dominant feature of his countenance was a lantern jaw that, in combination with his high forehead, tended to give his face a square, stolid look. He had wavy brown hair, deep blue eyes, and a blunt nose. His expression had the inquisitive, questioning stare that men acquire after years of police work. I had the impression that Breyer had sized me up within seconds.

"You say your name is Ball."

"That's right. I'm the nephew of Phyllis Hailley. She died earlier this week."

Breyer shrugged, then pointed the way into a room adjacent to the living room. "My den. Make yourself comfortable."

The walls of the room were covered with pictures and framed citations, obviously the souvenirs of decades of police work. In one of the pictures Breyer was being congratulated by a man I recognized as one of Murcer's former mayors. On one of the walls a shelf supported a glass case containing a number of trophies. Breyer sat down at a chair in front of his desk and swiveled around to face me.

My first thought on seeing Karl Breyer in the light was that I knew him from somewhere. I was about to mention the fact, but he spoke first.

"What's on your mind, Clint?" Breyer produced a pipe from the pocket of his jacket and began banging it on the palm of his hand. The combination of the pipe and the tweed jacket gave him the appearance of a middle-aged college professor.

"I'm in the middle of getting my aunt's affairs together, Karl, and some things have come up that I'd like to get straightened out."

"You been away a while, Clint?"

"I live in New York."

"What's your line?"

"Computers."

"I could tell you were a smart one as soon as I saw you. Smart people get out of Murcer, and it takes brains to handle the technical stuff."

"What I want to ask you about is a murder, Karl—one that took place twenty-eight years ago."

"Why ask me?"

"You worked on it." I reached for the package of cigarettes in my breast pocket. "You mind if I smoke?"

"Hell, no. Which homicide you asking about, Clint?"

"Someone killed a small-time mobster named Joey Hauck, shot him in his apartment. You remember the case, Karl?"

Breyer's big jaw clamped down on his pipe, and his eyes took on a faraway look. He frowned and then said, "They used to call him 'Joey Boy.' That the one you're thinking of?"

"That's the one."

"Yeah, like a lot of crumbs, he got himself knocked off. No great loss. Why are you interested in him, Clint?"

I had anticipated the question, but I had no good answer for it. I couldn't think of anything that wouldn't strain the limits of credibility.

"It's a personal reason, Karl."

Breyer was silent for a second. Then he sighed. "I recall that I worked that case, and I recall that we never closed the file. You tend to remember things like that. At least I always did. But I'd have to look it up to give you any further details."

Breyer got up and went to a small refrigerator in the corner of the room, from which he took two bottles of beer. He produced two glasses from an adjacent cabinet and handed me a bottle and glass. He poured a glass for himself and took a long swallow.

"Would you be able to do that, Karl?"

"Well, Clint, you got to understand two things. I'm retired now, so I don't involve myself in work the way I once did. And two, I should have at least some idea of what your interest is. That would make things a lot easier. Like, are you Joey Hauck's cousin, or son . . . or what?"

"I know how the police feel about amateurs mixing themselves up in police business. . . ."

Breyer grinned wryly. I could see I'd said the right thing. "All right, Clint. I'll see what I can do. But it might not be before the end of next week."

I stood up and we shook hands. I told Breyer I appreciated his efforts and would give him a call.

"One last thing, Clint," Breyer said when we were standing on the porch. "If I were you I'd knock off the coffin nails. Do what I did. Switch to a pipe."

"I've been trying to knock them off for years, Karl. I would if I could."

Breyer shook his head, turned, and went back into the house.

I climbed back into the rental Chevy, relieved that the visit with Breyer had gone well. Although his trophy-filled den indicated he had pride in his accomplishments, Breyer didn't give the impression of being the macho type, which is the one kind of policeman I tend to dislike. With brass all shining and uniform freshly pressed, they are the ones who fall in love with their own image of authority, and who sometimes have a need to hurt other people. The badge and the uniform can provide a man with a freedom from accountability that, on occasion, can have ugly consequences. And that may be one reason that many people, myself included, are just a bit wary of policemen.

Like many cities its size around the country, Murcer had always had difficulty recruiting men for its police force. Too often, people joined for the wrong reasons. The professionalism I had sensed in Breyer inclined me to believe that perhaps the city had been able to solve at least one of its long-standing problems.

I thought about getting something to eat but realized I wasn't really hungry. Although it was only quarter past eight, the streets were already empty and I was able to make it back to Waverly Street in less than fifteen minutes. Minutes after I had entered the house the telephone began ringing. It was a man's voice, a voice that reverberated with echoes of command. "Mr. Clinton Ball, please."

"This is Clinton Ball," I said.

"You're Phyllis Hailley's nephew, is that right?"

"May I ask who's calling?"

"This is Peter van Beldin. I want to talk with you, Ball. Personally." The van Beldin name was one of the oldest and most respected in Murcer. "You know where my office is, Ball? It's in the Braybar Building."

"Can I ask what you want to talk about, Mr. van Beldin?"

"I think you can probably guess why I want to see you, Ball, so cut out the crap. Come by my office at nine o'clock Monday morning. Or is that too early for you?"

"Nine is fine."

Van Beldin hung up.

I hauled the gin bottle out from behind the cereal box. It was down below half, and I made a mental note to buy another. I had a feeling I might be needing it.

The gin packed a wallop going down on my empty stomach. Although I had been back in Murcer for just four days, I was rapidly becoming an object of attention. Someone had cared enough to break into the house. And now I was being summoned for an audience with one of Murcer's most powerful businessmen, a powerful businessman who hadn't sounded very happy. I didn't know whether I should feel honored or only scared.

For as far back as anyone could remember, the name van Beldin meant wealth and power. And breeding with a capital *B*. There had been van Beldins in the area for four generations, and if Murcer had an elite, they were definitely it. The family controlled the Murcer Bank and much of the city's real estate, and was influential in local politics. The van Beldin home, an elegant estate just west of the city, was one of Murcer's showplaces, the centerpiece of which was an elegant Tudor mansion capable of drawing gasps of admiration from passersby. I remembered riding my bicycle out in that direction as a kid just to look at the horses that the van Beldins used to keep and breed in the paddocks behind their home.

But Peter van Beldin was a mystery. I assumed him to be the son of David van Beldin, the man who had been in charge of the family's holdings during the previous generation. I decided to call Sylvia. I found her number in the book and she answered on the first ring. I told her about the call I had just received from Peter van Beldin.

"It didn't take you long to move into the best circles. People around here would give their eyeteeth for a personal audience with Peter van Beldin. I'm impressed."

"He sounded upset, Sylvia, really angry. Is there anything about van Beldin I should know?"

"Well, he took control of the van Beldin family interests over ten years ago, after the death of his father."

"Age?"

"Early fifties. And, Clint, something else. Peter van Beldin wants to be governor. He's already thrown his hat in the ring for the nomination, and the way things stand, he's a good bet to get it."

"Why?"

"The perception of voters around the state seems to be that there's too much corruption in the statehouse. Someone like van Beldin—rich, on the stuffy side—might be just the kind of man people want. Morality looks like it might be a factor in the election this year."

I thanked Sylvia for the information.

"I can't wait to find out why he wants to see you."

"Meet me for dinner Monday evening and I'll be glad to tell you what happened."

"I'm working till seven-thirty."

I told Sylvia that I'd pick her up in front of the *Telegram* when she got off. Then I drank up the last of the gin, wondering all the while what it was Peter van Beldin wanted to see me about.

Most of the next morning—a gusty, cloudy Saturday—was gone by the time I finished breakfast and returned from a trip to the supermarket. Early in the afternoon I turned the black-and-white television set to a college basketball game, but after watching seven successive shots without a miss, I decided shooting baskets was easy and turned off the set. From the window I could see some of the neighbors at work—on their houses, on their cars, in their gardens. Mr. Hoffman was chipping paint from the frame around his door, so I went out to say hello.

Aunt Phyllis had always had her reservations about Mr. Hoffman—"a terrible busybody, worse than a woman," I recalled her saying once—but as a boy I had always found him approachable, not nearly as forbidding as most of the other people in the area.

Mr. Hoffman said he only needed five minutes to finish the job, and I told him to take his time. When he had gotten the last of the paint off, we carried his tools into the house and made ourselves comfortable at his kitchen table.

"The one thing I can't understand," Mr. Hoffman said after putting a pot of coffee on the stove, "is how a nice lookin' fella like you never got himself hitched. I married Ida—God rest her soul—when we were twenty-one. It'll be fifty-five years in June."

I took a bite from one of the cookies he had placed on the table. "I was due to be married in January, Mr. Hoffman, but at the last minute we decided—or I should say she decided—we weren't right for each other after all."

"I'm sorry to hear that."

"Breaking up wasn't easy. We'd known one another a long time, almost two years." I watched Mr. Hoffman pour the steaming coffee into two large mugs. At seventy-six his hand was steadier than that of many men half his age. "Actually, she met someone else. Her name was Doris."

Mr. Hoffman said something to the effect it was better to find out before the ceremony than after.

"I suppose. But to be honest, I haven't been the same since."

Mr. Hoffman took a long sip of coffee and looked at me searchingly over the rim of his cup. After a while he said, "Anyways, it's nice to see you lookin' so good. I never will forget the way you was as a kid. Quiet, but always with a mind of your own. Nearly drove your aunt crazy the way you'd never do what she told you."

I winced at the recollection. There was a lot of truth in that statement. For reasons I could never understand myself, I had always resented my aunt. I'd had a compulsion to disobey her.

"Been a while since you've been back, hasn't it, son?"

"Two years. Every time I made plans to visit something would come up."

"Sure. I know how it is. Work comes first." Mr. Hoffman pushed the plate of cookies toward me. "I suppose I'm one of the few people around who remembers your father. I remember we used to catch the same bus home when I was on the day shift. Big man, loud voice, but always friendly. Worked down the mill. I remember when he bought that house and when he died. And I remember when your aunt bought it just after he died. That was when she moved in to take care of you."

"You remember a lot more than I do, Mr. Hoffman," I said.

The old man smiled. "You'll have a lot of recollections when you reach my age, Clint."

"I'm not sure I'll reach your age, Mr. Hoffman," I said.

Mr. Hoffman asked if I wanted another cup of coffee, but I said no. A few minutes later I left and returned to Aunt Phyllis's house. I had to marvel at people like Mr. Hoffman. Amidst the change and flux taking place around them they somehow managed to remain unaltered. I couldn't decide whether such constancy was good or bad.

3

I drove into downtown Murcer on Monday morning with the rush hour hordes. The city's old narrow streets weren't built to handle heavy traffic. The result was that the trip took twice as long as it might have at any other time of day. I had visions of most of these drivers arriving at work worn out and snarling, year in and year out. It was a far cry from the way things had been when I was a kid. In those days, only the rich had cars—people like the van Beldins, in other words. The rest of us walked or took public transportation.

I parked the car on a side street two blocks beyond the court-house and had breakfast at the Mayfair luncheonette, where I was served by a sturdy girl with round glasses and thick eyebrows. She gave me a hint of a smile, and I was pleasantly surprised by the quality of the food—fresh coffee, warm toast, and eggs scrambled the way I like them. I didn't understand the language of the people behind the counter but I took it to be Greek.

Van Beldin's office was in the Braybar Building, still the most exclusive office building in Murcer, a six-story structure housing much of the city's "old money"—lawyers, real estate developers, stockbrokers. Van Beldin Enterprises occupied the upper three stories of the Braybar Building, and I entered Peter van Beldin's outer office at precisely five minues before nine.

I was just in time to observe van Beldin's elegant secretary perform her morning ritual—unlocking her desk drawers, dusting off the top of her desk, taking the cover off her electric typewriter, and finally, placing her very well-shaped rear end on the chair behind the desk. I identified myself, said I had an appointment with Peter van Beldin, and took a seat in a hardbacked chair opposite the door. A few minutes later I was told to go in.

My entrance was an unceremonious one—no handshake, no introduction, no small talk. I suppose when you are as important as Peter van Beldin it is not necessary to mince words or say things you don't mean.

Although he was seated when I entered, I guessed van Beldin to be roughly my height and weight—an inch over six and one-eighty. But the resemblance ended there. For better or worse. He'd had a lifetime to work at being someone important, and he was very good at the image business. Every aspect of his physical features—the graying brown hair, the slightly flushed, smooth-shaven face, the cold blue eyes, the expensively tailored suit—contributed to the image of the capable, self-confident businessman. He looked like the kind of candidate I might even have voted for myself.

"I'm not going to waste time with you, Ball, because as far as I'm concerned, I don't feel you're worth any more time than I absolutely have to give you. But I do want to let you know a few things, and I want to tell them to you personally. The first is, you are a son of a bitch. The second is, I intend to take any action possible, short of murder, to make your future life as unpleasant as possible. And not only will I feel perfectly justified doing so, my friend, I'm going to enjoy and relish every minute of it."

I was silent at first, the result of surprise at the directness of van Beldin's little speech.

"Come, come now, Ball. Is that all you can do? Stand there and look hurt. Has the cat stolen your tongue?"

"I hate to have to tell you this, van Beldin," I said, "but that carefully prepared little speech of yours doesn't compare with a reaming I once got from a master sergeant in basic training for not having my belt buckle properly polished."

"I figured you for a wise guy, Ball. I was right."

"One other difference you might be interested in. I deserved every bit of what I got from that master sergeant. I don't even know what you're talking about."

"Well, well. I hope I didn't injure your feelings. I expected you to play dumb, my friend, and I'm happy you haven't disappointed me."

"I haven't got the slighest idea why you called me up or why you called me in here."

"You're not as cute as you think you are, Ball, not by a long shot, and what I said before I meant. You'll be mowing lawns the rest of your life before I get through with you."

"Like I said, you're way ahead of me."

Van Beldin stood up, and I saw that he was a good inch taller than I was. "There's no way I'm going to give you the satisfaction of telling you what you're supposed to have done. We both know what you did and why. That's why." Van Beldin rubbed his thumb and forefinger together. "Why the hell does anyone do anything any more except for money?"

I could see he wanted to talk, so I decided to let him. I thought I might be able to pick up something the longer he went on.

"All right, people want to keep me out of the statehouse, that I can understand. You want to make yourself a little change peddling some information on the side. I can understand that too."

Van Beldin came around from behind his desk and stood squarely in front of me. His voice became lower, more controlled. Maybe some of it was theatrical and some of it was real. If the intention was to throw a scare into me, I won't say it didn't achieve some of the effect. "But there's one thing I won't forgive, and that's the reason I'll hound you and do my best to break you. You hit at me through my wife. You dragged Helen into something she had nothing to do with. That's why I wanted to talk with you today and tell you why I find you so sickening." Van Beldin turned around and once again stepped behind the desk.

"I still don't know what you're talking about," I said."

"Come off it, Ball. I know what Korban and his people must have paid you for that little tidbit of information. And I'm sure it will make you all very happy to know it's going to have the de-sired effect. . . . I'm withdrawing my candidacy." Van Beldin slumped back down into his chair. A trace of sadness crossed his face. "I'm going to make the announcement later today."

"I'm not up on local politics," I said.

"I'm supposed to believe you didn't know I was going to run for governor? Your audacity at least is refreshing, even if nothing else about you is."

"Good-bye, van Beldin," I said and turned to go. I hadn't sat down the entire time I was in van Beldin's office. Van Beldin slammed down his hand on his walnut desk.

"Just one more thing," he said. "In the event there's any fur-ther communication between us—something that I rather doubt —my lawyer will handle it."

I let van Beldin have the last word and headed for the door. Moments later I was walking up Stockton Street. The fresh air felt good. I walked to the corner and turned into the first gin mill I passed. It was a dark place with a long bar and pictures of boxers hanging on the wall behind the bottle display. A half-dozen regulars were perched on high stools getting an early start on the day. I ordered a double bourbon and a beer. After the bartender had brought the drinks and taken away the money, I stood looking at the glasses. I seldom take a drink before early evening, almost never before noon. The fact that I was standing in this place was evidence that Peter van Beldin had gotten to me with his threats. Although he was only a small-city businessman, I wasn't so naïve that I didn't know how far his influence might reach. I couldn't figure on lasting long at Precision Data, the computer firm I worked for, if he was permitted to make good his threats.

Somehow I'd gotten tangled up in something unpleasant, and I wondered what I would have to do to straighten things out. Whatever it was, I decided that straightening it out would even have to take priority over the question of Aunt Phyllis and the murder of Joey Hauck. I gazed down at the drinks I had ordered for another minute, then headed for the door. The bartender followed me out with a pop-eyed stare but didn't say anything.

I walked back toward the courthouse and the luncheonette where I had eaten breakfast. Once inside, I headed for the telephone in the back and put through a call to Sylvia at the *Telegram.*

"You're not calling to tell me you can't make it this evening, I hope? Not after I went and made a lunch-hour appointment with my hairdresser."

"No, nothing like that. What I'm looking for is some information. I thought you might get the morgue files on some people."

"Who?"

"Does the name Korban mean anything to you?"

"Warren Korban. A wheeler-dealer type here in Murcer. The word is he's worth millions, maybe more than van Beldin. You want his morgue file?"

"Yes. And I'd also like the file on Mrs. Peter van Beldin."

"Clint, I can't leave the office now. Where are you calling from?"

I told her.

"What I'll do is I'll send a copyboy down with the clips in a package. This is strictly against regulations, so take care of them, huh?"

I said I would, and twenty minutes later a longhaired youngster in his late teens entered the luncheonette. I waved him over, took the clips, and told him to return in an hour. Then I systematically went over the contents of the two files. I began with Korban's.

The first mention of Warren Korban in the Murcer *Telegram* was fifteen years before, when he was identified as the owner of a large tract of land north of the city that had been designated by the City-County Planning Board for improvement and development. Korban was described as being, at the time, the owner of a number of businesses in Chicago. Subsequent stories detailed the establishment by Korban of a real estate firm in Murcer, the acquisition of further property in and around Murcer, the erection of a number of shopping centers and office buildings. A small sheaf of stories recounted the building of a small industrial park, which subsequently attracted branches of larger businesses to the

Murcer area. Other little stories detailed what seemed to be a running battle between Korban's firms and a local environmental group that felt the rapid building was detrimental to certain wooded areas outside the city. I noticed that Peter van Beldin was one of the prominent members of the environmental group. Now and then Korban's name came up in connection with a charity event or a contribution to a worthwhile cause. All in all, it was what you might expect to read about a successful, influential businessman.

There was less to read about Mrs. Peter van Beldin. She'd been born Helen Nesbitt on a farm just outside Murcer. A short piece noted her graduation from Murcer General Hospital as a registered nurse. Some society items recorded her engagement and subsequent marriage to a Murcer doctor named Walter Lakeman. The most prominent item, though, was the account of her second marriage—to Peter van Beldin—which had taken place almost nine years before. In this story, it was noted that Helen van Beldin's first husband, Walter Lakeman, was deceased. More recent notices chronicled her work with charity and church groups.

An hour later the longhaired copyboy returned. His hair was dripping with water, an indication that it had again begun to rain. I gave him back the clippings and watched while he tucked them into one of his raincoat pockets.

"They won't get wet?" I asked.

"No way." His face lit up when I gave him a dollar bill.

He took the money up to the cashier, asked for change, and then walked over to a nook at the front of the store that held a couple of video games. He spent the next five minutes peering into the screen and simultaneously pressing a series of knobs and levers with a precision and skill worthy of a concert pianist. The thought occurred to me that at no time in history had young people been subjected to so many distractions as they were today and that, as a consequence, there probably had never been another era when it was so difficult to grow into a useful, balanced adult.

Finally, after having thrown in his last quarter, he turned, threw me a wave and a smile, and disappeared into the rainy street.

Two minutes later I followed him out to join the rain-drenched throng. I had with me as complete a list of my aunt's assets and debts as I could gather, and I negotiated the four blocks to Sonia Wegman's at a semi-gallop. I was nevertheless soaked when I arrived.

Her secretary announced me and waved me in.

My second meeting with Sonia Wegman somewhat altered the impression I had received the previous Friday. This time I was most struck by the contrast of her dark brown-red hair with the smooth pale whiteness of her skin. She had on a light gold blouse and a tan skirt. The impression of bigness was still there, but I noticed that everything was in splendid proportion—face, shoulders, breasts, legs—and the fact of her size detracted less on this occasion from her aura of femininity.

I told her that I had a list of my aunt's assets.

"And I have some forms for you to sign, Mr. Ball." I went over them, listening to her explanations, asking the necessary questions. When she'd finished she sat back in her chair, her manner changed, now less businesslike and more informal.

"Do you mind if I ask you what you intend to do when you've finished up with these matters here, Mr. Ball?"

"I'll be going back to New York. I've taken two weeks off to wrap things up here."

"Does that mean you'll be saying good-bye forever to Murcer?"

"I rather imagine it does," I said.

"I see." She looked thoughtful. "And how do you feel about that?"

"I guess I have mixed feelings," I said.

"I've often thought about leaving Murcer myself, but something always . . . got in the way. I had an offer from a large firm in Chicago just about the time my father died. Somehow I felt obligated to stay here. I don't know why."

"There are worse places than Murcer," I said, and I was glad when she smiled.

It had been only a brief conversation, but I had seen something in Sonia Wegman that I hadn't suspected was there. Maybe she wasn't quite the committed career woman I had first thought.

On the way back to the car I picked up some groceries, some beer, and a bottle of brandy. There wasn't much left of the afternoon by the time I arrived back at the house on Weatherly Street. I was relieved to notice that no one seemed to have entered while I was gone. I did some straightening up, showered, and killed the final empty half hour before I had to leave for my date with Sylvia by watching the evening news.

"You're a picture of loveliness," I told Sylvia seconds after she had climbed into my car.

"Flattery will get you absolutely nowhere."

"Will a juicy sirloin steak get me anywhere?"

"Food of any kind will get you somewhere. I haven't eaten since breakfast."

"My contacts here in Murcer, such as they are, tell me there's a reputable steakhouse about five miles out on River Road."

"Durango's. I haven't been there in ages, but it's always been good."

I put the car in gear. "I'll drive fast, so you don't have to suffer the pangs of hunger any longer than necessary, ma'am."

"Very thoughtful of you, kind sir. You'll receive your reward in heaven."

"In heaven? I was thinking—"

"I know what you were thinking."

Durango's was a long, low brick building with an orange roof. Its large parking lot was surrounded by a six-foot-high hedge. The fact that the lot was full on a Monday evening was one indication that the food appealed to locals as well as transients.

We gave the hatcheck girl our coats and were seated by an officious-looking man in a dark suit. In one corner of the room a piano player was running through a medley of show tunes. Beyond the piano bar, which was largely concealed from the diners, and on the other side of the room a bright fire crackled away in a brick fireplace.

We both ordered martinis. I took one swallow and couldn't contain a smile of satisfaction. I found it very pleasant being in Durango's with Sylvia, very pleasant indeed.

"I needed that," I said after putting the glass back on the table."

"Rough day?"

"Murcer certainly isn't the same place I remember as a boy."

"I find it depressing sometimes. The city doesn't seem to be changing for the better. And to think I used to believe in progress." Sylvia took a long swallow of her martini.

"Change is always hard to adjust to, Sylvia. Particularly after you've reached a certain age. But some of the changes I see in

Murcer I like. The city doesn't seem to be as stuffy as it once was."

"There seem to be more problems, though. Many more than when we were kids."

"True all over. In proportion, Murcer probably has the same headaches that afflict all the great cities—New York, Los Angeles, Chicago—drugs, street crime, transportation, schools."

"But in a place like this they should be more manageable."

"Why?"

"I don't know." Sylvia broke into a broad grin. "My God, I'm getting serious lately. I can't seem to be able to enjoy myself anymore."

"The best remedy for a dose of seriousness, I've always found, is a full stomach. Let's order."

We both selected steak, baked potatoes, and salad. I ordered a bottle of French wine, the name of which I didn't dare try to pronounce. We were drinking coffee when I asked Sylvia if she was still suffering from her attack of seriousness.

"No, now I'm suffering from a case of curiosity."

"About what?"

"About what happened today when you went to see Peter van Beldin."

I called the waiter over and ordered two brandies. "They're to fortify us," I said.

"That bad?"

"I'm afraid so." I then recounted the details of my visit to Peter van Beldin's office that morning. Sylvia's complexion went a shade paler in the course of the story.

"Do you think he'll really carry out the threats he made?" she asked when I'd finished.

"If he did, it wouldn't be the first time something like that was done. A man like van Beldin wields a lot of power—"

"Mr. Ball? Mr. Clinton Ball?" I looked up to see our waiter standing over me. "A message from the bartender. Someone would like to speak with you in the taproom."

"You're becoming well-known around here," Sylvia said.

I shrugged. "Excuse me a second," I said, and I followed the waiter out to the bar. The bar was situated in a long room beyond the last row of tables in the restaurant. The waiter pointed me toward the bartender, an angular man with thinning black hair who was standing behind the beertap wiping a glass.

"Did someone back here want to see me?" I asked.

"You're Clinton Ball, right?" When I told him I was, he gestured toward the door. "He's outside. He said for you to go out."

"Outside?"

The bartender nodded reassuringly. "He wants to talk private," he said in a quiet voice.

I walked over to the door, opened it, and stepped down three or four concrete steps. I looked around and was about to turn around and reenter the restaurant when a man, whose face I couldn't see, approached me from behind a nearby parked car.

"Hey, Mr. Ball. Hey!"

"What is this anyway? Who are you?"

"If you'll step over here, I want to—" And that was when he caught me. He was probably swinging a piece of hard rubber of some kind. The blow landed squarely against the side of my face and sent shockwaves of pain that engulfed my body from my feet to my head, and although the blow staggered me, I didn't go down. The shadow was now a man moving in on me like a fullback intent on picking up a couple of tough yards. When he hit me again I hurtled backward, going down against the wall of the restaurant in a heap and banging the back of my head as I did so. I was able to scramble back to my feet before he was able to come at me once again with his rubber weapon. This time I was able to duck it, and I heard it bang against the brick wall of the restaurant. I took a wild swing and caught him on the side of the face. He cursed. I took another swing, but he moved inside it and began delivering rabbit punches to my kidneys. As I sagged to the ground, he muttered something about "teaching me a lesson."

A second after I hit the ground, he aimed a kick at my face, catching me on the forehead above the left eye. He'd pulled his leg back for another shot when I reached out and caught the big boot with both hands before it could land. I gave a violent twist, and he went down with a loud thump.

"Sonofabitch!" he said. He didn't sound happy. We both made it back up but I noticed he was limping slightly. "You gonna pay for that, sonofabitch."

"Hey, what's happening over there?" The voice came from the last row of parked cars.

Then a woman's voice: "No, darling, don't go near them—"

The voice again: "Hey, you guys—"

"Over here," I called. I was very much in a daze. I thought I might be sick to my stomach. The other guy moved away in the other direction, away from the lights of the restaurant. He was quickly lost in the darkness. I stood leaning against the side of the building, holding a handkerchief to the side of my head.

The couple from the parked car moved slowly into the circle of light, eyeing me suspiciously. The woman was holding the man by the arm, trying to keep him back.

"Hey, fella, you all right?"

"Don't go near him, Tom," the woman said. "Maybe he has a gun."

"I'm not afraid," Tom said. He came around from behind the car and stood facing me.

I told Tom that I was all right and thanked him for coming over.

"I did the right thing, didn't I?"

"You did, Tom. You really did."

"I guess I spooked him, huh?" Tom said. He turned to the girl. "See, honey, I spooked the guy."

I could feel blood on my cheek, and the side of my face felt as if it had gotten in the way of one of Nolan Ryan's fastballs. After thanking Tom and his girl for the third or fourth time, I went back up the steps and reentered the taproom.

The bartender registered a look of alarm when he saw me. I ignored him and the other customers and headed straight for the men's room, where I spent the next ten minutes doing my best to repair the damage. The feeling of nausea passed, but I hurt all over. Whoever the guy had been, he had all the tricks down pat—how to sucker a person, how to get a lot of damage done in a short period of time, how to disappear. When I stepped back out, the bartender once again looked alarmed.

I walked over to the bar. Before I could say anything, the bartender said, "Management here don't want any fighting. This is a nice restaurant, a family place."

"Tell me about him," I said.

"About who?"

"About the guy who left the message he wanted to see me."

"I don't know no guy. What are you talking about anyway?"

I had been leaning over the bar and been feeling strongly tempted to throw a punch at the bartender when I felt a tug on my arm. "Clint! Clint! What happened? What happened to your face?" Sylvia stood there looking very troubled.

"I'll tell you outside, Sylvia," I said. "Let me pay the bill and we'll get out of here."

By this time I had become the center of a small knot of spectators—customers and restaurant employees. Even some of the kitchen help were standing by the door getting a load of the customer who'd gotten himself beat up. While Sylvia retrieved our coats, I intercepted our waiter and got the bill.

"By the way," I said after I'd overtipped him, "which customer was it that gave you the message he wanted to talk with me?"

"No customer, sir. Harry over there." He pointed to the bartender. "Harry said someone was waiting outside to talk to you. I'm sorry about—"

"No problem." I took Sylvia by the arm and we made as dignified an exit as the circumstances permitted. After we'd made our way outside, I detoured over to a window that gave me another look into the bar. The employees had dispersed, but Harry was in a heated conversation with our waiter. He seemed to be chewing him out for some reason.

"Feel better?"

I was flat on my back on the sofa in the living room of Aunt Phyllis's house, holding a cold compress against the side of my face. I was also nursing a bunch of very tender ribs, but our first diagnosis had determined that nothing had been broken.

"Much," I said. "My recuperative powers have always been extraordinary."

"Consider yourself lucky," Sylvia said. I'd told her the details of what had happened on the way back in the car.

"I'm not a very popular person in Murcer anymore," I said.

"The side of your face is going to be a problem for the next week. That's not going to do anything for your image."

"My image will have to suffer along with the rest of me."

"I don't know what else I can do," Sylvia said.

"Maybe if you kiss it, it won't hurt so much." She knelt down beside the couch and gently ran her fingers through my hair. Then she leaned over. She placed her lips on mine, then withdrew. I didn't try to prevent her from moving away.

"The old story," Sylvia said. "The patient trying to make it with his nurse." Then she bent over and kissed me again. This time she made no effort to pull herself away. Her lips were warm and giving. With my free hand I pulled her to me. The contours of her body were plainly evident as our bodies moved against one another.

"I'll bet you even believe I arranged to have someone take a poke at me in order to gain your sympathy."

"If you did, it worked."

4

When I awoke the next morning, the room was dark except for a crack of sunlight from behind the drapery, an indication that the day was well along. I raised myself to get a look at the clock, and immediately felt the bruised ribs. There was a note on the coffee table.

> *Clint, I tucked you in but couldn't find your teddy bear. Call me at the office when you wake up.*
>
> *Sylvia*
>
> *P.S. I didn't know how strong my maternal instincts were until last evening.*

The clock said 11:15. I'd slept for nearly twelve hours.

A ten-minute hot shower took the edge off the pain in my rib section, and a pair of aspirin eased the throbbing on the side of my face. I broke out a pair of new slacks, a checkered shirt, and a plain knit tie. A glance in the mirror told me I looked better than I had any right to expect. The visible damage consisted of a cut on my forehead over my left eye and a nasty bruise on my left cheek. Had he caught me an inch higher I would have had a classic shiner. I covered each of the wounds with a bandage. I looked as though I'd gone half a dozen rounds with Ali.

I started some coffee, scrambled two eggs, and toasted three pieces of bread. By the time I'd poured the second cup of coffee, I had my brain in gear.

This much seemed obvious: the guy who surprised me in the parking lot had been sent by van Beldin. This I supposed to be the opening salvo in the campaign to make my life miserable or whatever it was he intended to do to me. I considered what it was van Beldin thought I had done to queer his political chances. Supposedly, I had passed on some information concerning his wife to a man named Korban, one of his business rivals. My first thought was to confront van Beldin, but he'd only deny knowing anything about what had happened. And besides, I didn't want to give him the satisfaction of seeing the damage his bullyboy had done.

A second possibility was to report the incident to the Murcer police. But like so many small-city police forces, the Murcer officials would almost certainly be subject to the influence of the city's influential citizens—people like van Beldin, in other words. Such a move did not seem wise, at least not at the moment. That left me with one remaining possibility: to pay a visit to Warren Korban and see what he might be willing to reveal.

I dialed Sylvia and told her what I had in mind.

"Do you think it's wise? Korban has a reputation of being . . . a pretty ruthless person at times."

"What's he supposed to have done?"

"People don't amass a lot of money without doing all sorts of things."

"Tell me about it."

"A man of the world like you knows more about these things—"

"How about dropping over tomorrow night for something to eat? I'll show you firsthand what a man of the world is capable of in the kitchen."

I heard her laugh. It was a contagious, generous laugh, and I took it to mean yes.

The name of Korban's firm was in the telephone book. It was located at Korban Park, probably some kind of office complex he'd built himself. I put in a call, got Korban's secretary, said I wanted to see the boss, was told to hold on, was later asked what I wanted to see him about, said it was personal, was told to hold again, and was finally told to come by at three o'clock sharp.

I slipped on a solid blue sports jacket, which more or less matched the shirt and tie, ran a comb through my hair, and gave my face another once-over.

The weather, at least, had improved. A bright sun had taken the edge off the chill that had been so prevalent ever since I'd gotten back to Murcer. I decided to give the rental car some exercise and take in some more of the city in the two hours I had until my date with Korban.

The Murcer Pike had been widened since the days when I rode it as a kid on my bike. I took it going north. For a good distance the road fronted on used-car dealerships, liquor stores, fast-food places, and tacky little shopping centers. Beginning a couple of miles beyond the business strip, but still within the city limits, the developers had been busy. Four-story buildings housing so-called garden apartments predominated, and then gave way to clusters of ranch-style homes. This was the area that, according to the newspaper stories, had been largely built up by Korban. Acquiring this land had certainly been an act of great foresight. Clearly, he'd beaten people like van Beldin to the punch. That was quite a trick when you considered that Korban was an outsider.

I might have noticed him sooner if I hadn't been so preoccupied by the changes that had taken place over the last fifteen years in my old hometown. I was meandering, doing about thirty-five or so, and so was he. At times, wherever the road was straight, he'd drop back to where I couldn't see much more than a green blur in the mirror. Other times he'd close it up to fifty yards. I suppose that the aimlessness of my driving puzzled him. In any event, he got close enough at one point to let me see that he was driving a green Ford, a Galaxy. I was about fifteen miles beyond the Murcer city limits when I decided I'd seen enough. I pulled off the road at the entrance to someone's driveway, and waited until he'd driven past. Then I swung around and headed back toward town. I kept it at a steady sixty, taking some of the curves at an excessive speed, and keeping my eyes on the mirror the entire time.

Within five minutes the green blur reappeared in the rearview mirror. If I was doing sixty, he had to be doing seventy. I considered trying to shake him in downtown traffic, and then I wondered what was the sense. It was now about 2:30, so I headed toward my appointment with Warren Korban.

Korban's firm was located in a modern, four-story office building located on the outskirts of Murcer. An especially picturesque grove of woods had been decimated to make room for the structure and its neighboring parking lot. I pulled the rental car into a space adjoining the building and waited to see if the Ford would follow me in. It didn't.

The waiting room to Warren Korban's inner sanctum provided an interesting contrast to Peter van Beldin's outer office. Here the decor was modern, flashy, up-to-date—except for the magazines, which were three weeks old. Well, you can't have everything. But the most interesting contrast was provided by the secretaries. Van Beldin's had been lithe and prim. Korban's secretary was fifteen pounds too heavy, had bleached red hair, and wore too much makeup. Despite her lack of attractiveness, she exuded a muskiness that was not without its own fascination. While pretending to leaf through an article on micro-processors, I watched her rearrange the papers on her desk from one side to the other and then back to the original side again. Now and then I caught her glancing over at me, and I have to concede she at least had the good taste not to say anything about my face when I announced myself.

After I had cooled my heels for fifteen minutes, the red-haired secretary announced, "Mr. Korban will see you now."

Korban was a square, balding man with a fleshy face. He was seated behind a large desk that was piled with blueprints and an assortment of other papers. He wore a brown checkered sports jacket and a red and gold shirt open at the neck. He was chewing on the remnants of a cigar. I wouldn't have been surprised if he'd had a spitoon somewhere close by. He gave me a curious stare by way of greeting. I sat down without being asked.

"Your name is . . . Ball," Korban said flatly.

"Clinton Ball."

"What can I do for you, Clinton Ball?" Then, after a short pause he asked: "What happened to the face?"

"It's a long story. I'd rather not go into it."

Korban grinned. His smile had a wolfish, amoral quality. It was easy to see why he and van Beldin didn't get along. They were completely different types. "Sure, I understand," he said. "My secretary tells me you mentioned the name of van Beldin.

You want to talk to me about him?" Korban's tone sounded incredulous.

"I'm here because van Beldin has accused me of being part of some kind of scheme to smear him."

"So? Are you?" Korban flashed the wolfish grin again.

"No."

"So why come to me?"

"Van Beldin mentioned your name. He indicated that he thought I had passed on some kind of information to you that you were using to keep him out of the political race?"

"Now, why would I do a thing like that?"

"You tell me."

Korban began drumming his fingers on his desk. He was plainly a man with a short fuse. "I don't see where you're coming from, Ball. I don't see it at all."

"All right, maybe it is a little roundabout."

"Roundabout isn't the word. It sounds like you're trying to tie me up to something."

"All I'm trying to find out is why van Beldin thinks I'm in on a scheme to keep him out of politics."

"How the hell should I know that, Ball? I don't even know who you are."

"What is it that van Beldin thinks I told you?"

Korban's expression hardened. It took on the look of a man playing a poker hand with $10,000 in the pot. "I can see why someone decided to beat up on you. You're a troublemaker."

"Van Beldin said it had something to do with his wife."

Korban stood up and walked over to a small bar at the corner of the office. He squirted some carbonated water into a glass and drank it down. He didn't ask me if I wanted any. "I got to disappoint you, Ball. I don't know of any schemes to keep van Beldin from doing anything he damn well pleases."

"From what I hear, you and van Beldin don't get along."

"There're a lot of people around here I don't get along with. There're people in this city who had things tied up businesswise for the last hundred years. They've done their best to keep out new people and new ideas. Well, I broke through here, Ball. I got something off the ground, something big. And I did it without any help from van Beldin."

"I grew up in this town, Korban, so you don't have to tell me anything about local history. I know van Beldin, and I know who's been running the show here for three generations. But I don't live here anymore. Still, when I come back to visit, I don't like people threatening me, and I don't like getting beat up." I pointed my finger at my face. "When things go this far, I figure I have a right to know what's going on."

"You been to the cops?"

"I told you I grew up here. I know how the police think."

Korban nodded. "Okay, I understand the reason for your curiosity, Ball. But I still got to tell you what I told you when you came in here. I don't know where you fit in. And if that's not good enough for you, that's just too bad."

"It doesn't help a lot."

Korban settled himself back in his chair and lit up a cigar with a gold-plated lighter. He tossed the lighter back on the desk, leaned back and blew some smoke. "I don't have a clue as to why someone beat you up, buddy, not a clue. But what's between me and van Beldin don't really concern you. If, like you say, you don't live here, why not buzz off and forget it? Chalk it up to experience."

"It's a little too serious for that."

"What more can I tell you?" Korban put on his reading glasses and started ruffling through the pile of papers on his desk.

I got up and headed for the door.

"Give my regards to van Beldin when you see him," Korban said. Then he laughed at his own joke.

I drove the rental Chevy out of the parking area, all the time keeping my eye on the rearview mirror. The tail reappeared after I'd gone about half a mile. It was a little after four when I reached the downtown area of the city. The nice weather had brought out the shoppers, and the streets were even more crowded than usual. By the time I parked the car in front of a meter, I couldn't see any sign of my shadow. I figured I'd been able to shake him in the traffic.

I walked over to the Mayfair luncheonette, not so much because I was hungry but because I didn't feel like going back to Aunt Phyllis's place. There was something about that brooding structure that gave me the feeling of imminent disaster. Partly it had something to do with the less than happy childhood I had spent there. Partly it had to do with the gloomy old frame house itself.

The feeling I now had was similar to being in a small, bare

room with a dwindling oxygen supply and being aware that the walls were moving in from every direction. I was pushing for all I was worth against them but without any result. At least in the luncheonette I had people around me. The Greek waitress with the horn-rims took my order for a grilled cheese sandwich and coffee and shouted something incomprehensible to the man at the grill.

I was coming down with a classic case of paranoia, but I still felt it wasn't anything that a few straight answers wouldn't cure. At the same time I felt it was time for a change of tactics. The people of Murcer were proving themselves to be neither friendly nor cooperative. During my tour in 'Nam I'd spent some time as an interrogator, a job that teaches you certain things about the frailties and pressure points of the human animal.

Remembering some tricks I had once employed on a couple of infiltrators I couldn't keep back an involuntary smile, a smile from which any kind of civilized feeling was definitely lacking, and in between chomps on the sandwich I noticed the waitress staring at me in an odd way. A minute later she came by the table and slapped down the check, and returned to her post behind the counter. No offer of a second cup of coffee. Just get rid of the weird guy with the cuts on his face, thinking funny thoughts and laughing to himself.

I picked up a copy of the Murcer *Telegram* and, once back in the house, I opened a can of beer and read about Peter van Beldin's announcement to the effect that he wasn't interested in running for governor after all. It was the kind of news that wouldn't mean that much in other parts of the state, but in Murcer it rated the front page. According to van Beldin's statement, he had decided that his business ventures needed too much attention to permit the kind of vigorous, dedicated campaign the people of the state had a right to expect. Etcetera, etcetera.

I turned on the living room television, one of Aunt Phyllis's few concessions to the twentieth century, and watched a handsome TV detective single-handedly subdue and capture three desperate criminals. When, after five minutes, I felt myself yawning, I turned off the TV and set the alarm for ten o'clock that evening. My nap was dreamless, something for which I was very grateful.

*   *   *

I drove into a secluded roadside parking area a half-mile down the road from Durango's at precisely 11:20 P.M. Having put the rental Chevy in a dark corner well out of sight of the road, I hoofed it back to the steakhouse. All told, there were some twenty cars in the lot when I arrived, most of them belonging to late diners and largely clustered about the restaurant's gaudy front entrance. Around to the rear and not far from the door leading to the bar were five cars. I figured these to belong to the restaurant's employees. One of them was, in all probability, the property of Harry, your friendly neighborhood bartender. Good old take-a-message Harry.

Durango's dining room and taproom closed officially at midnight on weeknights. Give Harry twenty minutes to roust the last barflies and another thirty to rinse glasses and mop up. Figure Harry to emerge between a quarter-to- and one o'clock.

I watched the last customers straggle out. Noisy good-nights to one another, then the sound of car doors opening and slamming. Finally, the roar of engines. Then silence. Some time later waiters and busboys began leaving, mostly in small groups. Harry, bless his soul, was one of the last, stepping briskly out of the rear exit and striding straight toward a four-door Merc parked some fifty yards away. I let him get the door on the driver's side open before, moving silently, I stuck my aunt's revolver into the small of his back.

"No movement, no noise."

"What is this? Who the—"

I increased the pressure of the gun against Harry's back, directing him to get behind the wheel while I got into the rear.

"Just drive it out of the lot nice and quiet." I kept my voice low, nothing more than a throaty whisper. "Make a right onto the highway and keep it at twenty-five until I tell you to stop. If you're wondering what's pressed against your neck, it's a thirty-eight. Just enough to blow your brains all over this car. Now start the engine."

Harry made another attempt at conversation, but when he saw it wasn't going to change anything, he gave it up. When we reached the parking area, I told him to slow down and park the car. We were at a spot where no one could see us from the highway.

"Okay, wise guy, what now?" Harry was the picture of self-confidence.

"Just step out of the car real slow, Harry."

"Hey, I know you—"

"Sure, Harry, I hope you haven't forgotten already."

"Look, buddy, you got it all wrong. I didn't have anything—"

I pitched my voice low, kept it reasonable. "I thought you might want to tell me a few things, that's all. Like who it was who wanted to see me so badly last evening."

Harry looked at me and smiled. It was a smile with a lot of disdain. He looked down at the gun pointed squarely at his stomach and shook his head.

"Ya gonna shoot me if I don't tell ya? Or ya just gonna break my head?"

He was right, of course. Shooting Harry was out of the question. Neither was trying to knock the truth out of him going to accomplish anything. I decided to start feeling around, looking for the pressure points.

"What's it gonna be, hard man?" Harry started to laugh. "Ya mind if I smoke, hard man? One last butt before you knock me off?"

I took Harry's keys, walked around to the rear of the car, and opened up the trunk. I motioned Harry back to the rear of the vehicle.

"What's it now?" I could see there was just the faintest trace of alarm in Harry's expression. Just a little bit of uncertainty.

"Now you're sure, Harry," I said. "You're sure you don't want to tell me anything about the other night."

"Kiss off!"

"In, Harry." I gave Harry a shove toward the open trunk of the car. "In. We're going to take a ride."

"Now, hold on. Ya don't expect me to get into that . . . to get in there . . . that narrow space . . . not into the trunk—"

"In." I gave Harry a shove that sent him sprawling over the edge of the trunk.

"No, you can't . . . can't ask me . . . No way—"

Harry struggled to his feet with panic written all over his face. I was entirely ready for him when he made his charge. I stepped aside in the fashion of a matador, and when Harry was all but past me I brought the barrel of the gun down hard on the base of his neck. Harry pitched forward, stunned. I pocketed the gun and half lifted, half dragged him to his car where I deposited him

in the trunk. I had a feeling it might not be necessary to take
Harry for a ride, after all. By the time I hauled his legs over the
lip he was coming around, moaning and starting to move. I
slammed the door of the trunk closed, then lit a cigarette.

About three minutes later Harry gave his first yelp. And then
he started to pound. And then he yelped and pounded. I tossed
away the butt and lit another. I took a short stroll around the
little clearing. I kicked a beer can, then picked it up, walked with
it to a receptacle and dropped it in. I admired the moon, which
was bright and nearly full. For one brief second, I had the feeling
of once again being in Vietnam, a place where an awareness of
imminent danger had brought out a side of my character I had
not known existed.

I deliberately ground out the second cigarette beneath my foot,
a precaution I was certain would please Smokey the Bear. The
racket in the car had by this time subsided, the yelling and
pounding having given away to a hopeless sobbing.

I don't know what it's called, but I suppose it's a variety of
claustrophobia. It's an abnormal fear of dark, small, restricted
places. It's found most often in the elderly and persons who, for
some reason, believe themselves close to death. Psychiatrists
speculate that it can also be caused in the months just after con-
ception by some kind of shock to the young fetus. In any case,
Harry had it. I waited another minute and then opened the trunk
of the Mercury.

"Thank God. Thank you. Oh thank you." Harry started to
clamber out, but I stuck the barrel of the gun in front of his nose.
"Please let me out," he said, the panicky tone returning. I noticed the hostility was gone.

"You come out, Harry, when you're ready to tell me what I
want to know."

"Oh, yes sir. Certainly." Maybe the psychiatrists are right for
once. Even Harry's tone of voice now had a childlike quality to
it, as though he had regressed to some long-ago, bygone stage of
his existence.

So I let him climb out of the trunk of the Merc, and the two of
us stood eyeball to eyeball in the lonely parking area. I realized it
was no longer necessary to keep the gun pointed at Harry.

"Who was it that told you he wanted to talk with me, Harry?"

"The way it happened . . . uh . . . he came in, was drinking at the bar a while, had a couple of bourbons. Like he used to have, when he came in a couple of years back. We did a little talkin'. Like you know, a bartender's supposed to be friendly—"

"Keep going, Harry."

"Well, then he said he wanted to talk with one of the diners . . . urgent, he said, and private. Asked could I see this diner gets the message, he'd be . . . uh . . . waitin' outside."

"What did you say, Harry?"

"Well, I said okay, I'd see what I could do, like that. He said I should get the message to you and he'd be waitin' outside to . . . uh . . . talk with you private."

"Didn't this sound a little funny to you, Harry? This outside stuff?"

"Yeah, sure. He also said if anything happened I should forget he was at the bar."

"So why'd you do it, Harry? Why'd you set me up?"

"He give me a hundred. Then he give me the message with your name on it. And I give it to Joe. He was your waiter. He took you the message. You know the rest."

"You're forgetting something, Harry. You didn't tell me this guy's name. Who is this guy?" Harry stood there, some droplets of sweat on his forehead reflecting the moonlight. "Harry, you want to go back into the trunk?"

"Look, just don't tell anyone I told you. Dillerman . . . he knows people around here. That's how he got on the cops."

"That's his name? Dillerman?"

"Dillerman. Jerry Dillerman. Used to be a cop. Got kicked off a few years back. Back then he used to come in like maybe a couple a times a month. Chew the rag. Then after he left the force, he moved away, left Murcer. That's it. I can't tell you any more."

"You're not lying to me, Harry, because if you are—"

"No, no. Can I go now? My wife, she expects me."

"Harry, that wasn't nice taking the hundred from Dillerman. What would your boss say if he knew about that?" Harry shook his head and swallowed. "Tomorrow, Harry, first thing, I want you to donate that hundred to charity. You got that?" Harry nodded. "And get a receipt. Send me the receipt." I told Harry Aunt Phyllis's address. "All right, Harry," I said finally, in the tone of a stern parent, "you can go home now."

I tossed him the keys and watched him jump into his car and start the engine. Then he rolled down the window. "You know, when it's dark and cramped like it was . . . in the back . . . I just can't stand it. At night I sleep with the lamp on. My wife thinks I'm crazy. That's why I acted like I did, so excited I mean."

"Sure, Harry, I know."

He gunned the motor and roared off onto the highway toward home. Finding Harry's weakness was part luck, but as an old girlfriend once told me, I have an unerring instinct for the jugular. I had a feeling it was an instinct that was going to prove useful more than once before I finally left Murcer.

At twenty minutes to two, I pulled the car up in front of Aunt Phyllis's house, killed the motor, and climbed out. Weatherly Street was dead quiet.

A minute later I closed the front door behind me, and by the light of the street lamp outside, I took off the blue ski jacket and hung it in the front closet. I moved into the dining room, switched on the lamp—and that was when I saw him.

He was sprawled inelegantly on his back, over one of Aunt Phyllis's old dining-room chairs. I swallowed hard, stared for a second, and made a very determined effort to remain calm. It wasn't easy. Finding a corpse in your home in the early hours of the morning can affect your composure, no matter who you are.

I walked back into the living room, took a couple of deep breaths, and returned for a closer look. It was a face that was somehow familiar.

His mouth was grotesquely open, his eyes were staring sightlessly, his right arm was hanging limply. I felt around for a pulse, not really expecting to find one. I didn't. Two enormous red stains plainly visible on his yellow shirt told the story: gunned down at close range. The last time I'd seen someone dead of bullet wounds was in Danang, after one of Charlie's early morning surprise visits. I always have the same feeling. I'm glad it's not me.

This person didn't look like your ordinary garden-variety housebreaker. Not only was he wearing a tie, he had on a tweedy-looking sports jacket with matching pants and a pair of polished leather shoes. A pair of expensive-looking glasses lay on the carpet nearby.

I asked myself what I should do next. Call the cops? Call Sylvia? Dispose of the body? I went into the kitchen closet, hauled out the brandy bottle, and poured myself a generous shot. My hands, I was surprised to notice, were steady—the result no doubt of a clear conscience. It occurred to me that I was at least entitled to some I.D. I found it in the breast pocket of the tweed jacket—a card stating that my visitor was one Sidney Hockley, private investigator. His driver's license told me he was forty-five years of age, that he was a resident of Louis Drive in South Murcer, and that he'd received a $15 fine for running a red light six months before. In addition, he carried four credit cards, a Blue Cross membership card, and a picture of himself with a woman and two children. The billfold contained eighty-five dollars. It was a funny way for a conventional citizen and family man to buy the farm—in the home of a stranger at two in the morning—but maybe it's wrong to think of investigators as conventional citizens. I replaced the wallet and went back into the living room.

It came to me then where I'd seen Sidney Hockley. He'd been the guy in the green Galaxy. I'd gotten a pretty good look when I'd pulled off the road and watched him drive by. I rather imagined that same car was parked not far away.

It was time, I decided, to be a good citizen and call the police. But before doing so I climbed back up into the attic and carefully stashed Aunt Phyllis's gun in the little tin box in the hole where I'd originally found it. It had served its purpose this evening. I made certain Aunt Phyllis's letter, the anonymous letter, and the newspaper clippings were there as well.

At 2:05 I made the call to the police. At 2:10 I was aware of a blue light winking and flashing outside the house, then the clump-clump of feet on the wooden porch. I opened the door before they had a chance to ring.

There were two of them, one about my age and the other a little younger. I led them back to the dining room and watched as they worked to hide their surprise.

"You alone here?" the older one asked me after they'd poked around and conferred for a few minutes.

I said I was.

He asked me if I'd touched anything. I piously said I hadn't.

Then we went through the questions. Who I was, where I came from, how I happened to be living in the house, when I found the body. The younger of the two then headed outside to the patrol car and radioed in the information. Then they told me to sit tight while they did some more poking around. I watched from the doorway.

"You know this guy?" the older one asked.

I told him no.

"You never saw him before?"

"Not that I know of," I said.

He looked at me skeptically. "You have no idea what he was doing in your house?"

"None at all."

"Homicide'll be here in a while. You can tell the rest of your story to them." He looked me over calculatingly, obviously wondering to what extent he could trust me not to either turn violent or run away.

They arrived by ones and twos—the technicians, the photographer, the ambulance people, the coroner. They all shared a common mood, irritation at being roused out of bed. I couldn't say I blamed them. I asked the patrolman if it would be all right to brew a pot of coffee. His eyes brightened at first, but then he shook his head.

Some time after three, Lieutenant Gronski made his appearance. He was of average height but solidly built, with wide shoulders, a thick neck, short but powerful arms—a physical type that people often associate with football players. His black hair was cut short and was graying. He had wide set blue eyes, a broad flat nose and a thin mouth. He was wearing a flannel shirt and a pair of jeans with paint specks on them.

He looked around, talked to the patrolmen, gave the technicians some directions, told the photographer to make sure he got the scene from certain angles. Only after twenty minutes did he get around to me.

"You're entitled to have a lawyer present if you want one," he said.

"No problem, Lieutenant."

He nodded and took out a little notebook. The first thing he wanted to talk about was me—who I was, where I lived, why I was in Murcer, how I happened to be living in this house. He seemed impressed when I told him what I did for a living.

"Computers, eh? They'll end up taking over the whole world one of these days."

"Only if we let them, Lieutenant."

"How are we going to stop them? Tell me that."

Then we went over how I happened to find the body. It was all very relaxed and polite. Mr. Ball and Lieutenant Gronski. We could have been two business acquaintances discussing local politics at the club. But that mood came to an end when he asked the one question for which I didn't have a ready answer.

"Where were you during the time you were away from the house?"

I said that I went out for a drive because I couldn't fall asleep.

"You were driving the whole time? Three hours?"

"That's right, Lieutenant."

"Did anybody see you?"

"No."

"You stop for gas anyplace?"

"No."

"Are you in the habit of taking late-night drives, Ball?"

"Now and then."

"How'd you get your face banged up?"

"Murcer's a rougher town than I remember it."

"We got our share of hard cases, that's for sure. Are you saying you were mugged?"

"Not exactly." I told him how someone had roughed me up in the restaurant parking lot.

"Now, why would someone want to do something like that?"

"I haven't the slightest idea, Lieutenant."

"Anything like that ever happen to you in New York?"

"Never."

Gronski flipped back over the pages of the notebook looking over the facts he had taken down. He double-checked the name and address of my firm. "I have to ask you to stick around in Murcer for a little bit," he said. "You don't leave town unless you clear it with me first. Savvy?"

I told him I did, and he went back to talk some more with one of the patrolmen. By this time the technicians were packing up, obviously anxious to get going, and the ambulance attendants were standing by with their stretcher, waiting for a signal from Gronski to stick the corpse in the body bag and carry it off. A uniformed policeman came walking down the stairs, motioned Gronski over, and showed him something.

After a short conference with the polliceman, Gronski came

walking back to me. Between thumb and forefinger he was holding a gun, an automatic.

"You recognize this?" he asked.

"I never saw it before," I said.

"Officer O'Donnell says he found it upstairs in the bedroom,
under the bed."

I don't know if at that moment I turned deathly pale or bright
red, but I'm sure I registered some outward sign of shock. I
fought against a sudden wave of dizziness. Until that moment, I
had been able to maintain a decent calm in dealing with the situation. All at once, with Gronski holding the gun and looking at
me through narrowed eyes, I no longer felt so self-confident.

"Well?" Gronski was waiting for an answer. There was a
knowing smirk at the corner of his mouth.

My throat had gone dry, and the best answer I could muster
was a shrug.

Gronski nodded, as though that was the response he had expected. Then he said something to the policeman and they both
trooped off up the stairs, presumably to check where the gun had
been.

While Gronski was upstairs Razzilli arrived.

He came in with a bang, throwing the door open and tramping
through the front of the house into the dining room. "Goddamn
it!" he said. And he said it in such a way that everyone there was
compelled to take notice.

Six feet tall, he had broad shoulders, and curly black hair. His
cheeks were mildly scarred from an ancient case of acne and he
needed a shave. He wore a pair of horn-rimmed glasses that he
kept shoving back up the bridge of his nose, and had on a gray
top coat that was at least five years old and that hung unbuttoned
from his square shoulders. He stood staring down at the body
and saying "Oh, hell" over and over. When he turned away, the
ambulance attendants began placing the remains of Sidney
Hockley on their stretcher.

When Gronski reappeared, Razzilli started talking with him—
excitedly and loud enough that I could pick up snatches of
the conversation. He was asking questions and arguing at the
same time. When Gronski showed him the gun, he looked at it
closely.

"Where?" he said loudly. "In the bedroom? In the goddamned

bedroom?" He followed that up with some more profanity. Finally, he came over to me.

"I'm Razzilli," he said. "And I sure as hell know who you are."

"That saves me the trouble of introducing myself."

"Save the wisecracks, mister. You're gonna need plenty of smart answers for the judge and jury."

Razzilli had his face six inches from mine, close enough to indicate that he'd had some heavily seasoned food for dinner. I decided to take a walk across the living room. He followed me. "You're gonna hear plenty from me in the next couple of weeks, Ball. Sid and me were partners. And don't think because I'm private it's gonna make any kind of difference. You kill a cop, you kill a cop, private or otherwise."

"I'll take your word for it."

Razzilli had his face in front of mine again, and again I tried to move away. "I'm talkin' to you. Don't think I don't swing a lot of weight in this city."

I nodded.

"I oughta take you apart with my bare hands."

I didn't move away this time. I looked at him blandly, expecting him to throw a punch, tensing myself to deflect it, and hit back if necessary. The entire place went silent. Gronski stepped between us.

"C'mon, Rich," he said. "You know better than that."

"The way I see it, he's the one who wasted Sid. There's no question in my mind. Then he stuck the gun under the bed."

"Easy, Rich. We know how you feel, but this ain't going to get us anywhere."

Razzilli looked again at me. "You're between a rock and a hard place, Ball. The only thing is you're too dumb to know it."

Gronski took Razzilli firmly by the upper arm and marched him across the room. They spoke for a while. Razzilli let out a squawk. "What? You're not even gonna lock up the sonofabitch? C'mon, Paul, for cryin'—"

"Who the hell is runnin' this investigation, Razzilli?"

"But you got the gun. You got enough—"

"Don't tell me what I got or don't got." Razzilli turned away and threw a kick at one of Aunt Phyllis's small tables. The leg crumpled causing the table to fall on its side. Gronski came walking back to me.

"Was that necessary?" I asked.

"Rich and Sid were partners. Together over ten years. I guess you can understand how he feels."

"What's the verdict, Lieutenant?" I said.

"We won't be takin' you down, Ball. We'll have some more questions for you. Tomorrow, the next day. You don't leave Murcer."

A few minutes later they were all gone—cops, lab men, medical men. The house was again completely silent. Outside, the first streaks of red were slashing the morning sky. It was going to be a nice day.

Somewhere in the distance someone turned over his automobile engine, an early riser on his way to work. I walked back into the dining room. If it weren't for blood stains and a chalk marking on the rug, I could have believed it had all been a bad dream.

5

I tried reading. I drank three or four cans of beer. I smoked a lot of cigarettes. I finally dozed off but woke up a short time later. The clock said 8:10. I lay in bed thinking. I knew why Gronski hadn't arrested me. He'd undoubtedly staked a man out to keep watch on the house. In the mind of a policeman, there is nothing that can be regarded as a surer sign of guilt than flight. Had I packed a bag and ducked out the back door, the police would have felt they had a *prima facie* case to charge me for the murder of Sid Hockley.

Sorry, fellas. Not this time. Just because Hockley had been tailing me around the city for a couple of days doesn't mean I got mad enough to shoot him. Talk tough to him, maybe. Possibly even take a poke at him. But shoot him full of lead? No way.

After I'd showered and breakfasted, I did some housework. I

was able to get the chalk off the rug, but the blood wasn't so easy. I found working on the table to be good therapy. I glued and clamped it together. It wasn't going to be like new, but it would be serviceable.

Sometime after 10:30 the telephone rang.

"Clint, are you all right?"

"Fine, Sylvia. Having a second cup of coffee and wishing you were here."

"Clint, there's a story in the newspaper about a murdered man. It says he was murdered at your home."

"Did they spell my name right?"

"It's true then?"

I asked Sylvia to read the story. It was an accurate enough account of my discovery of the body embellished by a couple of quotes from Gronski. I told Sylvia it was true.

"My God," she said.

"Sylvia, I need a favor."

"What?" Her voice was small, faint, almost inaudible.

"Sylvia, I have to talk with someone who knows this city well, someone who's been around a while and who knows city government from the inside. Do you have anyone like that on the *Telegram?*"

She was silent for a time. "We may have." Her voice was hesitant. "Maybe a reporter—"

"That would be fine. Arrange a meeting for me with this person, Sylvia. For as soon as possible."

"All right," she said. Her voice sounded hesitant, reluctant. "Give me a couple of hours."

"Sylvia, we'll have to cancel this evening," I said. I could hear her sigh of relief over the phone. I couldn't blame her for not wanting to involve herself with me at this point. Not that I didn't need moral support, all I could get, in fact. But if Sylvia wasn't up to delivering it, I couldn't blame her. I only hoped she'd be able to dig up someone to talk with me.

Sylvia wasn't in the office when I called back a couple of hours later, but a secretary informed me that I had an appointment that evening at 6:30 with a man named Russell Kemner in a saloon called Metzger's. Metzger's I knew. A long bar. Sawdust on the floor. Fans hanging from the ceiling. Turn-of-the-century fixtures. Metzger's was already a Murcer institution back when I was a boy.

When I arrived that evening the well-to-do types were already there, standing three deep at the bar and regaling one another with tales of financial and sexual triumphs. The bartender pointed out Russell Kemner, a big, stocky, gray-haired man sitting silently in one of the booths staring into a glass of bourbon. The bitterness that seems to overtake newspapermen over fifty years of age was written in his face. I could have picked him out from the other drinkers without asking.

"Sylvia said some nice things about you," he said after I had introduced myself and sat down.

"I'm the guy who found the murdered P.I. in my home."

Kemner pursed his lips but said nothing. He regarded me questioningly, looking for some sign that would indicate to him whether I was guilty or innocent. "I'm a newspaper reporter, not a lawyer," he said.

In the course of their work newspapermen gain access to all kinds of information that they can't print—sometimes because of lack of verifiable proof, sometimes because of the libel laws, most often because the information is damaging to some powerful individual. Approached correctly, they can be abundant sources of information.

"Probably even more than legal advice," I said, "I need information."

"What kind?"

"For starters, I'd like to find out about someone named Jerry Dillerman."

"Mr. Ball, there are quite a few people in Murcer who can tell you about Jerry Dillerman. I'm kind of sorry if you had a run-in with him."

I pointed to my face.

"I figured." Kemner emptied the last of the bourbon from his glass with a long swallow and made a sign to one of the waiters. "Yes, Jerry Dillerman is easy to talk about. 'J.D.' everyone always called him. Stirred up quite a fuss during his brief tenure as a policeman."

I nodded, and that was all the encouragement Kemner needed to go on with his story.

"He'd been in a number of scrapes from time to time, but as it had to happen sooner or later, he finally went too far. Seems he collared a youngster out on the Pike one evening. The kid was speeding, at least that's what J.D. maintained. But when he wanted to write the kid up, the youngster started causing trouble, cursing and yelling, and again if we can believe J.D., even took a poke at him. Of course there wasn't anything J.D. could do at that point to quiet the fellow down short of beating a little sense into him with that little hard object the police carry. After that, he radioed for help and J.D. and another policeman carted the fellow in, booked him, and had him locked up."

Kemner paused and thanked the waiter who arrived at that moment with another glass of bourbon. He sighed deeply, as though just talking about Dillerman was proving to be a painful experience.

"What happened then was, someone went to look in on this fellow some time the next morning and he was out like a light in his cell—in fact, he was in a coma. Still in it, from what I understand."

"What happened?"

"Well, the scuttlebutt was, J.D. administered a beating to the prisoner that morning. He got off duty at two o'clock, so it's possible he could have done it. Beat him up according to scientific principles known these days to every police department and law enforcement agency around the world."

I nodded, recalling some of the methods we had at our disposal in 'Nam when we needed information quickly.

"There are ways to subject a man or woman to physical pain without leaving a mark on the victim."

I said, "But maybe he overdid it. Pushed the guy beyond the point where it's possible to come back." Again I thought of 'Nam and some of the results achieved by my more zealous colleagues.

"Exactly."

"You say that was the scuttlebutt."

"Yes, and no one who knew J.D. at all had any difficulty believing it. But there was an official inquiry into the matter. The victim had parents, and they hired themselves a lawyer. The police department had to do something."

"They couldn't prove anything."

"Precisely. Anyone visiting the cellblock has to sign in, and of course there was no record of J.D. signing in. There was medical evidence of internal injuries, but no sure way of telling how they had been contracted. And J.D. had some kind of alibi. These facts were all in J.D.'s favor."

"What were the facts against him?"

"Mostly circumstantial, I'm afraid. J.D.'s previous reputation and the fact that both J.D. and the victim were seeing the same girl."

"So he was acquitted."

"Officially, yes. But the feeling was, there were people in the department who knew what had happened. And there was talk a deal had been reached, that someone paid off the kid's parents. Part of the deal may have been that J.D. resign from the force. That's what he did a month later."

We were both silent for a moment, then Kemner said, "Have you been in the service, Mr. Ball?"

I told him I had spent a year in Vietnam.

"Then you may understand how I feel about the Jerry Dillermans of the world. I don't like them. I served in the Second World War, in North Africa, later in Italy and Germany. Got out a colonel. One of the reasons I was fighting was to keep the J.D.s from taking things over. But now I feel those German storm troopers and S.S. men didn't have anything on the good old J.D.s we have here at home. Same mentality, no feelings, and a positive love of hurting other people."

"And at the same time a tremendous interest in keeping their boots shining and their brass gleaming."

"You seem to know the type," Kemner said.

"I've run across a few in my day," I said. "You mentioned some kind of payoff to the victim's parents. Any idea who might have come up with the money? Or why?"

"Negative to the first question. The only reason why I could think of, maybe someone wanted to use J.D. as muscle. Trot him out when necessary; otherwise I can't think of any reason for anyone going to bat for him."

"Suppose, just suppose, you had to make a guess whether either Peter van Beldin or Warren Korban had made the payoff. Which one would you be inclined to favor?"

"Off the record now."

"Of course."

"I'd have to go with Korban. It would fit in closer with his way of doing things. Some people in this city—some of them quite ruthless themselves—have found themselves in over their heads when they tangled with Korban. I don't see van Beldin doing something like that."

I was silent for a moment, wondering whether I hadn't been

too hasty in concluding that van Beldin had been behind my getting roughed up by Dillerman. On the other hand, why would Korban have wanted to do it? He hadn't appeared to even know who I was when I appeared at his office the day before.

"Where can I find Dillerman?" I asked.

"No idea. After he quit the force, he left Murcer."

"How does Peter van Beldin relate to Korban?"

"You say you grew up in this city, Mr. Ball, so you must know a good deal about the van Beldins. Old money, conservative, ran the town, more or less, for three generations. Didn't really do all that bad a job of it."

"What happened then?"

"I just think that times caught up with them. Murcer went through a period of enormous growth during the sixties. Newcomers to the city think and act differently than people a generation ago. The times demanded different business methods."

"Korban's way of doing things?"

"He's rough, direct—and he operates in a lot of gray areas. And he deals in things like bowling alleys, bars, truck leasing, and so forth. I wouldn't be surprised if those things brought in more than his real estate and building operations."

"Anything else?"

"Essentially each is committed to a different philosophy of urban growth. Korban wants to develop outlying areas north of the city, which coincidentally happens to be that part of Murcer where he has most of his holdings."

"And van Beldin?"

"Van Beldin is committed to revitalizing the inner city, which has deteriorated terribly in the last fifteen years. He's very pious about it all, of course, espouses all the trendy arguments, addresses environmental groups when he can—all that sort of thing."

"Does the van Beldin family still own most of the downtown area?"

"Of course. So it's difficult to believe that his motives are pure."

"Still, you'd think there would be enough for both of them."

"Is it possible to have more than one queen bee in a hive?" Kemner smiled wryly. "We human beings are so arrogant. We think we're so different from the rest of nature's creatures. In the long run, a city like this can only have one top dog, one boss.

That's why van Beldin was so anxious to run for governor. If he'd gotten to the statehouse, he almost certainly would have been able to tie a can on Korban's tail."

"Why did van Beldin pull out?"

"Good question. If I find out, you'll be able to read about it in the newspaper."

I then asked Kemner about the Murcer Police Department.

"Today the Murcer Police Department is a superior organization, far better than most other departments its size around the country."

"It wasn't always that way," I said.

"No, it wasn't. Go back thirty, forty years and you might be justified in saying it was one of the worst. Things have changed."

"Why?"

"Partly, I suppose, because they are able to recruit the right personnel."

I asked Kemner if he knew Gronski, the homicide man.

"Of course. Gronski's a good example of the new breed. Very professional, also very career-minded. I wouldn't be surprised, one day, to see him move out of Murcer and into a top job in Chicago or Los Angeles."

"I met Gronski last evening," I said.

Kemner raised his eyebrows. "I don't envy you your situation, but Gronski's a good man. And Karl Breyer, who did the job before him, was another. A fine, persevering cop—very orthodox and completely honest. In fact, he taught Gronski a good deal. Gronski grew up without a father. From what I understand he still looks to Breyer for advice on tough cases."

It was after eight when I decided that Russell Kemner had told me all that I could reasonably hope to learn.

"Good luck," he said as I got up to leave. I paid his check at the bar and left him the way I had found him—staring into a bourbon glass and dreaming of a job on one of the big papers in Chicago, LA, or New York.

My first impression on getting outside was that it had once again turned cold. I put my head down and started walking up toward Stockton, where I knew I could hail a cab. I had gone roughly thirty feet when I became aware of them—approaching from the rear, one to the right, one to the left. The one on the left took hold of my upper arm with a very strong hand.

"Someone wants to talk with you, Ball," he said.

"Maybe some other time—"

"Knock it off."

No question that they were professionals. By exerting pressure on my arms, they were able to move me in the direction of a big Buick standing at the curb. One of them shoved me roughly into the rear seat and clambered in after me. The other went around to the driver's side, climbed in and started the engine. We took off with a loud squeal of tires.

Neither of them said anything. All I could see of the driver was that he was wearing a baseball cap and a leather jacket. The one in the rear was more suitably dressed for the occasion, with a green tie and a brown suit. He had curly black hair and very pale skin, and was good looking in an innocuous sort of way. His expression was very earnest. The trip lasted less than five minutes. We pulled up sharply in front of a nondescript office building, definitely one of the city's less impressive structures. Although it wasn't even nine, the streets were already deserted, and I had the feeling these guys could have killed me on this lonely street and gotten away with it as easily as they might have in the middle of a desert. But it seemed my friends had something other than murder on their minds, something for which I was deeply thankful. They hustled me out of the Buick and up to the second floor of the building. We walked quickly down a corridor past a number of offices until we stood in front of a door marked H&R SECURITY SERVICES, S. HOCKLEY, R. RAZZILLI, PROPS.

"The boss wants to talk with you," the curly-haired one said, and led me into the inner office. It was surprisingly well furnished—law books lining one wall, drapes over the windows, some nice paintings on the other wall. Razzilli himself was seated behind a broad desk working on some papers by the light of a shaded desk lamp.

He looked up. "Did he give you any trouble, Olson?"

"Naw," the curly-haired guy said.

"Too bad," Razzilli said. "That would've given you a reason to tag him a coupla times. Get a little back for Sid. Is he packin'?"

Olson ran his hands quickly up and down my body.

"Nothin', Rich. Clean." Olson walked out of the office.

Razzilli motioned to me to sit down. "I didn't get a real good chance to talk with you last night, Ball," he said, "so I set up this little meeting, alone, just you and me. I hope it doesn't inconvenience you too much."

"I suppose we're on tape," I said.

Razzilli worked his lower lip back and forth. "Like I said, since I was upset last night about my partner's death, it wasn't the right moment to ask you the questions I want to ask you."

"Is there any reason I should answer them?"

"Any reason why you shouldn't? Except that you're guilty of killing Sid?"

"You're not the police, Razzilli. You're just grandstanding, trying to beat out the cops, and show how good you are at solving crimes. Make like a cop, maybe get some headlines, good for business."

"I'll tell you the kind of headlines I'm gonna make. 'Clinton Ball Dies In Electric Chair!' I'm gonna help nail you for the murder of my partner."

I put my hand in front of my mouth, as if I was stifling a yawn.

"All right, did you or did you not know Sidney Hockley was following you as part of a properly initiated investigation by a client of this agency?"

"I'll take the Fifth."

"Why not tell the truth, Ball, if you're innocent the way you say you are?"

"What difference does it make whether I knew it or not?"

"Before he was killed, Hockley wrote up his report. He followed you to the office of Warren Korban. He indicated he thought you knew he was tailing you."

"So I knew. Does that mean I shot the guy?"

"Stranger things have happened in this business."

"I wouldn't know."

"Would you care to say why you visited Warren Korban and what you discussed with him?"

"I would not."

"It figures. Korban's business ethics are questionable. You would be tied up with him." Razzilli adjusted his glasses and read his next question off a piece of paper. "Where were you during the time Hockley was shot, from approximately eleven P.M. to two A.M.?"

"I told the cops where I was. Out driving."

"Out driving, he says." Razzilli got up, came around his desk, and stood glaring down at me. "Maybe Gronski accepts a wise-ass answer like that. I don't."

I stood up and we were in approximately the position we had

been in the previous evening, Razzilli ready to swing, me defying him to try it.

"I ought to break your neck right here, Ball. And I would except a low-life like you isn't worth . . . even talking to. Why am I wasting my time? The cops will fix you." Razzilli walked away, flung himself down on his chair, and let out a long sigh.

"Can I go now?" I said.

"Get out of here, Ball!" He reached down and flicked a switch that I took to be that of the tape recorder. "Get out of my sight!"

"You're going at this all wrong, Razzilli," I said.

"I don't need your advice."

"You need somebody to talk some sense into you."

"Yeah, sure," he said in a low voice. Again he told me to beat it, but this time his voice was quiet, almost subdued.

I walked out to the outer office where Olson and his partner were standing, each with a beer can in his hand.

"Your boss says I can leave." They looked uncertain but didn't do anything. Despite the chill in the air, I walked all the way home.

It had been a long day, but there was still something I wanted to do. I changed into the ski jacket and drove out to Durango's, where I parked in the rear and entered through the door of the taproom. I found a seat at the bar and waited for Harry to come serve me. Harry greeted me warily, and after he brought me a glass of beer, I asked him whether he had made the contribution to charity. He said he had.

"That was a nice thing to do, Harry," I said. "Don't you feel good about it?"

"Huh? Oh yeah, sure." He still looked wary. "You're looking better, Mr. Ball. You don't look so much like you were uh . . . beat up, like you did."

"And I feel better too, Harry." Then I motioned him to lean over the bar, so we could speak without being overheard.

"Harry," I said, "the cops might come out here with some questions. If they do, just tell them some guy here beat me up, that's all. No names. You never saw the guy before."

Harry nodded.

"Something else, Harry. You can tell them I stopped in here for a beer the next evening and asked you some questions. But we don't want to mention what happened outside. Because that's our secret. Nobody's got to know about . . . your little sickness."

Harry nodded enthusiastically.

I continued to speak very gravely. "We both tell the same story, Harry, no problems. Check?"

"Check, Mr. Ball."

I left Harry the balance from a five as a tip and walked out of Durango's taproom.

6

I woke up the next day to the sound of early-morning traffic. I ate breakfast more out of habit than out of hunger. While I was shaving, I noticed that the abrasions on my face were largely healed. At the same time I saw a certain gauntness that hadn't been there before. The events of the week were making their effect noticeable.

Up until two nights ago, or until Hockley's murder, I'd had the feeling that things would work themselves out. Now I wasn't so sure. I was getting jumpy. And I had a constant feeling of butter-flies in the pit of my stomach.

The sound of the postman jamming mail into the doorslot snapped me out of the reverie. Among the junk mail and a utility bill was an envelope without a return address. Inside, I found a receipt from the local Red Cross chapter acknowledging an anonymous $100 contribution. At least I'd been able to make a believer out of Harry, if nobody else.

At a few minutes after nine I got the phone call I'd been expecting—a police sergeant asking if I could come by headquarters at two o'clock to make a statement. I suppose it was my waning confidence that things were going to right themselves after all that induced me to call Sonia Wegman. She sounded genuinely happy to hear from me.

"I read about what happened in the paper," she said.

"You can understand the seriousness of the situation then." I told her about the call from the police. "I thought it might be wise to have a lawyer along."

"Of course. I'll be happy to accompany you." We agreed to meet in front of the Murcer Justice Building at ten minutes before two.

The building had been given a face-lifting and had been enlarged in size some time in the recent past. I assumed it was handling more business than it had previously. After reporting to a bored-looking desk sergeant, we were directed up a flight of well-worn steps to the second floor. We were met there by a detective, who guided us down a long corridor and into an antiseptic-looking room lit by fluorescent lights and furnished with a steel desk and some chairs. I couldn't help noticing the window had bars. In the corner of the room was a small sink, and I had visions of detectives using it to wipe blood from their hands after difficult interrogations. Minutes later Lieutenant Gronski entered the room, accompanied by a detective whose name I didn't catch.

After some very brief preliminaries, Gronski put a tape recorder on the desk and announced, "Subject: Investigation of murder of Sidney Hockley. Interrogation of Clinton Ball." He then gave the date, time of day, and noted the names of those present.

"You do know you have the right to remain silent, Mr. Ball," Gronski said.

Immediately I was glad of the fact I had asked Sonia to accompany me.

"Gentlemen," she said, "I'd like to point out that Mr. Ball has responded to your request to appear at police headquarterrs in order to make a statement because he wants to do all he can to aid this investigation and help apprehend the murderer of Sidney Hockley. Mr. Ball intends to answer all questions truthfully and completely." She then nodded to Gronski to begin the questioning.

After establishing my identity, age, place of birth, address and occupation, Gronski asked about the purpose of my visit to Murcer.

"I came here to close out the affairs of my aunt, Phyllis Hailley, who died last week."

"And during your stay in Murcer you have been staying at your deceased aunt's home. Is that correct?"

I said it was.

"Would you kindly state how you spent the day before yesterday."

I then went through the account of my ride into the country on the Murcer Pike, my visit to Korban, and my return home about five o'clock.

"Did you during this time, Mr. Ball, receive the impression that someone was . . . ah . . . observing you?"

Just then the door opened. Karl Breyer entered, made a brief nod to Gronski, and took a seat in the corner of the room.

"Yes," I said, "while driving on the Murcer Pike I became aware of a green car."

"What was your feeling about this?"

Sonia interrupted. "I don't feel that my client's feelings are especially pertinent."

"Well, Counselor, since the man following your client was the man found shot in your client's home, it might—"

"It might help to convict him?"

"I don't mind answering the question," I said. Sonia shrugged and I continued. "I was mildly annoyed by the intrusion in my personal life, but since I have nothing to hide from the law or from anyone else—"

Gronski cut me short with a wave of his hand. I glanced at Sonia, who responded with a quick nod, then at Breyer who, despite an impassive expression, seemed mildly amused.

Gronski picked up the questioning again, and for the next five minutes we went over the same ground we had covered the night of the murder. Finally, he asked where I had been between the hours of 11 P.M. and 2 A.M. on the evening Hockley was killed.

"During that time I was driving my car. I did, however, stop in at Durango's restaurant where I had a couple of glasses of beer."

Gronski looked surprised. He cleared his throat. "Will anyone there remember you?"

"I spoke with the bartender. He should remember seeing me. I asked him about the man who had roughed me up the previous evening."

Breyer nodded. "That should be easy enough to check."

Gronski looked disappointed. "Was the bartender able to help you?" His tone was hostile.

"No. He said he'd never seen him before."

Breyer motioned with his pipe. "What did you do afterwards, Clint? After you left the restaurant." Breyer's tone conveyed the impression he was trying to discover the facts, not trying to railroad me. Sonia must have picked it up as well, because when I glanced at her she nodded, an indication I should answer the question.

"I drove around a bit. I arrived home about one-thirty, quarter-to-two."

Breyer seemed satisfied, but Gronski's eyes flashed with hostility, as though he felt I was trying to make a fool out of him. Perhaps nailing the murderer was turning out to be more difficult than he had imagined. "Have you ever owned a weapon?" he said after a short but significant pause.

I said I hadn't.

"I'll ask you to step forward and look at this weapon." Gronski produced the automatic. "This weapon, a nine millimeter automatic, was found on the night of the murder in your home. Under the bed in the bedroom, to be precise. Do you recognize it?"

I said I didn't.

"Conclude interrogation," Gronski said. "That's it, Mr. Ball. You can leave, but what I said the other evening still holds. You'll have to remain in Murcer until further notice. After we have your statement typed, we'll want your signature."

"Wait outside a moment, Clint," Sonia said.

I left the room and Sonia emerged a few minutes later. I asked her if she felt like a drink, and she said yes. We left the Justice Building and found a small cocktail lounge in the next block. We both ordered Scotch and water.

"I don't suppose there's all that much keeping me out of jail," I said.

Sonia looked grave. "I imagine Gronski feels he should have more evidence before presenting the case to the D.A."

"How much more does he need? He's even got the murder weapon."

"Yes, but he can't prove you owned or ever possessed it. Anyone could have thrown it under the bed." Sonia's brown eyes looked out at me sympathetically from beneath hooded lids. The dull light of the lounge brought out the planes of her long face. It was a face not so much beautiful as unusual. I found it had a certain fascination. I enjoyed just looking at her.

"You haven't even asked me whether I'm guilty or not," I said. "Shouldn't you know that as my lawyer?"

"I don't have to ask," Sonia said.

"Is that very professional?"

"Of course not."

"Nevertheless, since I'd like you to represent me, I think I should tell you the entire story from the beginning—"

I was stopped in mid-sentence by the appearance of Karl Breyer, who at that moment entered through the front door of the lounge. He ordered a drink at the bar, took a swallow, looked around, and saw us. He picked up his glass and ambled over. I motioned to him to sit down.

We exchanged small talk for a few minutes, then Breyer said, "You can't blame Gronski for being upset. He's got a lot of people looking over his shoulder on this one."

"How's that?" Sonia asked.

"Hockley wasn't exactly a policeman, but as a private investigator he was close to being one, and people—"

"Murder is murder," Sonia said. "I suppose when you said he had a lot of people looking over his shoulder, you were including yourself."

"Of course. I worked homicide here in Murcer for over thirty years, and I still maintain an interest in what's happening. I have to admit this case fascinates me."

"Why?" I said.

"It doesn't add up. A guy like you, Ball, some kind of computer engineer, clean record. Gronski's gone over your background with a fine tooth comb, he can't find anything. No reason why you would kill Hockley."

"I didn't kill him."

"I don't think you did either. Still, Gronski can't figure you."

"What's to figure?"

"You getting beat up out at that restaurant, for one thing. Why did Hockley and Razzilli make you the subject of an investigation? Why did you come to me with those questions about the murdered racketeer? Stuff like that. You're too secretive."

"Did you ever look up that file?" I asked.

"As a matter of fact, yes. But there wasn't much to find."

Breyer started fussing with his pipe, putting in tobacco, lighting up. "It was one of those murders, motiveless, hard to figure." He looked at Sonia uncertainly. "I'll tell you about it another time."

I nodded.

"But I guess you've got more important things on your mind than that stuff you were asking me about last week."

"I guess I do," I said. I stubbed out the second cigarette I'd had since entering the lounge. Or was it the third?

"You know," Breyer said, "there's a lot of homicide men who would have you inside. You should be glad Gronski's running this case."

"My client wants nothing more than fair treatment," Sonia said.

"You did the right thing telling Gronski where you were at the time of the murder. Why didn't you tell him that on Tuesday? You'd've saved yourself some trouble."

I shrugged. "Natural reticence, I guess."

"You're still not saying why someone wanted to knock you around. There must've been a reason."

"I can't tell the police what I don't know myself." I couldn't keep a trace of irritation out of my voice.

Breyer waved away the smoke with his pipe. Then he stood up to go. "If I can be of any help along the way, don't hesitate to call me." Before leaving the lounge, he turned and gave us a final wave.

"He may be able to help," Sonia said. "He's still an important man around police headquarters."

"From what I understand," I said, "he's some kind of father figure to Gronski." I lit another cigarette. "The question now is, what do I do next? Should I just sit around and wait for Gronski to prove me innocent?"

"Knowing you," Sonia said, "you're going to do something."

"In leadership school in the army, they used to tell us that when the roof is falling in and you have no idea what to do, always do something. You probably won't make things worse than they already are."

Sonia smiled. It was a reassuring smile, full of sympathy and humor. Unaccountably, I felt better than I had at any time since finding Hockley's body.

We left the lounge and I accompanied Sonia back to her office.

It occurred to me there might be some sense in talking again to Peter van Beldin. While Sonia checked out some things with her secretary, I used her phone to put through a call to van Beldin's office. Because of the hostile reception I'd gotten the last time, I didn't identify myself right away.

"Oh, is this Mr. McDowd?" his secretary asked, obviously confusing me with someone else.

"I'd like—"

"I'm sorry, Mr. McDowd. I know Mr. van Beldin had you down for four o'clock, but he had to cancel all his appointments for today."

"Did he say when he might be back?"

"All I know is that Mr. van Beldin has been at the hospital all afternoon. Something to do with his wife. I can't tell you any more—"

"Thank you," I said and hung up. I then made another call, this one to Murcer General Hospital. The nurse on the admission desk said Mrs. van Beldin had made a suicide attempt, that she was in Intensive Care, that her condition was critical. . . .

I decided it might be a good time to talk with van Beldin. I said a quick good-bye to Sonia. Five minutes later I was in a cab on the way to the hospital.

A sign on the wall in the main lobby indicated that visiting hours were 10–noon and 6–8 P.M., but I entered the place as though I'd worked there all my life, and no one questioned me. On the second floor I asked an inoffensive-looking aide where I could find Intensive Care. She turned out to be not so inoffensive, after all, and told me to inquire downstairs at the main desk. I told her I already had but had gotten lost.

"They said Mrs. van Beldin—"

"Oh, you're looking for Mrs. van Beldin." It hadn't taken me long to discover that merely to mention the van Beldin name brought special favors. "She's down in the west wing. Straight ahead as far as you can go and left. ICU. You'll see it marked."

I thanked her and followed directions. At the ICU station I told the head nurse my name and that I was looking for Mr. van Beldin and that it was urgent. Without looking up, she told me Mr. van Beldin was in conference with Dr. Schwartz, Room 212. I found Room 212 and waited outside.

Less than five minutes later a haggard-looking Peter van

Beldin emerged from Room 212. He looked surprised when he saw me although I had the impression he was unable to place me at first.

"How is she?" I said.

"What do you care? You don't even know my wife. You're the cause—"

The blow was a roundhouse right, one of those wild swings third-grade kids throw back and forth at one another in the schoolyard while the teacher's back is turned. I had no trouble stepping inside it, with the result that van Beldin's forearm slammed against the side of my neck. I grabbed his left wrist with both hands and twisted around and up. I went just far enough, so that he let out a quick yelp of pain. Then I let him go. I looked both ways along the corridor. No one had noticed.

"I said: How's your wife?"

Van Beldin glanced at me dully, rubbing his wrist. "She's in a coma. They won't know how she is until they can determine how much she took. Pills and booze. That damn Valium. Now let me pass, Ball." He made an attempt to walk around me, but I got myself in front of him.

"Tell me what happened, van Beldin."

He ran his fingers through his damp hair, then sighed. "I got home for lunch a little after twelve, the usual time. No sign of her. Looked all over. Finally found her in the bedroom. I thought she was sleeping at first, just napping, but then I saw the pill bottles and an empty Scotch bottle. I screamed at her. Nothing. No response. Gave her mouth-to-mouth, kept her breathing. The maid called the ambulance."

"Is that all?"

"For crying out loud, Ball, isn't that enough? Doctor says her condition's grave, but her air passages are open, and that's supposed to be a good sign. I can't tell you any more than that."

Just then the head nurse from the station came bustling up to us. Concern and sympathy for the town's leading citizen were written all over her face. "If you care to, Mr. van Beldin, you can use the hospital cafeteria. I know you've had a wearing day."

I answered for van Beldin. "Thank you, Mrs. Stephens," I said, reading her name off the tag on her uniform. "How do we get there?"

She gave us directions—"down the corridor to the elevator,

and the elevator down to the basement. Today they have the pea soup. Very good." She exuded cheerfulness. Again I thanked her, took van Beldin firmly by the upper arm, and led him down the corridor.

"Gotta get home," van Beldin said. His voice was empty, without emotion.

"I'll see you get home," I said. "First we want to clear up a few things."

"I'm not in the mood."

"You'll feel better with something in your stomach." He didn't say anything more. He was really shot, and who could blame him? There must be few things worse than hearing your wife has just tried to commit suicide.

I sat van Beldin down at a table in the hospital cafeteria and returned a few minutes later with two large bowls of pea soup. Strangely, van Beldin did look better after he'd had the soup. I picked up a couple of cups of coffee and offered him a cigarette. He took it eagerly. Having people wait on him was something he accepted unthinkingly. Being rich is never having to say thank you.

"All right, Ball, what the hell do you want to see me about?" He'd accepted my offer of a light, now he was attempting to reassert himself. Dynamic businessman once again regains control of situation.

I decided to speak to him in the manner of a schoolmaster addressing a slow pupil. "First question: Why did you read the riot act to me in your office?"

"Oh hell, Ball, you know the reason—"

"I told you then I didn't know the reason, and I still don't. When you tell me, then I'll know."

"Okay, I'll spell it out. Why shouldn't I? How did you expect me to react? You go to Korban with information about my wife, information that he uses to keep me from running for office. He knows that if I ever made it to the statehouse he'd sure as hell have to clean up that act—"

"What kind of information do you think I relayed to Korban, van Beldin?"

Van Beldin was silent. He looked me in the eye, pursed his lips. Then he said it. Reluctantly. "Information to the effect that my wife once . . . committed a murder." He stubbed out the last of his cigarette in the ashtray and shoved back his chair as though he wanted to leave.

"Not yet. Give me the rest of it."

He started fumbling around in his pockets for another cigarette. I gave him another one of mine, but I let him light it himself this time. Finally, he said, "Over twenty-five years ago my wife killed some guy, a petty gangster, someone named Hauck. As you already know, she was helped by your aunt . . . Phyllis Hailley. I happen to know you know all about it."

I tried not to let any surprise show. "What makes you think I know, and what makes you think I passed information on to Korban?"

"Hell, I know you know, Ball. Sid Hockley reported it. Said he'd seen the gun and some newspaper clippings describing the murder in your home. You had to know."

So that was it. Hockley had been the one who had entered the house on the afternoon after the funeral.

"Razzilli's been talking to the cops," I said.

"But not about that. Do you think I want the world to know my wife's a murderer? Use your head, Ball."

"So Hockley was working for you."

"Damn straight! And for all I know you shot him!"

"Even the police aren't sure about that."

"That's not what I hear.

"No? What do you hear?"

"From what I understand, the only reason you're not already in jail and charged is because Karl Breyer put in a good word for you with the homicide man—"

"Gronski?"

"Yes."

I made a mental note to say thank you to Breyer when I saw him again. "I suppose you're getting regular reports from Razzilli," I said.

"Razzilli's a good man. So was Hockley. They've done a lot of work for me over the years. Trustworthy and discreet."

"What've they ever been able to dig up on Korban?"

"Not enough," van Beldin said glumly.

"I still don't see why you jump to conclusions. Why assume I was the one who passed on the information about your wife to Korban?"

"Who the hell else, Ball? This murder takes place—how long ago? twenty-seven, twenty-eight years?—and suddenly you come back to town and Korban knows all at once. Besides, who else knew about it except you?"

I saw how van Beldin had it figured. From his perspective, the pieces fit. The only catch was, I hadn't been the one.

"Were you the one who turned Dillerman loose on me?" I asked.

"Dillerman? Who's Dillerman? Never heard of him."

"Jerry Dillerman. He worked me over at Durango's Steak House last week." I pointed to my face.

"I don't know anything about that, Ball."

"Listen, van Beldin. It wasn't me who gave Korban the information about your wife. I don't know who it was, but it wasn't me. You understand me?"

He looked at me with glazed eyes. I couldn't be sure how much attention he was paying to me or to what extent I was getting through to him. I had the feeling his mind was partly upstairs, with his wife. Or maybe it was that things had started moving too fast for him. Prep school, the university, the protective environment of the small city had shielded van Beldin from reality for a long time. Nothing in his well-ordered background had prepared him for people like Korban or for a suicide attempt by his wife. It was just as well that he wouldn't be going to the statehouse. The country has enough of his kind holding public office already.

"One thing more I want to know," I said. "Why did your wife and my aunt kill this guy Hauck? It sounds crazy."

"Christ, Ball, I only got the story out of Helen a few days ago. All I learned was what I could pry out of her. You don't think she told me the goddamn story before she married me, do you?"

"All right, all right." A couple of nurses at the next table were beginning to stare at us curiously. "What were you able to find out?"

"She said . . . I can hardly remember. She was crying, all upset." Van Beldin was torn between two emotions: pity for himself and sympathy for his wife. She'd complicated things for him, but she'd obviously suffered herself. I could clearly see the reasons why Helen van Beldin had attempted suicide. People have knocked themselves off for less compelling reasons.

"Was there anything else she said? Think, it's important, van Beldin."

"Yeah, she said it had to do with the doctor. They had to protect the doctor."

"Which doctor?"

"Hell, I suppose it was Lakeman, Dr. Lakeman. She was his nurse at the time, and she later married him."

Dr. Lakeman. A name out of the distant past, a name that rang a faint bell. He'd been a general practitioner in Murcer back when I was small. I remembered Aunt Phyllis bringing me into his office. A massive man with a flushed face and a trim mustache. A man with large hands but with the gentle touch of a young girl. A man who laughed readily and inspired confidence that you'd soon be healthy. He'd been Murcer's best-known physician. Then I recalled having seen his name in the newspaper clippings on Mrs. van Beldin.

"She admired the guy. Hell, I guess she loved him. She married him when he was almost sixty."

"Then what?"

"He died. Left Helen a young widow. My first wife and I had split. I met Helen at a charity affair, something for the orphanage. We got married." Van Beldin shrugged his shoulders and ran his fingers through his hair. "She was referring to old Lakeman, all right. She was crazy about the guy. Used to talk about him by the hour. I got sick of hearing about him, to be honest."

I decided to call it a day. Van Beldin looked beat, emotionally drained, but I don't suppose I looked any better. He said he was going back upstairs to see how his wife was. We parted at the elevator, neither of us bothering to say good-bye.

It took me nearly half an hour to locate a cab and make it back to the house. I was looking forward to some peace and quiet, but I suppose I should have known better.

There were three of them—Gronski, the detective who had been at the interrogation, and a third guy who at that moment came sauntering around from the back of the house. Gronski and the other man were half standing, half sitting on the porch railing. Gronski gave a friendly wave as I climbed the porch steps. I said hello.

"We said we'd be in touch," Gronski said pleasantly.

I shoved open the front door and the three detectives trooped into the house behind me. Gronski then produced a number of sheets of paper. One was a transcript of the statement I'd made earlier that day at headquarters.

"First off, we need your signature on this. Second, Judge McIntyre was kind enough to agree that there was probable cause enough to permit us to search your premises. It's a warrant."

"I thought you fellows did a pretty good job of it the other night." I noticed that the two detectives were already started. One was standing on a chair, peering into the shelf of the dining room closet. The other had disappeared upstairs. Gronski threw himself down on the big chair in the living room. I watched him as he took out a pipe and began filling it with tobacco from a pouch.

"Calms the nerves," Gronski said after getting it lit. "A pipe helps a man to think clearly. It's one of the things I learned from Karl Breyer back when he was still working homicide. Of course I learned a lot from him."

"Like what?" I sat down opposite Gronski on the couch.

"Karl was the best homicide detective this city ever had. Very capable, very effective. Working under him was the best training I could have had to break into this job."

I could see Gronski wanted to talk, so I didn't try to interrupt him.

"What puzzles me, Ball, is how a fellow like you—law-abiding, quiet, educated—how a fellow like you ever got himself into such a tangle. We ran a check on you, and everything you told us checks out."

"You sound surprised."

"Maybe I am, a little." Gronski sighed, paused, exhaled smoke. "Nice job. Even got yourself a bank account. It doesn't add up."

"I'm just lucky, I guess."

Gronski's eyes flashed. "Don't let's have any of that." He paused again. "You know what I think," he said at last. "I think you're not telling us the whole story."

"Care for something to drink, Lieutenant? A beer maybe?"

Gronski scowled. "No thank you."

I got up, went into the kitchen, and came back with a can of beer. Gronski looked at me, sneering.

"You've got your pipe, and I've got my can of beer, Lieutenant. It helps me to think."

"There's a line between self-confidence and arrogance, Ball. If I were you, I'd try my best to find out who my friends are. You may be needing them—real soon."

It was a perceptive remark. Finding out who my friends were was a top priority. But even more important was finding out who my enemies were—particularly the individual who had shot Hockley and tossed the gun under the bed.

I took a swallow of beer. I was aware of one of the detectives opening and closing drawers in the bureau upstairs. I was glad Aunt Phyllis had the foresight to make sure people wouldn't find things she didn't want them to find.

"Now, you say that the only reason you're here in Murcer is to wind up your aunt's affairs, sell the house, probate the will, that sort of thing."

"That's correct, Lieutenant."

"And then you're thinking of pulling out, going back to where you came from."

"Makes sense, doesn't it?"

"And when did you say you arrived in Murcer?"

"I got here a week ago. By the time I got here my aunt, unfortunately, had already slipped into a coma. She died two days later."

"Did she leave any valuables around, or any large sums of money that might attract outside interest?"

I had to hand it to Gronski. He was getting warm. I supposed it might only be a matter of time until he found out Aunt Phyllis's secret. But he wasn't going to find out from me. I told him I didn't know of any money or valuables.

"The question is, what was Sid Hockley doing in this house anyway? Was he searching for something?"

"Beats me, Lieutenant. Have you tried asking Razzilli?"

"He's clammed up too." We were both silent for a couple of minutes. "Then the other problem," Gronski said finally.

"What's that?"

"How come you wouldn't tell us right away that you'd been out to Durango's the evening of the murder? How come you gave us that song and dance about driving around for three hours?"

"I guess I wanted to play down what happened out there."

"The bartender says he remembers you coming in, having a couple of beers, asking about the guy who slugged you." Gronsksi stood up. "But I have a feeling we'll catch you out one of these days, my friend. I have that feeling."

It took a while, but Gronski's detectives finally completed their search. It would have required a much more thorough combing of the house to find the gun and the newspaper clippings Aunt Phyllis had left behind. One of her qualities had always been thoroughness.

Gronski's remark about discovering who my friends were started me thinking. I wondered who I could truly trust. I could see that Gronski was eager to build his case and that, in the absence of a better suspect, he would very likely charge me. If what van Beldin said was true, it was only the restraining influence of Karl Breyer that was standing between me and the Murcer jail. I supposed I couldn't really blame Gronski. He was just doing his job.

I ran down the list of people I knew.

Sonia was supportive, but distant, and at times difficult to communicate with. Sylvia was more open, but she had become wary when she thought I might be involved with the murder of Hockley. Breyer, the former policeman, was shrewd but was probably trusting to instinct more than anything else when he'd advised Gronski against locking me up. Razzilli was obsessed with finding his partner's murderer. Van Beldin was hiding at least one family skeleton and who could say how many more. Korban was plainly someone who would do anything for money. . . .

I was nearly through my third can of beer and still deep in thought when the telephone began to ring. I hoped it would be Sylvia. I tried to keep the excitement out of my voice as I picked up the receiver and said hello.

It was Sonia.

"I remembered what you said about not liking to cook, and I picked up an extra-large steak this evening at the supermarket and . . ."

Even with all the talk of a new morality, women have difficulty asking men for a date.

". . . and I was wondering . . . I suppose you're busy this evening, but I thought I'd ask anyway. Oh hell, Clint! Do you want to come over for supper, yes or no?"

"Yes," I said. I said it quickly, without thinking. I knew I didn't want to spend the evening alone.

The steak dinner was good. The impression that I received of Sonia over the course of the evening was that she was an uncomplicated woman, an unusual quality to find in a woman who had studied law. Or was I being naïve? As Sonia brewed coffee, I wondered to what extent she was satisfied with her life and her career. I also wondered about why I found Sonia so intimidating. She was formidable in a way Sylvia was not. I had involved myself with Sylvia almost without giving the matter a second's thought. But such a thing was impossible where Sonia was concerned. There was, despite her genteel, soft-spoken manner, something about her that forced me to take her very seriously. And this quality made me uneasy.

When she had returned, I commented to Sonia on the fact that I found her apartment so comfortable.

"I've lived here for a year and a half, ever since Dad died. I was reluctant to sell his house at the time. Now I'm glad I did."

"I still haven't gotten around to listing my aunt's home," I said.

"I suppose it holds memories for you."

"But not really many happy ones. Living in that house with my aunt was never really very . . . satisfactory."

"Growing up without parents is difficult."

"Yes, but it was more than that. . . . My aunt was a fine woman, but her attitude was . . . strange."

"In what way?"

"One thing that always bothered me was the fact she would never mention my father, or permit me to."

"Why not?"

"I suppose she just didn't care for him. I imagine she thought her sister, my mother, threw herself away on him. Once she told me my father never took proper care of me."

"What did you think?"

"I had no complaints. Of course I wasn't very old at the time."

"How well do you remember your father?"

"Not really well, although some incidents stand out. My impression is he cared for me a great deal." I felt myself hesitate. "But he was scary when he got mad."

"In what way?"

"I recall once he gave me a present of a small toy automobile. But in taking the present out of the wrapping, I dropped it and broke it. He slapped me violently. I cried of course. A half hour later he took me to the toy store and bought me a new auto and an ice cream to boot."

"What happened to your father?"

"He was beaten to death one evening in Murcer. Probably the result of some kind of robbery. Or perhaps he'd gotten someone very mad at him. His body was found in an alley in the city. The police never discovered who did it."

"How awful."

"I was too young to feel the full impact. And I was fortunate. My aunt immediately took me in."

"Did you like her?"

"She wasn't a warm person. She always called me 'Clinton,' never anything but 'Clinton.' 'Clinton, do this, Clinton do that.'"

"She sounds old-fashioned."

"It wasn't the best relationship."

"Maybe you're being too hard on yourself."

"I had a need to defy her. One winter, when she specifically told me to stay off the ice on the river, I made it a point to go down and play on the ice. I fell through. I was lucky. A couple of fishermen got me out in time. A few more minutes and I would have frozen."

There were other things I wanted to say. I wanted to tell Sonia about the dream, the recurring nightmare that always ended with me being beaten by a person whose face I never could clearly see, the nightmare that always ended with a sensation of falling. . . . With an effort of the will I cut myself short. "I don't know why I told you all that."

"There is something I would very much like you to tell me," Sonia said. "What did Karl Breyer mean when he said you'd gone to see him shortly after coming to Murcer?"

Earlier in the evening I had given Sonia a run-down of everything that had happened to me, only omitting to tell her about Aunt Phyllis's letter and the murder of Joey Hauck. But, like Gronski, Sonia had sensed that the pieces did not fit together.

"That was a private matter," I said. "It had absolutely nothing to do with the murder of Hockley."

But even as I said the words I knew they weren't true. The fact that van Beldin had assigned Hockley and Razzilli to shadow me because of the guilty knowledge shared by his wife and my aunt was an indication that everything had some kind of connection. It was probably unfair to Sonia not to tell her more, but I still wanted to preserve my aunt's confidence if I could.

While Sonia was in the kitchen reheating the coffee, it suddenly occurred to me how I might be able to shake up certain individuals around the city, one in particular. I suppose I was smiling my sinister smile as Sonia reentered the room because, when I looked up, she was standing there with the coffee pot staring at me, much as the waitress in the luncheonette had stared at me.

"Clint!"

"Excuse me, Sonia, I was thinking of something."

She shook her head. "This mess is bound to clear up in time," she said. "Try not to let it bother you."

"I don't think it will clear up by itself. I think I have to help clear it up."

Sonia sat back down on the sofa. As she did so, our thighs touched. It was momentary, casual touching, yet I felt there was a design to it. I acted upon an impulse. It wasn't much of a kiss, probably acceptable even to the television censors. We were both seated upright on the sofa and only our lips touched. There was no grappling, no shifting of positions, no bodies pressed hard against one another. But the kiss had an urgency to it nevertheless.

But it was an urgency I chose to ignore. I didn't want a woman, I wanted Sylvia. I stood up. Sonia looked at me in surprise.

"We don't want to jeopardize the lawyer-client relationship," I said.

Sonia winced, then smiled.

"Bad joke," I said.

"You've cracked worse," she said, and we were back on the friendly but distant terms that had characterized our association from the beginning.

I drank the coffee and turned down the offer of a drink. We

made some polite conversation and then, pleading fatigue, I left. I rode home with thoughts of Sylvia on my mind and the taste of Sonia's lips on my mouth.

7

The fact was I did want to make an early start the next day. I figured I knew Razzilli's type—a self-made man with his own business. He would probably be an early riser. I set the alarm for seven, and at exactly 7:45 I parked the Chevette on the street opposite his office and waited. I turned on the radio and listened to as much of the Top Forty as I could stand before turning it off. At 8:10 Razzilli, dressed in the same dirty white raincoat, turned into a cafeteria two doors away from the entrance to his office building, and three minutes later came out carrying a small brown paper bag, which he held gingerly with his hand underneath. Hot stuff.

I gave him two minutes to get upstairs and take his coat off. Then I followed him in.

There was no one in the outer office, so I barged right into the inner sanctum. I figured it wouldn't hurt any to surprise him. I was right. He had his teeth into a french cruller, and when he saw me, he started sputtering.

He took the cruller out of his mouth and wiped his lips with the paper napkin. I plunked down in the chair facing his desk and said good morning.

"Make yourself at home." There was a look on Razzilli's face suggesting he felt sick to his stomach. It was hard to say whether it was contrived or genuine. I had the feeling he turned it on at will for unwelcome visitors—for people like me, in other words.

"I'll let you finish your breakfast," I said.

"I've got a lot of patience, Ball. But it doesn't extend to the man who murdered my partner. Get out of here."

"Isn't it time you stopped acting like the injured party, Razzilli? Isn't it time you started acting grown-up?"

"Who's talking about acting grown-up? I spent last night with Sid's wife and two kids tryin' to cheer them up, helpin' to straighten things out. I come into work the next day and the first person I see is you. Oh brother!"

I didn't figure trading insults with Razzilli was going to get either of us anywhere. So I got right to the point.

"I had a talk with van Beldin yesterday."

"So what did he tell you? To get lost?"

"Did you know van Beldin's wife had a hand in killing a man twenty-eight years ago?"

Razzilli had his container of coffee at his lips when he put it back down again. "Did van Beldin tell you that?"

"That's not all he told me." I took out a cigarette from a crumpled package in my jacket pocket. I didn't bother to offer Razzilli one. I knew he wouldn't take it. Razzilli gazed at me speculatively, not saying anything. After I got the cigarette lit, I said, "Somehow Korban got hold of this information and used it to keep van Beldin from entering the race for governor."

"If van Beldin told you all that, he must be losing his mind." Razzilli lifted the coffee to his lips and again set it down without drinking. "Why was he talking to you?"

"You should be able to figure that out. Van Beldin told me because he knows that when his wife committed the murder she wasn't acting alone. My aunt—Phyllis Hailley, my late aunt—was involved. One or both of them fired the shots that killed Joey Hauck. Why they did it still isn't clear. If Mrs. van Beldin doesn't pull through, we may never know."

"Fine, Ball. So you got van Beldin to open up to you about his private affairs, admit that there's a skeleton in the family closet. What do you want, a medal?"

"Van Beldin called me in to see him one week after I arrived in Murcer. He was so mad he could hardly see straight. He wouldn't tell me what the problem was, only that he was going to get back at me for what I'd done to him. He thought that somehow I'd found out about his wife through my aunt's involvement and that I'd passed the information on to Korban."

"Didn't you?"

"No."

"The hell you didn't." He picked up the cardboard cup, took a swallow, made a sour face. "Hockley saw newspaper clippings describing the murder and the gun—"

"I was reading that material for the first time. I didn't pass information on to Korban."

"That's not the way we figured it."

"You figured wrong."

Razzilli gave me a hard look. I couldn't tell what he was thinking. He tapped his glasses back up onto the bridge of his nose. He dropped the cardboard coffee cup into his wastebasket. "Information like that would have been worth plenty of money to Korban. He knew that van Beldin could never let a story like that get any circulation. It'd drag his family's name into the newspapers, make him look like a real horse's ass. Hell, there's not even a statute of limitations on murder. His wife could be tried." Razzilli licked the sugar from the cruller off his hands.

"An ambitious D.A. could make a name for himself," I said.

"I wonder why the hell she ever killed that guy anyway. He was a nobody, a crummy, small-time hood. You don't figure a woman with her background to even know punks like Hauck existed."

"And what about my aunt? Where does she fit in?" I leaned over and crushed out the cigarette in an ashtray on Razzilli's desk. "Van Beldin said she mentioned Dr. Lakeman. I vaguely remember him."

"Hell, Ball, half of Murcer knew old Lakeman. Mrs. van Beldin was married to him for a time. Before that, she was the nurse in his office. After Lakeman died, she met van Beldin. It don't make no goddamn sense at all."

"There's something else, Razzilli," I said. "Last week someone tried roughing me up out at Durango's. When it happened I thought it was one of van Beldin's goons. According to him, it wasn't."

"We don't operate like that, Ball. It wasn't anyone in this agency, I can tell you that."

"I know who the guy was."

"That's nice. Why don't you find him and kick his ass like he kicked yours?" Just then Razzilli's secretary poked in her head and said good morning. She looked surprised to see me there. Razzilli gave her a wave, and she shut the door.

"The guy's name is Dillerman. You may have heard of him."

"Old J.D. One of Murcer's real hard cases. I'm surprised you're still alive. Maybe you're tougher than I thought."

"You ever run across Dillerman?"

"Not personally, but in this business you get to hear things. Dillerman grew up in Murcer, went to 'Nam, was in the Green Berets, I think. Came back, became a policeman, got in a jam, got kicked off. Where he is now, I got no idea. The guy's a flake."

"He was here in Murcer last week. I'm still carrying one of his souvenirs. We find Dillerman, and maybe we can carry this thing a little further."

"We? You and me? You're outta your mind."

"You say you want to find your partner's murderer, right? There's some kind of connection between me getting beat up and the rest of this. It doesn't make any sense otherwise."

Razzilli was quiet for a while. He took a pack of cigarettes from his jacket pocket, lit one, tossed the pack onto his desk and leaned back in his chair. "I'm not convinced, Ball."

"You think you could find Dillerman?" I asked.

"No sweat. We can find anybody. The question is, do we care enough to want to find Dillerman?"

"There's something else," I said.

"What's that?"

"Korban. Get him to open up, say where he picked up the facts he used on van Beldin."

"I thought you guys were buddy-buddy. Didn't Sid follow you out to Korban's place?"

"I was only there because your boss had mentioned his name to me. Naturally, he denied trying to use any leverage on van Beldin."

"Naturally." Razzilli made a wry face. He was having trouble giving up his pet theory—that I had relayed the information to Korban. Razzilli thought about that for a while too. Without saying anything, he flipped through a small address file on his desk. Then, after tapping his glasses back on his nose, he picked up the telephone and started dialing.

"This is Richard Razzilli. Is Mr. van Beldin there?"

A second later he said, "This is Razzilli, Mr. van Beldin. How's Mrs. van Beldin?"

He listened for a few seconds, nodded, mumbled, then said, "I've been talking with Ball, Mr. van Beldin. In fact I have him here in my office right now. He says he spoke with you yesterday. . . . Yes. . . . He maintains he's innocent. . . . I can't say at this point. . . . Uh-huh. . . . What I would like to know precisely is, when and how did Korban indicate that he knew about what . . . uh . . . Mrs. van Beldin is supposed to have done." Razzilli listened for a moment. Finally he asked, "Another thing. Ball has some suggestions concerning how we might proceed with this thing, and I wanted to get your approval. . . . Uh-huh. . . . All right, if you say so, Mr. van Beldin."

Razzilli was less obsequious and more himself when he once again turned his attention to me. "Van Beldin says he received a phone call from Korban telling him to meet him in the bar of the Harmon House Hotel. Korban wouldn't say what it was about, only that it was urgent. Van Beldin went." Razzilli sighed, reached out for his pack of cigarettes again, and extracted one. "He says they sat at a table in the corner of the bar and Korban let him have it. He says they only talked for about ten minutes. They both hate each other's guts. Anyway, Korban said he didn't want to see van Beldin in the statehouse. His leverage, he said, was his information that van Beldin's old lady—uh, Mrs. van Beldin—had murdered a man twenty-eight years before. That was it."

"That was two days after I got back to Murcer."

"Yeah, we checked your arrival time with the airline. That much figures. You could have run with your little tidbit to Korban. With your aunt dying, you didn't have anything to lose."

"Korban didn't seem to mention my aunt."

"No, only Mrs. van Beldin. But, naturally, van Beldin pumped his wife. She tied your aunt into it. Then we got onto you."

Razzilli took an electric razor out of the drawer of his desk, plugged it into a socket in the wall behind the chair, and ran the machine back and forth across the stubble on his face. He rubbed his fingers against his face to check if he'd missed anything and, evidently satisfied, he unplugged the razor and put it back into his drawer.

"What else did van Beldin say?" I asked.

"Van Beldin says I should use my own judgment."

"Which means?"

"I'm gonna use my own judgment."

Razzilli came around from behind his desk and I followed him into his outer office where Olson, one of the operatives who had corraled me for Razzilli two nights before, was leaning on the switchboard talking quietly to the secretary. They stopped talking when we came out and Olson took his hands out of his pockets and pulled himself up to his full height, about five-ten. I said hello, to show there were no hard feelings, and he mumbled something back.

Razzilli gave each of them some instructions and we walked in silence out of the building. I told Razzilli I had my car across the street, but when I pointed the Chevette out to him he shook his head and said, "No way anyone's gonna get me into one of those scooters." We walked around the corner to an outdoor parking area where Razzilli had a Buick Electra parked.

Razzilli skillfully guided the big car through the city's downtown traffic snarl.

"What we do," Razzilli said, "we give Korban a little push, let him know we're out here."

"Do you think it's worth it?"

"Sometimes you got to push, feel around for the weak places, wait for something to give." Razzilli cursed when the driver of a small bakery van halted for a delivery directly in front of us, causing him to swing the car into the outside lane. "Sometimes you get lucky."

The lobby to Korban's office building was humming with activity when we got there. Well-dressed business types carrying attaché cases moved back and forth, in and out. We went through the automatic glass doors and, after talking with a receptionist, headed down the carpeted hallway toward Korban's office. The same red-haired secretary was on duty and she greeted me with the same question delivered in the same tone. "Who may I say is calling?"

We were in luck. Just as we were identifying ourselves for her benefit, the Great Man himself emerged from his inner sanctum. All six-foot-three, two-hundred-and-thirty pounds of him. He was wearing a green and red plaid jacket, something Peter van Beldin wouldn't have been caught dead in. He looked at us inquiringly. He knew each of us individually; what caught his attention was the fact that we were together. After a brief pause, he nodded his head, and pointed the way back into his office.

"You're famous," Korban said to me once he had the door closed. "I been reading about you in the papers. I hope you're not trying to involve me in any of your troubles?"

"I can't do that," I said. "If you're involved, it's because you involved yourself."

Korban pointed to a couple of chairs. "What's your problem?"

"Maybe it's this way, Mr. Korban," Razzilli said. "Maybe we all got problems."

Korban shook his head. "I'm not buying that. Ball has problems, with the police wondering whether he committed murder. And you've got problems. Your partner is the guy who got killed. And your employer, van Beldin, he's got problems. His wife's in the hospital still in a coma, from what I hear. Me, I don't have any problems."

"Things may not be as peaceful as they seem," I said.

"How so?"

Razzilli took over. He was good. He reminded me a little of one of the TV newscasters, the one who does the documentaries and asks all the loaded questions. "Let me lay it out for you, Korban. Last week you arranged a meeting with Peter van Beldin at the Harmon House. This was some time after van Beldin had announced he was going to enter the gubernatorial primary. I think we can assume you wanted in the worst way to prevent van Beldin from entering the race."

"Let's say," Korban said, "there are people who I would rather see in the statehouse."

"You're still with me. All right. At this meeting you tell van Beldin you don't want to see him in the race. He's enough of a pain in the ass for you as it is, without throwing political clout around as well. You tell him you want to see him drop out of the race. If he doesn't, you're gonna spread around a little story that's bound to make him very very unhappy—that his wife once killed a man. It was a long time ago, but it's sure to make lots of waves if it ever comes out."

Korban pursed his lips and made a steeple out of his hands. The motion looked affected, as though he'd picked it up from a movie or TV show. But if Razzilli was getting to him, it didn't show. He still appeared very assured.

Razzilli kept talking. "What we would like to know is, what was the source of this information concerning van Beldin's wife?"

"You guys gotta be kidding." Korban shook his big bald head, as though he'd just heard an absurd joke. "I don't know what van Beldin's after now, and I don't see how you fit in this, Ball—"

"For one thing," Razzilli said, "van Beldin didn't send us. He told us the story, that's all."

"I don't get it then, not at all."

"This is it, Korban," Razzilli said. "There's a connection between whoever told you about Mrs. van Beldin and whoever it was who shot my partner."

"How close?"

"Close enough so that the cops are gonna be interested when they find out."

"Is that right?" Korban suddenly looked more interested. He took his hands out of the steeple position and began rubbing his finger across his chin.

"If you're clean," Razzilli said, "you've got nothing to worry about."

"I'm supposed to believe that? After you been workin' for van Beldin all these years, I'm supposed to believe that?"

"I'm giving it to you straight."

"You guys been poking around, trying to dig up every traffic ticket I ever got—"

"This has nothing to do with van Beldin," Razzilli said. "We're looking for the murderer of my partner."

Korban nodded in my direction again. "You sure he's not the one?" There was a trace of a smile on his face.

"If the cops thought that, they'd've charged him by now," Razzilli said. I was surprised by the vote of confidence from Razzilli. I wondered to what extent he was convinced and to what extent he was saying it for Korban's benefit. At the very least, I figured I should buy him a drink later.

"How do you figure a connection between where I got my information—and I'm not sayin' I ever got this information—and your partner's murderer?"

"Someone wants Ball out of town, out of circulation. We figure it's the same one who shot Sid. That's all we can say."

Korban sat impassively with his hands back in the steeple position for a long time. Then he reached over to his desk, took out a big cigar, and lit it. "I ration myself to two of these a day," he said after he'd blown out a cloud of blue smoke. "What's in it for me if I happen to . . . ah . . . divulge where I obtained this information?"

"We turn up the killer, the cops never learn you tried to pressure van Beldin. I'm not saying it's a punishable offense, but who knows?"

Korban stood up, came around from behind his desk, and said, "Been good talking to you fellows." He opened the door for us himself. "Good luck in your search."

We got out of Korban's office and his building as fast as we could walk. Razzilli burned some rubber driving the car out of the lot.

"Well, now we wait and see," Razzilli said after we'd driven a block. Then he punched the radio button and tuned in some rock music. We drove the rest of the way back to his office without speaking.

Before getting out of the car, I thanked Razzilli for the vote of confidence. He shrugged his shoulders. "Just don't ever give me reason to regret it," he said.

"I'll buy you a drink," I said.

"Hell, I'll let you buy me lunch. Do you know Louise's up on Sixth?" I said I'd find it. "Meet me there at twelve-thirty."

I had two hours to kill and spent them walking the streets of Murcer. Occasionally, I found a store or business I recalled as a child. The old stationery store where I used to buy paper and writing supplies for school was still there but with a new proprietor. The ice cream store on the corner of Stockton and Court had become a fast-food outlet specializing in chicken. A good portion of the buildings in the center of the city, I noticed, were unrented and empty stores dotted each block. Commerce had moved to the suburbs, to the shopping centers, industrial parks, and small office buildings that now ringed the city, most of them owned by Warren Korban.

But as I walked the downtown streets I wondered whether I hadn't moved too fast where Razzilli was concerned. His partner had been shot, and he clearly believed I was the murderer. The extent of his sudden cooperation puzzled me. I wondered whether he wasn't being too nice and whether he might not be ingratiating himself with me for some specific purpose—like framing me for the murder or even putting me out of circulation altogether. I wondered whether I might be blundering into something by meeting him for lunch. At the same time, though, I knew I would have to take some risks and that, as I was told in leadership school, doing something is always preferable to doing nothing.

Downtown Murcer was a depressing place. But if the city had its problems, I had my problems too. And they were crying for fast solutions. When Razzilli arrived at Louise's I was already there, seated at a corner table and sipping a glass of wine.

"I don't know if you like Italian food, Ball, but this place has the best in town. In fact, this is the kind of business I'd love to get into myself. Shut down the agency, open up a little place like this. My wife's a great cook. That's my dream."

Razzilli was wound up tight. I watched him order a martini, drink it down within minutes, and order a second. After we'd been served, I asked him about Korban.

Razzilli put a large forkful of fettuccini in his mouth. He eyed me deliberately before answering. "I'll tell ya, van Beldin had us workin' on Korban so long, I thought I knew more about him than he knew about himself. He was lookin' for stuff, anything we could find to cut him down to size. That was the phrase van Beldin always used—'cut him down to size.'"

"What did you find?"

"Not all that much, really." I watched Razzilli wash down another mouthful of fettuccini with a swallow of white wine. The alcohol seemed to have relaxed him and made him talkative. "Korban was born in Wisconsin. Father died young. Mother took him and a brother to Chicago when he was four or five years old. He grew up there. Quit school at fifteen. You know the type—not dumb, just tired of being poor all the time."

"He wanted to start making money."

"Sure. Why the hell not?"

"How'd he make out?"

"It took a while to learn the ropes. Hustled odd jobs a while. Then an uncle got him a union card. That's how he got into construction."

"Then what?"

"Why the hell am I tellin' you this?"

"You want to find who murdered your partner, right?" I didn't mention to Razzilli that he'd had too much to drink. "Korban fits in some way. He's got to."

"Yeah. Well, he must've saved up a little because he got out of construction after a bit and bought himself a laundromat. Or was it a car wash? Anyway, he built that up, got a few more, then sold out. Used the money to get back into construction, but with his own firm."

"This was Chicago. How did he manage to get to Murcer? Murcer's always been a closed town."

"Yeah, same people have run it for a hundred years."

"People like van Beldin. How did Korban buck the odds?"

"Sixteen, seventeen years ago Murcer was booming, like the rest of the country. The city was growing, expanding. There was a lot of pressure to bring in industry, create jobs."

"At about that time I went off to college."

"Well, you can see the difference between then and now. Anyway, the City-County Planning Board did a lot of redistricting, set up all kinds of surveys and studies to find the best land to set aside for industrial development. Tried to do things quietly, of course. There was a lot of discussion back and forth between the commissioners."

"Natural."

"Sure. There was money to be made. Everyone wanted a piece. What the Planning Board did was set aside S.I.D.s—"

"S.I.D.s?"

"Special Improvement Districts, areas designated for development of some kind, either residential or commercial." Razzilli spooned out another generous portion of fettuccini for himself and started munching on a piece of bread. "All of these S.I.D.s were north of the city. That's the direction that the expansion went."

"That was all farmland when I was a kid."

"And it should've stayed farmland, if you want my opinion and the opinion of a lot of other people around here."

"Where does Korban fit in?"

"That's just it. After all this was pushed through, people thought a couple of those farmers up there were going to become millionaires." Razzilli paused. "What they found out was, most of these old geezers had optioned out their acreage to—"

"Don't tell me, let me guess."

"Korban had some sort of real estate company in Chicago by this time. That company held options to buy just about all the land that was rezoned."

"Too good to be true."

"Sure. Except for one thing. The chief planner, a guy named Stanley Hanks, was perhaps the most respected public servant the city of Murcer ever had."

"I know the name," I said.

"He was the moving force behind getting the land to the north of the city redistricted. Got some aldermen to switch their votes, called in a couple of favors. They needed a two-thirds vote."

"I can imagine some people here didn't take it lying down."

"You're right, and van Beldin was one of them. His holdings were largely to the west and the south. And of course within the city itself. There was talk of an investigation, but nothing ever came of it."

"So that's how Korban got his start here," I said.

"And what a start. Since then he's made Murcer the headquarters of his whole operation. Now he manages, builds, wheels and deals. Yeah, the business situation here is a whole new ball game with him around."

"You'd think he had enough by now," I said and motioned to the waiter for the bill.

Razzilli shrugged. "Guys like him don't know the meaning of the word." When we were out on the street again, Razzilli said, "By the way, I got a man checking out Dillerman. I thought you'd like to know."

"Keep me posted," I said.

"It's the least I can do for a guy who bought me lunch."

I watched Razzilli move off down the street, weaving the slightest bit as he went. I wondered to what extent the run-down on Korban at lunch had been genuine or just part of an act to put me off guard.

8

I picked up my car across the street and drove through the downtown traffic to the Murcer General Hospital. At the station outside the Intensive Care Unit I found Nurse Stephens entering some figures in a large book. She recalled having seen me with Peter van Beldin and was happy to talk.

She made a wry face when I asked about Mrs. van Beldin's condition. "She's holding her own, I guess you'd say. The vital signs are still like they were. One positive development is that she's no longer in a coma."

I nodded knowingly.

"We'll have a better idea in a day or two," Nurse Stephens said. "Now it's too early to tell. These things, they can go either way. Either you get a complete recovery or . . ."

"I understand," I said. I left Nurse Stephens to her figures and went back downstairs to the hospital parking lot.

I kicked myself for not having tried to talk with van Beldin's wife sooner. Although he had mentioned his wife when I spoke to him in his office, I hadn't made the connection between her and the rest of it.

Just as I started the car engine, an ambulance came roaring out of the intersection and into the bay in front of the hospital's emergency ward. I watched as the attendants worked to haul the patient out of the vehicle and into the building. An accident victim, someone with a coronary—or a drug overdose? These days in Murcer the last possibility was as likely as either of the first two.

I thought about stopping at Sonia's office but then rejected the idea. I knew she had some papers she wanted me to sign, but I decided to let the matter wait another day.

The last of the afternoon sunlight was already gone as I pulled the Chevy up in front of Aunt Phyllis's house. The old place had the appeal of a Transylvanian castle. I was already halfway up the walk before I saw him—Karl Breyer. He was standing in the middle of the garden gazing down at the flower bed adjacent to one of the big maple trees.

"They don't get the nourishment they should over here," he said. "The roots of the tree will take the vital ingredients from the soil and prevent the flowers from growing properly." He shook his head, then stuffed his hands into his jacket pockets and walked out to the front. He stuck out his hand. "I don't want to sound like a know-it-all, but one subject I know something about is gardens. I love flowers."

"I haven't been paying as much attention to the house as I should," I said.

"Easy enough to understand. You've got a lot on your mind."

"One thing before anything else, Karl," I said after we were in the house. "I want to thank you for putting in a good word for me with—"

Karl cut me off with a wave of his hand. "No need. I just don't think you did it, Clint."

"I didn't do it, but I want to say thanks anyway." I turned on some lights and poured a couple of beers. I asked Breyer what was on his mind.

He let out a long sigh. "Nice place your aunt had. Comfortable. You grew up here, right?"

I said I did.

"No parents, just your aunt."

"Just the two of us. Not another living thing, not even a canary. She didn't like pets."

"Yeah." Breyer sighed again. "I can guess how it was."

"Can you?" I said.

"My dad, he immigrated here from Hungary after the First World War, got himself a job down at the old cardboard factory. They made boxes there. It's hard to believe now, but they had some bitter strikes in Murcer during the twenties and thirties. Companies did whatever they wanted in those days. Anyway, during this one strike management tried to break it up with some out-of-town goons. They showed up carrying lead pipes and baseball bats and tried to break the picket line. My dad, stubborn old hunky, wasn't moving, you know? One of them smashed him on the side of the head with an iron pipe. He died in the hospital two days later. I was seven at the time."

"I see what you're getting at," I said.

"You've got the look, Ball. I saw it that first night. I kind of knew. You're carrying around a lot of grief from when you were a kid."

"You can spot these things, Karl?"

"You're a cop, you notice certain things about people." Breyer paused. "Or maybe I've got the same look. It was just me and Mom all those years."

I got up and came back with two more beers.

"But I'll tell you something else," Karl said. "Maybe we got more determination than other people."

"Good for us, right, Karl?" I was working to keep the conversation casual, but deep down I knew what Karl was talking about. We'd been through the same kind of things. And licked it. Maybe it was the similarity in backgrounds that gave Karl an insight into me that others didn't have. People like Gronski—and Sylvia.

"I mean it, Ball. When I went into police work, I said I was going to be the best. And I was. I made a name for myself during the years I worked homicide. Not bad for a poor kid from Old-town."

"I see your point," I said.

"And it's the same with you. You got out. You did it because you wanted to do it."

"I knew what I wanted, Karl. Something better than what I had." I raised the beer can. "Cheers, Karl."

"The real reason I came out here was to answer those questions you asked me about the Hauck murder—that is, if you're still interested."

Damn right I was interested.

"I don't know why you want to know about something like that, but I looked up the file for you. I probably can't tell you a lot you don't already know." Karl put his glass down on the table and leaned forward. "This Hauck was a small-time hood who never amounted to much. Part of the proof of that was this third-rate rooming house he was living in when he was killed. A real shambles, that place was. The way we reconstructed the murder . . . someone came to his door, someone he knew probably. He let them in with no idea naturally of what they had in mind. He closed the door and then—bang!—someone shot him. Or I should say bang! bang!—'cause he was shot twice."

"Sounds cold-blooded."

"Murder is always cold-blooded. Anyway, one of the funny things was, he was shot once from the front and once from be-hind. Coroner surmised the second shot was fired into his back while he was lying on the floor."

"Making sure?"

"It was a funny thing to do because the first bullet caught him right in the chest and broke open his heart. Killer must've known he was dead from all the blood over the place. Anyway, he put a second bullet into Hauck, like you say, maybe to make sure."

"Were there any suspects?"

"Since it had to have been someone he knew, we went after everyone who ever had anything to do with Hauck. Everyone got a real going-over, but we came up empty just the same."

"You never got on to anyone?"

"No, sir."

"The reason I ask, Karl, there was a story in the *Telegram* at the time saying you were expecting to crack the case."

"Could have been. Maybe a reporter jumping to conclusions. Anyway, the file's still open, officially anyway."

"I don't suppose anyone's all that interested in it now."

"I don't think anyone was all that interested in it then. Whoever knocked off Joey Boy did the city a favor. I worked the case—professional pride, you might say—but I had lots more important stuff. And besides, either you crack 'em quick or not at all."

I thanked Karl for his efforts.

"If I was you, Clint, I'd be more concerned about cracking the Hockley murder. You're not out of the woods yet, you know."

"At least I'm not in jail."

"Gronski's workin' his tail off. Someone's gonna be in jail. Once Gronski gets his teeth into something he won't let go." Karl removed his pipe from his jacket pocket and started filling it. "If I tell you something in confidence, can you keep it quiet?"

"I might."

"That's not the best answer, but I'll tell you anyway." Karl got his pipe lit and exhaled a cloud of blue smoke. "Gronski likes Razzilli."

I lit up a butt of my own. "That surprises me," I said.

"Why? Why should it surprise you?"

"I don't figure him for the type of guy to murder his partner. He's not a saint, maybe—"

"Your problem, Clint, is, you've led a sheltered life. You don't think like a cop. You look at it the way we look at it and it makes a lot of sense."

"How do you look at it?"

"First of all, don't let all that screaming and yelling about his partner fool you. Or all the talk about how he's gonna nail the guy. That's all smokescreen."

"It fooled me."

Karl looked at me hard. I could feel the condescension. "The word is, Razzilli was making it with Hockley's wife. Ever since the murder, he's spent every night over at her place—"

"According to Razzilli, he's been helping her out—"

"Come off it, Ball." Karl's tone again brimmed with condescension. "Whenever Razzilli comes over she packs the kids off to her sister's. Then they go at it hot and—"

"Okay. You don't have to draw me a picture."

"What they've been doin' is plannin' where to spend the insurance money."

I shrugged my shoulders. I felt stupid. Razzilli had been trying to get me jugged for his partner's murder and here I was defending him.

"There's more," Karl said. "The agency. With Hockley dead, Razzilli won't have to work another day in his life."

"How's that, Karl?"

"They had a standard partnership agreement, but with an interesting clause. Razzilli gets the entire agency now that his partner's dead. And don't think that business isn't a moneymaker. Background, domestic surveillance. He's got half a dozen operatives workin'. And they're not afraid to charge, believe me."

I remembered what Razzilli had said in the restaurant about giving up his business. Maybe that had been his plan all along. Once he owned it all, sell out. It also explained Razzilli's drinking. The fact that the police hadn't charged me right away was making him nervous. He didn't like the idea of a continuing investigation. I told Karl that what he said seemed plausible.

"Razzilli almost had a fit when Gronski didn't arrest you on the spot," Karl said.

I nodded, recalling the argument on the night of the murder between Razzilli and Gronski. "Razzilli could even have planned it by having Hockley tail me—"

"Sure. Then he tells him to enter the house while you're out. Then he goes in himself, shoots Hockley, and plants the gun."

It now seemed that trying to get close to Razzilli hadn't been such a bright idea, after all. All I'd done was put myself in more of a bind. "What do you suggest, Karl?"

"What I suggest is, you be careful of Razzilli. Any contact you have with him, you report it to Gronski or to me. Because if Razzilli's the one, he'll be doing everything possible to set you up. You're a pigeon, made to order. Whoever shot Hockley tried

to frame you once. Why shouldn't they try it again?" Karl looked
at his watch and got to his feet. "This took longer than I thought
it would. I gotta run."

I thanked him for taking the trouble to come out."

"Like I said, Clint, I know the way things were when you were
growing up, and I can see the problems you got now. I don't
figure you for a murderer."

"Thanks again for the vote of confidence."

"When I worked homicide, I saw a lot of people get in trouble
through no fault of their own. First your aunt dies, then you get
beat up, then you find a dead man here in your house. I dunno. I
never used to let other people's headaches get to me."

"Maybe you're mellowing with age, Karl."

"And maybe I'm getting soft in the head." We shook hands
and Karl made his way down the steps. "And don't forget what I
told you about the plants. And the lawn." Then he turned and
moved away into the darkness of Weatherly Street.

I had received the impression from Karl Breyer's visit that the
police no longer considered me their only suspect in the Hockley
murder. The news, I thought, was worth passing on to Sylvia. I
put through a call to the *Telegram*. She listened cautiously as I
told her what Karl had said.

"That's fine, Clint; I'm really glad to hear it."

"I thought it might be worth a celebration. Perhaps dinner
tonight."

"I'd like to, but I'm tied up."

"Tomorrow?"

"Clint, these last few days have been hectic. Can I get back to
you in a day or two?"

"Sure, Sylvia. I'd like to see you again. I want you to know
that."

"I'll call, Clint. I really will."

After I hung up the phone, I felt more than ever the urgency
of the situation. I thought back to the breakup with Doris late
last year. It seemed every time I got close to a woman I cared
about, something happened to upset the situation. It had become
more than just a question of satisfying the police of my inno-
cence. I wanted to erase all doubt in everyone's mind that I had
anything to do with the murder of Sid Hockley. I wanted van
Beldin to know I had nothing to do with Korban's attempts at

blackmail. But of course it was Sylvia's opinion of me I was most concerned about. If there was any doubt that I missed her and wanted her back in my life, it had required only the sound of her voice to erase that doubt. I had winced when Karl Breyer referred to me as some kind of pigeon. I didn't like the idea of people thinking of me in those terms, I didn't like it at all.

I spent the better part of the next hour going through drawers and closets deciding on what was worth keeping and what should be either thrown or given away. I had filled close to twenty boxes full of clothing and knicknacks when the telephone rang for the first time. It was Sonia.

Her voice had an edge of tension, of forced casualness. "Clint, I just happened to receive two tickets for the Murcer Light Opera Company for this evening's performance. A client couldn't use them and—"

"I don't think so, Sonia," I said. "I'd like to, but I can't."

"I understand, Clint." There was a sound in Sonia's voice that was more than sadness; it was something more like despair, and it made me immediately sorry I had said no. "Sonia I—"

Sonia interrupted me before I could change my mind. "There are some papers you have to look at and sign in connection with the probate. Please come in on Monday." She hung up abruptly.

I went back to sorting out my aunt's possessions, but not with very much enthusiasm. Shortly before ten, the telephone rang again. It was Razzilli.

"You got time tomorrow night?" he asked. When I said I did, he said, "Van Beldin wants to see us. At the country club out on the River Road. You know where it is?" I said I did, and he said to be there at 6:30.

"Anything up?" I suppose my wariness of Razzilli came across in my tone of voice.

"You'll find out tomorrow night. Be there. On time." Razzilli's tone was abrupt and his voice just a bit thick. I got the impression he had been drinking again. I wondered where he was calling from, and I restrained a sudden impulse to ask how Mrs. Hockley was.

After Razzilli hung up, I put through a call to Karl Breyer. He listened without interrupting as I told him of the call from Razzilli.

"What do you think, Karl?" I asked.

"Offhand, Clint, I can't say. It's possible that both Razzilli and van Beldin are in on something . . ."

"And Hockley found out?"

"Or maybe it's van Beldin wanted Hockley killed."

"Why would he . . ."

"Just guessing now. Maybe Hockley discovered something about van Beldin's wife, maybe something to do with her trying to kill herself."

Karl's remark triggered a sudden thought. Could Hockley have discovered something about Mrs. van Beldin's involvement with the murder of Joey Hauck? All of a sudden I felt eager to find out why Razzilli and van Beldin wanted to see me. I said as much to Karl.

"Fine, Clint. But like I say, keep your wits about you. And pass on whatever you find out to Gronski."

"I'll be in touch," I said.

9

The next day, Saturday, I was able to complete the job of sorting and packing and was even able to make arrangements with some local charities and junk collectors to carry off that portion of Aunt Phyllis's belongings that I couldn't keep, which was practically everything. All that really remained to do was complete the probating of the will and the selling of the house. And to get Gronski's permission to leave Murcer. In any event, I felt better than I had the previous evening, less inclined to be pessimistic. Maybe things were going to right themselves after all. As I showered, I sang and resang the lyrics to as many Victor Herbert tunes as I could recall. By a few minutes after six I was in the rental Chevy on my way out to the River Club.

A stern-looking flunky in a green uniform with polished gold buttons held the oak door of the River Club for me, and after I'd mentioned Peter van Beldin's name, another flunky, this one in a red uniform with polished gold buttons, removed my topcoat and pointed me toward the restaurant. Van Beldin and Razzilli were already there, and after I had identified myself for the benefit of the head waiter, a man in a blue uniform with polished gold buttons and braid on his shoulder, I was escorted to a table in the corner of the dining room.

"Good to see you again, Ball," van Beldin said and gave my hand a mighty squeeze. I knew I was once again in the company of a confident, take-charge businessman. I said hello to Razzilli and ordered a Scotch and water. Van Beldin did most of the talking and he kept the conversation light throughout the meal. Only when we were drinking coffee did he finally turn serious.

"Rich and I had a long conversation yesterday morning, Ball. He's of the mind that you didn't have anything to do with the murder of Sid. Also that you weren't responsible for feeding information concerning my wife to Korban." Van Beldin deftly removed a silver cigarette case from his breast pocket and offered each of us one. After we'd all lit up, van Beldin continued. "So I think any misapprehensions or misunderstandings that may have existed among us should now be regarded as a thing of the past." Van Beldin poured a glass of brandy for each of us from a bottle on the table and raised his glass. We drank.

"My primary concern now, of course, is the health of my wife. I visited the hospital today and Dr. Schwartz was guardedly optimistic. Helen's out of the coma, thank God." Van Beldin's little speech was so smooth I wondered if it had been rehearsed.

Both Razzilli and I said we were glad to hear of the improvement in Mrs. van Beldin.

"However, there are some major problems. One thing is her involvement in the murder of this racketeer—what's his name?"

"Hauck, Joey Hauck," Razzilli said.

"I'd prefer that didn't come out."

I said, "But since Korban knows the story, and someone told it to him, it may not be possible to keep it quiet."

"I realize that very well," van Beldin said curtly. He didn't like people raising points that could be considered bothersome. "Nevertheless, let's make it one of our objectives, shall we?"

"It could be considered, under some circumstances, as with-holding evidence of a felony," Razzilli said.

I didn't say anything.

"Of course I don't have to remind you, Ball, that your aunt was a party to this . . . ah, gruesome deed. I wouldn't think you'd want the story to become public knowledge."

"What do you have in mind?" I asked.

"I'd like to clean up this affair, get to the bottom, find out everything that happened and why."

"Aren't the police hard at work on that?" I asked. For some reason the remark sounded ingenuous.

"It's not that I have anything against the Murcer Police De-partment," van Beldin said. "It's just that I'll feel easier if we conduct our own investigation. This way I'll be surer that there hasn't been some kind of cover-up."

"It might be a good time," Razzilli said, "to go over every-thing we know, put it all together."

They both looked at me, as though they were waiting for me to begin. "Just what are you thinking of?" I asked, trying to stall.

"Tell us what you know," van Beldin said.

"Where should I begin?" I took a swallow of brandy, then watched as van Beldin refilled my glass.

Razzilli glared at me, his face glowing with impatience. "Start with Day One, why don't you? For cryin' out loud, Ball."

At that point I couldn't see any reason for not telling them what I knew. In all likelihood they knew much more of the story than I did. "My knowledge of the affair began with the discovery of a letter written by my aunt in which she indicated she'd com-mitted some 'horrible deed' a long time ago. She indicated in the letter that she'd hidden a pistol and two newspaper clippings de-scribing the murder of Hauck—"

"All right," van Beldin said. "That's what Sid saw when he . . . ah . . . entered your house. That much we know."

"A couple of nights later," I said, "last Monday actually, I was eating at Durango's Steak House and someone lured me out to the parking lot and tried roughing me up."

"Why do you think?" van Beldin asked.

Razzilli said, "We gotta assume the guy didn't want to kill you. If that was the case, they only wanted to run you off. Send you back to where you came from."

"It only got me mad," I said.

"Well, you reacted different from most people there. People with any sense don't like violence, don't want anything to do with it—"

"Are you trying to say I don't have any—?" Once again I was ready to take a poke at Razzilli, River Club or no River Club.

"Gentlemen, gentlemen." Van Beldin placed a restraining hand on my shoulder. Razzilli raised two fingers, signaling peace, but I had a feeling that behind the horn-rims and the fixed expression he was grinning. Anyway, I decided at that moment not to let this guy get under my skin anymore with his smart-alecky remarks.

I said, "I was able to find out the name of the guy who roughed me up. It's Jerry Dillerman."

"That's progress," van Beldin said approvingly.

"We're already looking for him," Razzilli said. He spoke calmly, as though he and his crew were miles ahead of everyone else.

"The next night," I said, "I came home to find Hockley's body in my aunt's home."

"He'd been tailing you all day," Razzilli said. "He must've broken in while you were out."

"He'd broken in once already," van Beldin said.

"He must've had a good reason to go in again," Razzilli said. "But I can't think of what it could've been."

I said, "You were his partner—"

"Mr. Ball has a point there, Rich," van Beldin said quickly.

"Whoever shot him tried to frame me. They went upstairs and tossed the gun under the bed."

"Let me pick it up from there," van Beldin said. "The murder took place twenty-eight years ago this month, years before I met Helen. At the time Helen was working as the receptionist for Dr. Walter Lakeman, a general practitioner here in Murcer. As we all know, Dr. Lakeman was one of Murcer's most respected citizens—not only a capable, understanding medical man but also a warm, wonderful human being. Helen married him some four years later, almost twenty-five years ago now. They remained married eight years, until the death of Dr. Lakeman. In speaking to her, I got the idea that he was somehow . . . well, involved in the murder." Van Beldin paused. "But when I tried to press her, she wouldn't say anything more."

"How do you explain her attempt at suicide?" I asked.

"I could almost believe her attempt to take her own life was a way of preserving the memory of Dr. Lakeman," van Beldin said.

Razzilli interrupted. "One thing that might help, Ball, is if you could tell us how your aunt connected to either Mrs. van Beldin or to the doctor."

"I remember my aunt taking me to Dr. Lakeman a few times when I got sick. I vaguely remember a big house . . ."

"Exactly right," van Beldin said. "A big house, hedges in the front, a sloping lawn, a shingle by the gate."

I said, "As far as I know, my aunt was one of Dr. Lakeman's patients, that's all. I can't say how she knew Mrs. van Beldin." I thought for a moment. "Maybe my father took me to Dr. Lakeman. I can't remember too clearly. He died when I was five."

Just then I felt a rush of nausea, a result of the excitement and uncertainty I always felt when I mentioned my father.

Van Beldin and Razzilli both looked at me queerly.

"How old are you, Ball?" Razzilli asked.

"Thirty-three," I said. I emptied the last of the brandy glass. "Why?" The warmth of the liquor felt good in my stomach.

"I was thinking the same thing," van Beldin said. "Exactly when did your father die?"

"He died in January. It was twenty-eight years last January."

I could see both of them thinking, doing some rapid mental calculations. Van Beldin broke the silence.

"In other words, Ball, your father died just two months before Hauck was killed. And you went to live with your aunt directly afterward."

"She took me in. Then we moved to my father's old house."

"How did your father die, Ball?" van Beldin asked.

"Really, all I know is what my aunt told me, and she never liked to speak about my father. She never liked him." I reached for the brandy bottle, but van Beldin beat me to it. He refilled my glass and shoved it back toward me. I felt a slight tremor in my hand as I lifted the glass to my lips. "I don't think anyone knows exactly what happened. His body was found in an alley just off Bedford Street—"

"I never heard of Bedford Street," van Beldin said.

"It's behind the freight yards, bars, and cat . . . uh, brothels mostly," Razzilli said.

"He'd been beaten up, that was clear. Either he'd been mugged or he'd gotten into a barroom fight."

"Was he a boozer?" Razzilli asked.

"According to my aunt, he was a boozer and a brawler."

"What killed him?"

"Probably a blow to the temple with a sharp instrument of some kind."

"What kind of occupation did he have?"

"He'd gone to sea as a young man, but after he met my mother he settled down. He worked at the textile mill."

It was like a third-degree. They were shooting questions and I was answering, all traces of reluctance having long since disappeared.

"What else can you tell us?" van Beldin asked.

"Not much about my father. Walks in the woods when I was small, bouncing on his knee . . ."

"In that letter your aunt wrote to you, she said she did it for you. What do you make of that?"

"I don't know."

"It all ties together," Razzilli said. "It'd be too many coincidences otherwise. Your father dying, maybe murdered. The women killing Joey Hauck two months later. It lies dormant twenty-eight years, then your aunt dies and you come back—and it starts to unravel."

"But how does Korban fit in?" van Beldin asked.

"Or Lakeman?" Razzilli said. "Your wife seemed to be protecting Lakeman. His aunt was protecting him. What the hell was there to protect everybody from?"

"God knows," van Beldin said. I took out my handkerchief and wiped perspiration from my forehead. I felt as though someone had just turned up the thermostat by ten degrees.

Van Beldin poured himself another glass of brandy. I could tell something was on his mind from the fact that he didn't offer either of us any, just sat there holding the glass in one hand and the bottle in the other, and staring into space.

I knew it was time to go home.

I arrived home feeling empty, emotionally, spiritually and physically. I had the feeling I needed to talk to someone, but I didn't know who to call. For company, I turned on the local FM station, but they were playing Grieg; I had enough troubles of my own without confounding them with Peer Gynt's, so I turned the radio off. I sat down at the kitchen table with half a tumbler of brandy. I wanted to forget. Things had welled up out of my subconscious over the course of the evening, things I had kept submerged for years. I stared at the brandy glass for a full ten minutes. It took an effort of will, but I got up and poured the contents down the sink.

Ever since the day of my aunt's funeral, I'd had the feeling that I was involved in something, something messy and chaotic. Maybe I'd been involved for a long time but had always been too dishonest or too weak to admit it. I thought of the words Aunt Phyllis had written in the letter—*what I did I did for you*—and I knew that my failure had been my refusal to admit my own responsibility. But what was I responsible for? The succession of events of the last eight days, the twists and turns, reminded me of the time I had fallen through the ice into the river after disobeying my aunt. I had struggled to climb out, but each time, after lifting myself up to a certain point, I would slide back into the icy water. If it hadn't been for the two fishermen, I would have died from the cold. I wondered who could help me now.

I had ambivalent feelings toward everyone in Murcer—toward Razzilli, van Beldin, Sonia, Karl Breyer, Korban, Gronski—even toward Sylvia. And I'd always had ambivalent feelings toward Aunt Phyllis. And of course my father. . . .

I hadn't thought about my father for years. Somehow Aunt Phyllis had instilled in me the idea that it was wrong to speak of him or to even think of him. But I still recalled how, as a youngster, I would lie awake nights in the darkened bedroom nourishing the handful of memories of my dad—the tramps through the woods, the sled he'd given me one Christmas, the sound of his laughter. Whatever else there had been I'd blocked out of my mind.

After a long time I roused myself and trudged upstairs. I undressed and threw myself on the bed, more conscious than ever of being alone. . . . And then I was aware of someone, an enormous, powerful presence, and this person was very angry with me. One blow glanced off my head, but the next struck me solidly on the eye. And then there was a succession of blows, and shouted curses. I tried to cover my head with my arms, but it didn't help. I staggered away and was then aware of falling down a long flight of steps, and of bumping my head and arms as I rolled and tumbled. The physical pain was intense, but even worse was the emotional pain. . . .

When I awoke, I was drenched in sweat. The bedroom clock indicated it was twenty minutes past one.

10

"You know, there are some guys got a genius, a real genius, for getting themselves into hot water. And let me tell you something else, Ball, the jails of this country are filled with guys like that, guys with this genius I'm talking about." Detective Lieutenant Paul Gronski was sitting behind his desk in his office at police headquarters, and I was sitting opposite him. It was half-past nine the following Monday morning. "In some ways, these guys aren't any worse than most of the other people walking around on the outside. It's just that they got this genius I'm talking about, a genius for trouble."

"How does this affect me, Lieutenant?" I knew well enough what Gronski was getting at, but I decided to let him build up to it in his own way.

"Ever since you've been back in Murcer, Ball, there's been trouble, and you've been in the middle—"

"I don't know if that's fair—"

Gronski raised his hand. "I'm not saying you're responsible for anything, not yet anyway"—then he flashed his knowing smirk—"but I think you could've handled things better."

"For instance?"

"For instance, you've got a tendency to hold out, to keep things to yourself. I still don't believe you've told us the whole story or anywhere close to the whole story."

I said, "I've been keeping you up-to-date where Razzilli's concerned." The remark was in reference to the fact that I'd given Gronski a rundown on my Saturday evening meeting with Razzilli and van Beldin. But Gronski sensed I wasn't telling him everything. The unexpected twist in the discussion late in the evening—the references to the Hauck murder, the involvement of Dr. Lakeman and my father—had caught me by surprise. I couldn't tell Gronski anything that might lead him to discovering the circumstances behind the Hauck murder. The result was I had been able to tell him very little.

"I'm supposed to believe van Beldin and Razzilli got you out to that swell club just to buy you dinner? To talk about old times? Come off it, Ball!" Gronski threw his pen down on the desk. He seemed frustrated.

"I'm cooperating where I can, Lieutenant."

"Where you can! What the hell's that supposed to mean?"

"It means—"

"Listen, Ball. What I told you out at your house still goes. I think you're holding out. Even if you didn't commit the murder, withholding evidence can—"

"You don't have to explain the law to me, Lieutenant."

Gronski didn't like being interrupted. He stood up from his chair and came around from behind his desk. "This investigation is continuing. And the way it's going to end, my friend, is with someone in jail for murder."

I could see what Karl Breyer had meant when he said that once Gronski had his teeth into something he wouldn't let go. Gronski walked over to the office door and opened it. He stood holding it open until I walked through it.

After leaving police headquarters, I walked over to Sonia's office where we spent twenty minutes going over some of the details of my aunt's estate. It was a dry process, and wasn't made any easier by Sonia's insistence on keeping things extremely formal. I'd gone from being Clint to once again being Mr. Ball.

When we'd finished discussing the will, I told her that I'd just come from police headquarters where I'd been talking with Gronski. I said that I'd received the impression from Gronski that I was no longer the primary suspect. "I suppose I should be grateful for small favors," I said, trying to steer the conversation into a lighter vein.

"I'm very happy for you," Sonia said. She laid her reading glasses on the desk and stood up from her chair. She put out her hand. "You shouldn't need me to represent you anymore."

"Is all this necessary, Sonia?"

"All what?"

"All this formality. What's the point of it?"

She answered in her most clipped, businesslike tone, a manner lawyers probably pick up in law school. Perhaps there's a course in it. "I just wanted to say a proper good-bye, wish you all the best."

"I suggest dinner this evening."

"No, not tonight."

"Tomorrow then?"

"Not ever. I'll send you a bill when we've completed the probate. There are still a few details."

I walked out of the office without saying good-bye. I supposed there was a smirk of satisfaction on Sonia's face, but I didn't turn around to look.

I needed some blades, soap, and cigarettes, so I headed up to the big drugstore on Stockton Street. I picked up a newspaper, then walked down to the Mayfair luncheonette and ordered a cup of coffee at the counter. The Greek waitress with the heavy eyebrows set down the cup in such a way that the coffee sloshed into the saucer. In reaching for the cream I put the sleeve of my jacket into a piece of jelly that I hadn't noticed. On the way out I was bumped by a fat man who didn't take the trouble to excuse himself. Little things were getting to me.

Or was it that the world was changing? People seemed to be becoming more haphazard, more careless, more selfish. Or maybe they'd always been like this and I'd never noticed. Sonia's behavior, in particular, bothered me. I liked Sonia, but the simple fact was I liked Sylvia more. I loved Sylvia. I wanted to marry Sylvia.

I thought about what Karl Breyer had said the other evening about the police shifting their attention to Razzilli. Gronski had hinted at the same thing today. Obviously, Breyer and Gronski had done a lot of talking, with Breyer feeding a lot of angles into the investigation. He was in a position to influence Gronski's thinking, a fact for which I was very grateful. Maybe Breyer only liked me because he discerned a similarity in our backgrounds, but whatever the reason, he had been responsible for keeping me out of jail. At the same time I wondered whether I wasn't being premature in thinking I still wasn't a primary suspect in the murder of Sid Hockley. I had an uncomfortable feeling that in Gronski's mind I was still the logical choice.

The chances were I hadn't done much in the last few days without the police having a good idea of what I was up to. They'd probably even had someone following me on Saturday evening when I'd gone out to see van Beldin and Razzilli. Maybe van Beldin and Razzilli were involved in something together. Maybe van Beldin was more interested in seeing his wife dead than alive. Or maybe, as Karl had suggested, Razzilli had pulled the trigger and was only waiting for a chance to take off with Hockley's wife. This last surmise seemed to be the most logical. I'd never had any reason to like Razzilli, and the thought that he'd tried to frame me by tossing the murder weapon under the bed made me see red.

It certainly appeared that, as Gronski had said, I had a genius for trouble. Well, if someone had singled me out to be a pigeon they'd made a wrong choice.

Gronski was right, of course, about withholding information, but Aunt Phyllis hadn't told me the story of the murder so I could run with the information to the police. Then there was the fact that I'd always been wary of the police. Maybe that was the real reason I hadn't said anything to Gronski or Breyer about Dillerman. Or maybe it was because I was still mad about getting knocked around at the restaurant, and I wanted to get back at Dillerman in my own way. After that, I told myself, the police could have him.

I thought about calling Sylvia and asking her to lunch but dropped the idea. The chances were she would only say no anyway. I walked down a couple of blocks and turned in at Razzilli's office.

Razzilli's secretary told me he was in conference with a couple of his operatives, but that it probably wouldn't be long. I killed ten minutes with a three-week-old copy of *Newsweek*. Finally, two men emerged, and I got the go-ahead.

Razzilli was in his shirt-sleeves looking over a sheaf of papers. He nodded toward the chair and said, "Just the man I wanted to see."

"Anything interesting?"

Razzilli looked at me and lowered his voice. "You find Jerry Dillerman interesting? Because if you do, you may get a chance to talk with him."

"Where is he?"

"Olson's located him, in Chicago. You feel like taking the plane out there?"

I responded without thinking. "Sure. Jerry and I go way back."

"The first plane for Chicago out of here tomorrow is at seven-thirty. Meet me at the airport. And, Ball, don't mention this trip to anyone. We want to keep it between the three of us."

After getting home, I decided to follow Karl's advice and do some work in Aunt Phyllis's garden. While pulling crabgrass and pruning bushes, I thought about my promise to Breyer and the possibility that I might be walking into some kind of trap by accompanying Razzilli to Chicago. On the other hand, if Razzilli was on the level, Dillerman might provide some interesting answers. In any event, the exercise had a beneficial effect: that night I slept like a child.

The travelers moving through the Murcer City Airport at seven the next morning were mostly business types. Men wearing dark suits, carrying attaché cases, looking self-confident, traveling in pairs and small groups, speaking to one another in hushed tones. Make the trip to Chi, close the big deal, have a good meal, catch the late plane back to Murcer.

I found Razzilli at the United counter. He was easy to pick out from the rest of the group. Flannel shirt, checkered sports jacket, a slightly skewered look that indicated he wasn't a morning person. We had twenty minutes until boarding and decided to kill them over a cup of cardboard coffee at a stand-up counter in the cafeteria next to the boarding lounge.

"I was talking to van Beldin last night. The reports on his wife are good. They think she'll pull out of it, maybe with no serious damage."

"Good news."

"Not if she ends up standing trial for murder."

"That's only if the cops get word."

"They'll reopen the case if they learn the facts, depend on it. I can see the headlines from here. 'Wife of Prominent Citizen Found Guilty of Murder.' Everyone'd stand to gain—the cops, the D.A., the newspapers, the gossip hounds."

"How do we keep the lid on?"

"Korban's the weak link. Van Beldin told me last night he's gonna try and work out some kind of deal."

"I didn't know these guys would even talk with each other, much less deal."

Razzilli took a swallow of coffee and looked at his watch. "Ball, these business types'll deal with anyone as long as it's to their advantage. I've seen it dozens of times. Van Beldin and Korban may look like they're coming from opposite directions, but there's one quality they have in common. They like to make deals."

I drained the last of my coffee and stamped out my cigarette. "Don't say any more. You might shatter my faith in human nature."

The flight to Chicago took just under an hour and a half. O'Hare was a different place from the Murcer Airport. All types of people, speaking half a dozen languages, were moving through the terminal, seemingly unconcerned about anyone's business but their own. We made our way through the mob scene to one of the car rental booths, where Razzilli signed us out for a Chrysler. Before leaving the airport, Razzilli put through a call to somebody from a phone booth.

"We gotta talk to a guy before we go look up Dillerman," Razzilli said as we drove along the highway connecting O'Hare with the city.

Razzilli knew his way around Chicago. We fought the weekday traffic, finally ending up in a maze of small streets on the city's South Side. We parked on a side street in front of what looked like an abandoned tenement, then walked back to a broad avenue. It was a couple of minutes after ten. We turned right and halfway up the block stopped in front of a place called Elwood's Lounge. We went in.

The early morning trade had already begun. A couple of girls with hard-looking faces seated at the bar looked at us defiantly. Two men at a table halted their conversation and made wry faces. The bartender stopped wiping whatever he was wiping, then started wiping it again. A silver-haired man in a gray suit got up from a table in the rear where he had been going over cash register tapes and stood at the end of the bar, challenging us to come talk with him. Ignoring the bartender and the customers, Razzilli walked straight toward the man, who seemed to be the manager or the owner. I followed.

"I'm Razzilli, down from Murcer," he said. He stuck out his hand. The man ignored it.

"So you're Razzilli, and you're down from Murcer. Do I know you?"

"Harold knows me. Where is he?"

"You got an appointment with Harold?"

"Yeah, I got an appointment with Harold," Razzilli said, successfully mimicking the silver-haired man's high-pitched voice.

The man's eyes flashed with anger, but before he could say anything, a door at the back of the lounge opened, and a man who must have weighed three hundred pounds appeared and waved.

"It's all right, Milt," he said. "I know these guys."

Fat Harold motioned us into the back room and gave each of us a pat on the back. He seemed so happy to see us I felt like I was his long-lost son. "Don't worry about Milt. He's mad at the world. Been that way ever since his wife left him. Ran away with a furniture salesman. Can ya imagine?"

"Yeah, I can, as a matter of fact," Razzilli said without smiling.

Fat Harold burst into laughter. After a few seconds he started wheezing and gasping for breath. "Same old Rich."

"He thought we were cops," Razzilli said.

"Never," Fat Harold said. "Yiz look too honest." Then he started laughing again, so hard this time that tears rolled down his cheeks, and he was finally forced to sit down. I felt that I was witnessing a practiced routine, a kind of ritual the two of them had played before in one variation or another.

We sat down at a large round table at which Fat Harold was having breakfast. One plate held the remains of scrambled eggs, sausages, and home fried potatoes, and Harold was in the process of digging into a stack of pancakes swimming in syrup. He poured each of us a cup of coffee and went back to the pancakes. The coffee was good.

"Get you guys anything?" Harold asked between bites.

"Na, we ate on the plane," Razzilli lied.

"It's good, I can tell yiz," Harold said.

"It looks good," Razzilli said.

"I get it sent in from across the street," Harold said.

Harold was enjoying breakfast so much I felt guilty about disturbing him. We sipped the coffee and watched him eat. When he'd finished the pancakes, he opened a roll and smeared a couple of pats of butter on it, then ate it in two bites. As he ate, he exchanged small talk with Razzilli.

When he'd finished eating, he leaned back, sighed, and took out a toothpick. He looked sad. Mealtime was over, and it would be a couple of hours before he could start gorging himself again.

"What brings you down, Rich?" he asked finally.

"We're looking up a guy, and we want a little background before we go talk with him," Razzilli said.

Harold's piggy eyes narrowed, becoming almost invisible behind the rolls of facial fat. His face didn't look amiable anymore. "Who's the guy?" The tone of his voice became crisp, businesslike.

"Dillerman, Jerry Dillerman. Comes from Murcer."

"Sure," Harold said. "Was a cop up there. Christ, they'll take on anybody, I guess."

"He got kicked off, left town. The word is, he's operating down here. We wanna know what he's been doing, how he stands."

Harold looked at me. "This guy working for you?"

"Yeah. He's all right."

Harold poured himself another cup of coffee. Each of his stubby fingers wore an expensive ring, jewelry worth enough to keep a family of four in groceries for a long time. "Has Dillerman done anything I should know about?"

"All we know, he beat up my man here a little while back."

Fat Harold looked at me, obviously searching for signs of physical damage. "You're still in one piece. Most people don't survive so well, Dillerman roughs 'em up."

"Somebody spooked him," I said. "I was lucky."

"Ball can take care of himself," Razzilli said. Harold looked at me with respect in his eyes. I decided I owed Razzilli another lunch.

"There's not too much I can tell you, Rich," Harold said. "Dillerman ran a few errands for me, but that was a while back."

"Like what kind of errands?"

"He muscled a couple of guys for me. That's what he does best. Except I could never be sure he wasn't gonna kill the mark." Harold reached into his pocket and, with some effort, removed a handkerchief and wiped his forehead. "He gets carried away once he gets started. I mean, what do I need that kind of trouble for?"

"Anything else?"

"We cleaned out a warehouse once, color TVs, I needed bodies. I used him on that one."

"He's freelance then."

"Hell, yes. He ain't connected, if that's what you're worried about."

"Something like that," Razzilli said.

"You wanna talk with the guy, no problem. You can do whatever you want with him. Nobody'll get excited, his mother maybe."

"Good deal."

"Between you and me, I wouldn't touch the guy with a ten-foot pole. He comes across like . . . off-the-wall."

"Yeah," Razzilli said, "that's the way people up in Murcer felt about him too."

Harold wheezed and grinned. "In fact, I might go so far as to say Chicago would be a better place to live without the likes of Dillerman."

"Chicago is a fine city," Razzilli said.

"It is," Harold said solemnly. "And we do our best to keep it that way."

"It maybe wasn't necessary this time," Razzilli said, "but you can never really tell." Razzilli was guiding the big Chrysler through more of Chicago's urban tangle. We were still on the South Side but I wasn't sure where. "It may seem kinda funny to an outsider, exaggerated even, but they all take it serious."

"I never would have believed it," I said.

"Ever feel you led a sheltered life, Ball?"

I didn't say anything. I looked out at the streets, which were strewn with garbage and teeming with people. A man heaved a paper bag with a bottle in it against an ancient building, and the bottle broke. Nobody took any notice.

On a narrow side street Razzilli pulled the car up at a fire hydrant and killed the engine. "You game for some action?" he asked.

"Don't ask dumb questions."

"Just making sure."

Two minutes later someone walked over to the car, opened the door, and climbed into the rear seat. It was Olson.

"Where is he?" Razzilli asked without turning his head.

"I haven't seen him today," Olson said. "He got in late last night. Probably still sleeping it off."

"Which one's he in?"

"The two windows over the bakery are his. It's 2-F. Let me know when you get in."

Razzilli and I left Olson in the car and made our way across the street to the entrance of the tenement. The door to the building was ajar, and once inside we were assaulted by the ancient structure's fetid air—a combination of cooking smells, urine, and lack of oxygen. The stairs creaked as we went up them. The only light was from a small bulb screwed into a ceiling outlet over the second-floor landing. We found 2-F and then posted ourselves on opposite sides of the door, Razzilli toward the end of the corridor, me on the landing.

"We wait till he opens up," Razzilli said. "Safer that way."

It was the better part of a half-hour before the door to 2-F was opened. A man wearing only a pair of white jeans and carrying a bag of garbage came out moving in my direction. Before he was fifteen feet from the door, Razzilli moved in behind him, spun him around, and shoved him back toward the door of the apartment all in one motion. The bag of garbage fell and scattered over the floor.

"Inside," Razzilli said. His voice was part growl, part hiss. Razzilli showed Dillerman his gun, then moved around behind him. Dillerman looked at me as I approached from the other direction, then back at Razzilli.

"Who the hell are you guys?"

"Shut up and get inside." Dillerman moved slowly into the apartment with Razzilli behind him. I followed them in and shut the door.

Dillerman was a type some women would go for. Wavy blond hair, cut fashionably long, fair skin, a hawk-shaped nose, a square jaw. But the more perceptive woman would see the emptiness in the blue eyes and the cruelty in the defiant curve of the lip. And she would politely excuse herself and make a beeline for the door.

Physically, Dillerman was impressive—six-two, roughly two hundred twenty pounds, a broad upper torso, the bulging arms of an iron-pumper. On his chest he had tatooed his initials and, below them, a picture of an eagle with its wings partially spread. He dominated the room just standing there. He didn't have to move or say anything.

Suddenly, he broke into a smile. "Say, I know you guys. For a minute I thought you were someone else. You guys are down from Murcer, right? What's the name?"

"You're a bright boy, J.D." Razzilli moved across the room and pulled the shade up and down a couple of times. Dillerman followed him with his eyes, observing his movements closely. He looked back at me. "I'm Razzilli and you remember Mr. Ball here, don't you, J.D.? You had him paged one evening at Durango's."

"I'm not sure."

Razzilli motioned to Dillerman to sit down at the table and spread his hands out in front of him.

"That cut over his eye, it's almost healed now, but you gave it to him."

"Uh-uh. No way. Not me. I ain't been out of Chi, not since Christmas. I ain't been near Murcer."

"Mr. Ball thought you might want to tell him why you went to all that trouble to cause him discomfort." Dillerman made a move with his left hand. "Keep your hands right where they are, J.D." Razzilli stepped around in front of Dillerman, aimed the gun. "You don't open up, I might be tempted to shoot down Old Baldy."

Dillerman smiled again. He had a fine set of white teeth. "Shit, you wouldn't do that, Razzilli. You'd make a mess here in the apartment."

"Who sent you up to Murcer to beat up on Ball, J.D.?"

"I told you. I ain't been up there." Dillerman gestured with his hands, and Razzilli aimed the gun directly at Dillerman's throat.

"Safety's off, J.D. Don't make me nervous. You could end up as an accidental death, a statistic. You know how many people get killed with guns through carelessness every year?"

Dillerman's hands were large, meaty extensions of his powerful forearms. Even at rest on the table they appeared dangerous. Dillerman glared at Razzilli but didn't say anything.

Razzilli handed the gun to me, and then he started looking around the apartment, poking into drawers, closets, examining whatever was lying on the chairs and the room's one table. He disappeared into the bedroom and came out a couple of minutes later.

"You ain't gonna find anything here," Dillerman said.

Razzilli turned his attention to Dillerman and smiled. "Ball was in 'Nam too, J.D."

Dillerman smiled back. "No shit. I was with the Hundred-and-First Airborne. We were—"

"Tell me about it," I said. Dillerman's smile vanished.

"Ball don't care about your war stories, J.D. He wants to know why you gave him a going-over last week."

"I already told you guys—"

"Ball was with an interrogation team over there. The stories he told me about getting information out of people, they make even me shudder." I wondered where Razzilli got his material. I hadn't told him anything.

Dillerman smiled again, but it was a smile of disdain. "We're in the States now, buddy." Dillerman's body was tense, as though he were a cat awaiting his chance to spring. He eyed me intently, gauging his chances, wondering whether I was capable of pulling the trigger.

Razzilli walked toward Dillerman, leaned down on the table, and spoke softly to Dillerman. "You wanna try something, J.D.? Go ahead. Ball here would like nothing better than to shoot some lead into you. He still remembers what you did to him at Durango's. What he'll do is he'll go for your leg, make a cripple out of you. Like you tried to do to him." Razzilli's face was inches from J.D.'s, much nearer than I would have dared.

J.D. mouthed a curse. He did it slowly and distinctly. Despite the lack of sound, his meaning was unmistakable.

Razzilli moved away, shaking his head. "You're not going to be so attractive to the ladies, after I sic Ball on you."

Dillerman twitched nervously. He didn't like the idea of any damage being done to that big, beautiful physique. "How many times—"

"You're the guy," I said. "It was dark but you're the guy."

"Positive I.D.," Razzilli said.

"He don't know what he's talkin' about," Dillerman said to Razzilli.

Razzilli sat down on the arm of the room's one upholstered chair. "I look around at this place and it makes me sick. You haven't come very far in the world, J.D., you know that?"

"What's it to you, Razzilli? What do you care?"

"I care. I'm like a bleeding heart. I always wanna see people from our town of Murcer make good. It hurts me that you're living in a stinking hole like this."

"I'll bet," Dillerman said.

Razzilli got up and walked around the room. "Look, cockroaches in the sink. And this room hasn't had a paint job in—"

"Screw you, Razzilli. You and your friend both. I don't have to listen to this—"

"To show you my heart's in the right place, J.D., and to show we don't hold grudges, look what I'm gonna do." Razzilli took out his wallet and slipped out two fifty-dollar bills. "Look, J.D. Look at this, a pair of U.S. Grants. All you gotta do is tell us— who wanted you to come up to Murcer and beat up on Ball?"

Razzilli dangled the bills casually in front of Dillerman's face. Dillerman made a thin line out of his mouth. "I wasn't in Murcer," he said in a low voice. "Haven't been back there."

"You're a chump," Razzilli said and slipped the money back into his wallet. At the precise moment that Razzilli had his hand in his pocket, Dillerman made his move. He upended the table and shoved it hard in my direction. Moving around the table with catlike rapidity, he came up on me from behind. He delivered a karate chop to my upper arm, sending a searing charge of pain down my right side and causing me to drop the gun. Still on my knees, I tried to recover the gun from under the upended table. Out of the corner of my eye I could see Razzilli moving in on Dillerman from the other side. He didn't get very far. Dillerman hit him hard in the pit of the stomach and followed the blow with a knee to the same place.

I took advantage of Dillerman's preoccupation with Razzilli to shove him hard toward the corner of the room. I caught him off balance and he stumbled against the sink, the violence of his impact causing him to smash some of his stacked dishes. I dove down behind the upended table again in search of the gun as Dillerman came roaring back at me, mouthing curses similar to those I'd heard in Durango's parking lot.

An empty beer bottle came rolling across the floor, and Razzilli picked it up, swung it at Dillerman's head, but caught him only a glancing blow. It hardly fazed him.

I aimed a fist at Dillerman's stomach but missed and caught him in the chest. It was like striking a brick wall. Razzilli took another swing at Dillerman with the beer bottle and caught him this time full in the face. The glass shattered and Dillerman's face was suddenly a sodden, bloody mess, but the pain only served to anger him more. He set himself, crouched, and hit Razzilli, a shot that crumpled him in a heap.

By this time I had retrieved the gun from beneath the table, but before I could bring it up, Dillerman had me from behind. He had one of those mighty arms around my neck and was squeezing with all his strength. I dropped the gun and tried kicking, but it didn't help. I aimed a punch toward where I thought the pit of his stomach might be, but it missed. The pressure was relentless, unyielding, and the shortage of oxygen made me breathless. I fought the pressure of his arm with my free arm but with no effect. I couldn't breathe. Then there was an enveloping blackness. . . .

The pressure eased.

"What the hell!" Olson said. He was standing there with a gun in his hand. He'd obviously slugged Dillerman with the butt.

Dillerman was in a heap next to the overturned table, the features of his face covered by slowly oozing blood. Razzilli was sitting on the floor emitting sounds that were half gasps and half moans. I staggered to my feet and shook the cobwebs out of my head. I felt a ferocious pain in my left temple. I staggered across the room, threw open the window, and drew in great quantities of air. The stuff had never tasted so good.

"I think I decided to come up here at just the right time," Olson said.

"That's . . . what I . . . pay you for," Razzilli said in between groans. He got to his feet and staggered uncertainly toward the bathroom. I followed him in, and we took turns splashing water on ourselves. After we'd made ourselves reasonably presentable, Razzilli went back out, and stood looking down at Dillerman.

"He's alive," Olson said, "but his days as a matinee idol are finished."

"I think it's time we left this burg," Razzilli said. "We'll leave the mess for the cleaning woman."

We drove back to the airport in silence. We turned in the rental car, and since the next flight to Murcer wasn't until three, we went into the big O'Hare restaurant for lunch. The table linen and hovering waiter gave me a reassuring feeling—as if I'd just returned to civilization after a long absence.

"So what did we find out?" Olson asked after we'd each ordered steaks.

Razzilli poured a glass of beer and took a long swallow. "Not to mess with J.D. without having a regiment to back you up."

"We knew J.D. was a hard case, Rich. Don't tell me you guys came up empty after all the trouble I had finding the guy."

"Not completely empty," Razzilli said. He reached into his pocket and laid a small pink piece of paper on the table. At the top were some printed words: BIDE-A-WHILE MOTEL. "It's a receipt," Razzilli said. "It was in a drawer in the bedroom."

Olson looked at it. "It proves Dillerman was in Murcer last week. He stayed there two days."

I said, "I wonder why he wouldn't talk. Who's he tied up with that's so important?"

Razzilli looked at me menacingly. "I don't know, Ball. But whatever the reason, it's got something to do with you. That much I'm sure of."

"That's the way you figure it?" I said.

"Yeah." Razzilli drained his beer glass with one long swallow and waved his empty bottle at a passing waiter. "That's the way I figure it. No offense."

I didn't say anything. From the slant I had, it was more and more beginning to appear as though Razzilli was the one at the bottom of things. What I needed, though, was some time to figure out why, if he was the guilty one, he had gone to the trouble of staging the visit to Chicago.

At that moment the waiter appeared with the steaks. Razzilli and Olson began eating like starved wolves, but I just picked at mine. I wasn't hungry anymore.

11

The desk clerk at the Bide-a-While Motel had almond-shaped eyes, pointy ears, and resembled some kind of rodent, a weasel maybe, or a squirrel. He was perhaps thirty, but because of thinning brown hair and a gaunt, emaciated face he loooked at least five years older. In a practiced voice he asked us how he could help us.

After Razzilli identified himself, his expression took on a speculative, calculating air. He didn't say anything. Razzilli took out a twenty and laid it on the counter. The clerk glanced quickly down and then back up.

"We'd like some information on a guest who stayed here last week," Razzilli said.

"I'm sorry. We're not permitted—"

"I understand perfectly," Razzilli said.

The clerk moved away and began shuffling some papers. A guest approached the desk, asked the clerk about a message, and left. Razzilli and I didn't move. Razzilli sighed, then removed another twenty from his billfold, and placed it next to the first.

A minute later the clerk returned. He glanced down at the money. "I'd like to help you, really I would but—"

Razzilli took out a ten and silently laid it on the counter. The clerk's eyes brightened perceptibly.

"It's against the rules, you understand," he said, "but—"

"The name is Dillerman," Razzilli said. "He was here last week, two days. Can you tell us if he made any phone calls from his room?"

Without a word the clerk disappeared into a back room. He came back a moment later and shook his head. "No calls."

"You happen to remember anything about this particular guest?" Razzilli asked. "Like if he met someone, had visitors, or whatever."

The clerk said he didn't recall Dillerman, but that he'd stayed in Cabin Number Six, and that he'd ask around. But that the asking would take time.

"You get back to me with anything, and it's another payday." The clerk nodded, deftly picked the bills off the counter, and placed them in the lapel pocket of his suit jacket. Razzilli gave him his card.

"Call me at this number," he said. "And one other thing. If this guy ever comes back here, let me know right away."

"I surely will," said the clerk.

"You talk about inflation," Razzilli said when we were back in the car. "I remember when ten dollars was enough to get you chapter and verse on whoever and whatever in this city."

"Those were the days," I said.

"No they weren't," Razzilli said and gunned the engine. "In those days I was so poor I had to beat information out of people."

Razzilli let me off at the house shortly before seven. I spent a few minutes in the shower and put on some fresh clothes. The clock said 7:25. I didn't feel like rattling around the old place for the rest of the evening, so I decided to act on impulse. Fifteen minutes later I was seated in the car in front of the *Telegram* building. I had been waiting perhaps twenty minutes when Sylvia appeared, moving rapidly through the big glass doors. I jumped out of the car, opened the door, and made a low bow.

"Clint! What are you—"

"I could say I just happened to be in the neighborhood, but it wouldn't be true. Would you care for a ride?"

"I'd love one," she said and with an enormous sigh plumped herself down on the seat. "I'm dead."

I drove out to a diner on River Road, where amidst crowds of teenagers and loud jukebox music, we ordered soup, hamburgers, french fries, and coffee.

"I've missed you," I said as I loaded down an order of french fries with several gobs of catsup.

"My husband used to be a catsup fiend. I can't stand the stuff."

"For you, fair damsel," I said, "I'd give up anything, but catsup never."

"Come to think of it, maybe the reason he went so heavy on the catsup was to disguise the taste of my cooking."

"I've always enjoyed living dangerously."

Sylvia looked at me questioningly. When she spoke her voice was serious. "Clint, there are some things I think I should know . . ."

"I suppose you mean in connection with the Hockley murder."

"Well, yes, that. And other things. The incident out at Durango's. When that happened I thought it was . . . well, a case of mistaken identity, or something."

"I won't forget how you nursed me back to health that evening, Sylvia. I thought that might be the start of . . . something between us."

Sylvia fingered the top button of her blouse, buttoning it and unbuttoning it. "I thought so too. But when . . ."

"When Hockley was murdered in my aunt's home you began to reconsider."

"Do you blame me?"

I paused before answering. The jukebox played loudly in the background, some kind of country song. "No," I said finally. "Not really."

Sylvia reached across the table and placed her hand on mine. "I'm sorry, Clint."

"I didn't murder Hockley, Sylvia." Sylvia had compelled me to say it. I had hoped I wouldn't have to.

"But you must know more than you're telling." Sylvia withdrew her hand. I watched as she raised her coffee cup to her lips. Just looking at her gave me pleasure. The thought occurred to me that my aunt's confession was becoming an impossible burden. I felt a strong temptation at that moment to tell Sylvia the entire story. Sylvia spoke first. "You're too secretive, Clint. Just like when you were a child—"

"Sylvia!"

"I'm sorry."

We were silent for the next five minutes. I wolfed down the hamburger, but Sylvia only picked at her food in a preoccupied, disinterested fashion. "Take me home, Clint," she said finally. Her voice was faint, hardly audible over the sound of electric guitars on the jukebox.

"When will I see you again?" I asked Sylvia as we stood before the entrance to the small apartment building in which she lived.

"Call me in a day or two. Maybe things are moving too quickly." She hesitated. "And tomorrow's a workday. . . ."

"I understand."

After placing the key in the lock, she turned and said, "Clint, I *do* like you." Then she moved inside and let the heavy metal door close behind her.

On the drive home I thought about things from Sylvia's point of view. She still wasn't eager to involve herself with me. I supposed that her marriage had made her more cautious of entanglements than she might have been otherwise. Nevertheless, I was confident that once I could tell her the entire story, I would have no difficulties breaking down her barriers of reserve. I thought about how much less complicated my personal life would be if Sylvia would show the same confidence in me that Sonia had shown.

The depth of my feeling for Sylvia surprised even me. We had, after all, only been together a half a dozen times. I had, of course, known there was something missing from my life ever since the breakup with Doris, an incident that had left me feeling more alone and more empty than at any time previously. Sylvia represented something I had lost when I lost Doris. She represented something I very much wanted and very much needed.

I spent most of the next morning working in Aunt Phyllis's garden, pulling weeds and trimming plants and hedges. While I worked I considered reporting the trip to Chicago to Breyer and Gronski, then decided against it. I knew it would mean involved explanations of how I had gotten on to Dillerman and eventually a confession that I had been withholding information. I decided the matter could wait. In the course of the day I received two telephone calls. The first was from Sonia's secretary, asking me to come by the office and sign some paper in connection with the estate. The second was from Razzilli.

"Things may be breaking, kiddo," he said.

"How so?"

"Van Beldin's arranged a meeting with Korban at five-thirty this evening. He wants both of us there. For moral support. Can you be in his office an hour before?"

I said I could.

"And, Ball, bring your best table manners. We're meeting at the White Lotus Club."

"I'll bring my appetite too," I said and hung up before he could get in the last word.

* * *

Razzilli and van Beldin were already in van Beldin's office when I arrived there that afternoon. Van Beldin started talking as soon as I sat down.

"I have to admit I was skeptical at first, but Richie here persuaded me that you should be present when I meet Korban this evening. You don't have any objections, I hope."

"On the contrary."

"That's what we thought. We agree, too, that you have a perspective in this thing that might be helpful in analyzing whatever he has to tell us."

"Not to mention that you seem to be in it up to your neck," Razzilli said.

I was about to reply, but van Beldin spoke first. "I suppose I don't have to tell you gentlemen that it's costing me to do business in this way. Korban's not making things easy."

"What he means," Razzilli said, "is Korban's agreed to tell us how he got the information concerning Mrs. van Beldin, but he's not doing it for nothing."

"He's asking for significant concessions on my part," van Beldin said. "I'm supposed to arrange a line of credit for him with the bank, I'm supposed to give up my opposition on environmental grounds to the development of certain lands. All in all, I'm going to look like a fool when the news of these things gets around."

"I can see that you're being put in an uncomfortable position," I said.

"There's no sacrifice I won't make for my wife," van Beldin said. Razzilli nodded seriously and looked toward the window. "I only hope that whatever Korban has to tell us brings us closer to the solution to this thing."

"There's something else you wanted to tell Ball, Mr. van Beldin," Razzilli said. "About your wife."

"Yes, of course. My wife's condition has improved to the point where she's permitted visitors. She's asked to see you."

"To see me?" I couldn't keep the surprise out of my voice.

"She says she wants to talk with you about . . . your aunt."

"I see."

"To be honest, we've tried to dissuade her, but she's been insistent. She says there are things you should know, things she can't tell anybody else." Van Beldin shrugged his shoulders. "She also says she wants to see how you turned out."

Razzilli looked at his watch. "Time to move," he said.

"There's one other thing," van Beldin said. "Whatever is said this evening is in the strictest confidence. Nothing is repeated to anyone, ever. We want to keep the lid on, if it's at all possible."

The White Lotus was a businessman's club of relatively recent vintage, an establishment that had sprung up to fill the social needs of successful people who couldn't gain membership in Murcer's older, more exclusive clubs. I was sure that van Beldin was entering the White Lotus for the first time. I suspected that, for van Beldin, meeting his rival on his rival's own turf was more galling than any financial concessions he might have to make.

The club was sedate enough. It was located on a side street not far from Murcer's central business district, and was shielded from the street by a large iron gate and a six-foot hedge. The only indication of its function was a small metal plaque attached to one of the pillars of the gate.

Korban met us downstairs at the reception desk. Personal greetings, cordial handshakes, a brief description of the building's layout. Then he guided us up a broad, heavily carpeted staircase into the second-floor lounge.

He said, "I've reserved a table for dinner at six, but we can perhaps settle some preliminaries here." Razzilli and I took the hint and wandered off to play a game of billiards in the next room while the business wizards smoothed out the details. I imagined Korban would have some way of guaranteeing what he was going to get from van Beldin in exchange for his information and his silence.

At six Razzilli and I entered the main dining room, a cavernous, high-ceilinged chamber with white-uniformed waiters scurrying back and forth. The head waiter was all deference and led us to a table Korban had doubtless specified in advance—in the farthest corner of the room and well out of earshot of any neighboring diners.

The small talk continued throughout most of the meal, and I could see that van Beldin was getting edgy. But Korban was determined to do things his way, and it was only after he had ordered himself an exotic dessert that Korban led into the subject.

"We all agree," he said, "that nothing of what I say this evening goes any farther—"

"We've already said that," van Beldin said impatiently.

Korban nodded. Then he began his story.

"I'm going to give you fellows the framework, the facts, and then you can ask questions when I'm through." He blandly forked up a mouthful of dessert and wiped his mouth. "It's no secret to you guys that I was working out of Chicago before I came to Murcer. I was doin' this and that. Tried a bunch of things, finally got into construction. Then I began buying and selling real estate. Nothing big, understand." Korban pushed away the empty plate, reached for a glass of water. "It was through a real estate transaction that I first met Jack Hoglin."

A waiter approached, removed some plates, and refilled our coffee cups. Korban waited until he had withdrawn to continue. "Anyone ever heard of Hoglin?"

We shook our heads.

"Should we have?" van Beldin asked.

"The reason I'm asking," Korban said, "Hoglin was a lawyer. He was born in Murcer and grew up here." Korban picked up the salt shaker and began toying with it absentmindedly. "Anyway, Hoglin was interested in some of the things I was doing, and I think he kinda liked my style—anyway, after a time he lent me some money to move on certain things. You get the picture?"

We all mumbled that we did.

"Well, it was maybe nine, ten months later him and me became partners. Except Hoglin didn't want his name on anything. He wanted to keep a low profile."

Razzilli asked why.

"Taxes, probably," van Beldin said.

Korban scowled. He didn't like other people answering questions that were directed at him. "Taxes, maybe, but Hoglin was into all kinds of things. With him you never knew."

"I've met the type," van Beldin said. There was a touch of disdain in his tone. Korban raised an eyebrow but didn't say anything.

"What was the financial arrangement?" Razzilli asked.

"Fifty-fifty off the top. Jack got his in cash. Anyway, it got so after a while that we were working only on his information. He knew people all over. The guy was a magician. We made a bundle."

"All right, all right," van Beldin said. "But what's the connection with what we want to know?"

Korban ignored the interruption, paused, drank some coffee, and took out a handful of cigars. Except for van Beldin, who seemed to be dying of impatience, we all lit up. "Like I say, Hoglin knew people all over. Most of our deals were around Chicago, but we also got into stuff in Phoenix, Reno, and LA. Then, like seventeen years ago, Jack comes to me with a story about Murcer."

"What kind of story?" Razzilli asked.

"He said there was something over here he wanted me to see. So the next weekend we drove over. We drove out to the country north of the city, and Hoglin tells me how this land is gonna be designated for Special Improvement Districts—"

"S.I.D.s," van Beldin said.

"Murcer had to expand. Things were booming all over. All this land was gonna be developed commercially, residentially, Jack said. This was the land that the Planning Board was gonna designate, except that nobody knew it yet."

"How did Hoglin know?" I asked.

"Hoglin never said where he got any of his information, and I never asked him. But he said it was a sure thing. He suggested we take options on the land, anything we could get north of the city."

"And you did," van Beldin said.

"We sure as hell did," Korban said coolly. "What would you have done?"

Van Beldin didn't say anything.

"That's how I got my start in Murcer. Less than a year later the whole area was rezoned, just like Hoglin said it would be. And we had options on the whole thing." Korban couldn't keep a trace of smugness out of his voice.

"Then what?" Razzilli asked.

I was getting the feeling that Korban was telling the story to indicate to us how smart he was. We were all still looking for the connection between these facts and how he got to know van Beldin's wife had murdered Joey Hauck. But one thing was sure: He was going to tell the story in his way.

"Anyway, a lot of that's ancient history, and I didn't do anything illegal," Korban said.

"Maybe you didn't, but what about your partner?" van Beldin said.

Korban shrugged. He exhaled a large cloud of blue smoke and gazed into the distance. "Be that as it may, that's how I got my start in Murcer."

"It's a nice story," van Beldin said. He made no attempt to keep the irony out of his voice. "Poor boy makes good. So what else is new?"

After pausing a moment to allow a hovering waiter to move out of earshot, Korban continued, ignoring van Beldin's interruption. "I guess it was late last year when I first got the word about . . . Mr. van Beldin here making plans to enter politics on a statewide level. At first, I didn't think that much about it, figuring that like most candidacies it wouldn't amount to much." Van Beldin gritted his teeth but remained silent. "But after the first of the year, sometime in January, it began to appear as if Mr. van Beldin's candidacy had a lot of support, and that he had a good chance to get the party nomination for governor. After that, of course, you would have to figure that his chances of making it to the statehouse were considerably better than fifty-fifty."

"And that's when you began to worry," Razzilli said.

"That's when I began to worry. Somehow I didn't feel that Mr. van Beldin in the statehouse would be all that sympathetic to my interests and goals. In fact I had the impression that Mr. van Beldin might do his damndest to run me out of Murcer entirely."

Van Beldin gazed at Korban impassively. He drummed his fingers on the table but didn't say anything.

"So what I did," Korban continued, "I passed the word. Anybody who could come up with a way to knock off van Beldin, keep him from running, it would be worth twenty-five grand."

Razzilli pursed his lips and made a low whistling sound. "What were you figuring?" he asked.

"Some kind of dirty tricks. You know, like the kind of stuff they were pulling off in Washington back in the seventies. Or maybe something like that newspaper publisher did when he got Muskie crying in New Hampshire. Along those lines."

Van Beldin nodded. I had a feeling he was working to keep back his anger.

Korban looked at van Beldin amiably. "It's done all the time." He gave the impression that dirty tricks, political or otherwise, were all in a day's work as far as he was concerned.

I asked Korban what kind of response he'd got. I couldn't see any connection between these events and what we had come to hear, but I found the story fascinating just the same.

"I'm getting to that now," he said. He exhaled cigar smoke and carefully placed his cigar in the ashtray at the center of the table. "About two weeks ago, I got home one night late, maybe a few minutes after eleven. I was in the house less than five minutes when the phone rang, my private line. Someone asks if I was Warren Korban, I said I was, and this individual asks me how I'd like some information that might prove very valuable to me. 'What kind of information?' I ask. Then this individual says, 'Information that would prevent Peter van Beldin from running for governor.'"

Van Beldin frowned and shifted nervously.

"So I say, 'Does the bear shit in the woods?' And he says it's gonna cost. And I say there's a going rate. And he says, yeah, he heard about it. Twenty-five grand. Then we go back and forth a little more, and we both agree that twenty-five grand is a fair price, and finally I ask how I'm supposed to know this information is reliable and whether it's worth the money. And he says, 'I got information to you once before and that was reliable.' I ask him what that was." Korban paused, looked each of us directly in the eye. "Then the voice on the phone says, 'I'm the guy got the word to you on the S.I.D.s.'"

"Was this Hoglin?" van Beldin asked. He looked like he was ready to leap out of his chair.

"It wasn't Hoglin," Korban said matter-of-factly.

"How do you know?" I asked.

"Hoglin's dead. He died eight years ago."

We sat there, the three of us, not saying anything and watching Korban calmly exhale cigar smoke. Korban enjoyed being the center of attention, and he was playing his little part for all it was worth. Finally, Razzilli asked, "Did you recognize the voice?"

Korban shook his head. "He took precautions to make sure I wouldn't. He was good too. I couldn't tell whether it was a man or woman."

"Oh come off it now," van Beldin said. "Anyone can tell—"

"Mr. Korban's entirely correct," Razzilli said. "There are certain small devices available that, when you speak through them, deprive a person's voice of its identifying characteristics."

I placed the cigar I had been smoking in the ashtray. It had gone out and no longer looked very appetizing. I looked across the table at van Beldin. For once, he was speechless.

"Anyway," Korban said, "this must be the person who got the information on the S.I.D.s to Hoglin fifteen years ago."

"And he's still around," van Beldin said.

Razzilli asked Korban how the information was relayed to him.

"On the phone. He told me if I was interested, report to the post office the next day. There'd be a letter for me, personal delivery. The letter, he said, would contain the information and the instructions for payment. Naturally, I went." Korban reached into his jacket pocket and produced a folded piece of paper. He passed it around for each of us to read:

> On March 5, 1955, Helen Nesbitt, who is now Mrs. Peter van Beldin, shot a man named Joseph (Joey Boy) Hauck in his home at 236 West Baker Road. The murder was never solved. At the time Mrs. van Beldin was employed as a nurse for Dr. Walter Lakeman.

Below the note were instructions to send $25,000 in cash to a Chicago postbox number within the next seven days. I noticed there was no mention of my aunt having been involved in the murder. The note told Korban only what he needed to know to get at van Beldin.

"You sent the money?" Razzilli asked.

Korban nodded. "You kind of get a feeling for certain things. Whoever this was, I felt he knew enough about me to cause problems. I think I did the right thing."

For the first time I began to see a pattern. Maybe there had been someone selling information around Murcer for a very long time. Even Korban wasn't too sure about how to handle the situation.

"Someone seems to know where a lot of bodies are buried," van Beldin said.

"Not only that," Razzilli said. "Someone knows who turned the bodies into corpses. People like that can be very, very dangerous to us, the living."

"Amen," Korban said and made a sign to the waiter.

A certain amount now seemed clear. Find out which individual knew in advance which property was going to be rezoned into S.I.D.s a year before the vote actually took place. That individual was the same person who had known that Mrs. van Beldin had been involved with the murder of Joey Hauck. It now seemed altogether possible that this was the same person who had shot Sid Hockley and tried to frame me by tossing the murder weapon under the bed. There was also the possibility this was the same individual who had sent Dillerman around to beat me up in Durango's parking lot—maybe because I had found out that my aunt was also involved in some manner that still wasn't clear.

After Korban had signed the bill, van Beldin announced he was going home, and we bid him good-bye in front of the club. Razzilli and I were still wide awake, so we picked up a six-pack and walked over to his office.

"It almost has to have been someone on the Planning Board," I said.

Razzilli took a piece of paper out of his desk and read off a list of nine names. "That's the list of the commissioners on the Board when they voted. Three are dead, one's in a nursing home, one's living in Florida."

"That leaves four possibilities."

"But the catch is, none of these four could have swung the vote all by his lonesome."

"A couple of days ago you said the person responsible for swinging the vote was the Planning Commissioner."

"Right. So we're back to him, Stanley Hanks. The only problem is he died six years ago. So it sure as hell wasn't him who made the call to Korban." Razzilli leaned back in his chair, put his feet on his desk, and took a swallow of beer. "And there's another problem we don't want to overlook."

"Which is?"

"Of all the people you can think of, he's the last, the absolute last, who'd've sold out—"

"I don't believe in saints, Razzilli."

"Don't interrupt. Not only was Stanley Hanks honest, his family had money."

"But he had influence."

"He had influence, one, because he was so damned honest,

and two, because he was an engineer who understood zoning problems—access, water tables, construction, even things like pollution. Three, he cared. He never made a decision without examining it and considering it very, very carefully."

After talking it over, Razzilli and I agreed to divide the work. The next day we arranged for him to talk with a couple of the surviving commissioners. I said I'd go out and talk with Mrs. Hanks, Stanley Hanks's widow. That settled, Razzilli got up and came back with a couple of more cans from his office refrigerator.

"You know, Ball," he said after sitting back down, "I feel bad about what happened yesterday. That was the first time I ever hit anybody like that."

"Dillerman, you mean."

"I've been in fights, free-for-alls, but I never hurt anybody like I hurt Dillerman. I have to admit that it's been bothering me."

"Was there a choice?"

"None, none at all. But that still don't mean I'm not sorry."

The only light in the office was from Razzilli's desk lamp, and it cast some strange shadows across the room. The shadows highlighted his round glasses and unkempt hair in such a way that he looked like some kind of animated figure from an old black-and-white movie cartoon. Out in the street there were no more traffic noises. The citizenry of Murcer had packed it in for another day. We drank our beer, neither of us saying anything. We were both thinking about what had happened at Dillerman's apartment the previous day.

"It was my fault," I said after a while. "I had the gun."

"Nobody's fault." Razzilli tossed his empty beer can at the wastebasket six feet away. It missed, and rolled across the rug, stopping at the far wall. Razzilli shook his head and sighed. "What I'm saying, we shouldn't've left him there like that, bleedin' and all."

"What then?"

"We shoulda got him to a hospital, shoulda talked with him. It wasn't right." There was the sound of a couple of hisses as Razzilli popped the tops on the two fresh cans and passed one over.

"Look what he did to me," I said pointing toward the cut on my head. "He's an animal. Besides, we tried talking with him."

Razzilli shrugged. "Don't make no difference. I was in charge. I didn't handle it right."

I was having difficulty reconciling Razzilli's soft-hearted sentiments with the image of the hard-nosed private investigator. I wondered whether he might not have used Dillerman as some kind of fall guy, as part of a scheme to get my confidence before setting me up for something. Finally, I said, "Maybe you should go into the restaurant business after all."

Razzilli smiled, something he seldom did, and it gave a serene quality to his expression. I wondered whether the fact I was sitting alone with him in his office trading confidences didn't mean I was being a prize fool. Korban had said that the person on the phone had effectively disguised his voice, perhaps by the use of some special device. Such a trick would surely be in the repertoire of a private investigator like Razzilli. In addition, a man in Razzilli's position would have been in an ideal position to pick up information concerning the city's plans to rezone its lands. . . .

"When are you heading back to New York, Ball?"

"On the weekend—early next week if I can get another couple of days from the firm."

"Did I ever tell you I was born in New York, Brooklyn actually?"

"I didn't know. How'd you happen to land here in Murcer?"

"I joined the navy when I was eighteen, right out of high school. I was stationed for a couple of years out at Great Lakes. We used to go into Chicago all the time. One night at a dance I met this girl from Murcer, eventually married her. She suggested coming to Murcer after my discharge. Been here ever since, twenty-five years." Razzilli tilted his beer can to his lips and took another long swallow. "But you know, after all these years I still miss Brooklyn."

"How do you explain that?"

"Where I grew up, everybody was Italian, and I mean everybody. We musta had thirty, forty relatives all living within five blocks of us—aunts, uncles, cousins, in-laws, you name it. It gave you a good feeling."

I nodded.

"It must've been real tough on you, alone like that."

"You don't miss what you never had."

"I dunno if that's true. There's some things everyone's gotta have." Razzilli leaned back in his chair, put his feet back up on his desk. "You've done real well for yourself. I admire you. I know how tough it must've been to fight your way up from nowhere."

"I had the desire. I was still young when I realized I wanted certain things, things I didn't have as a kid. It didn't take long to figure out that it was money that bought these things. That's why I went to college and that's what kept me there. That's what kept me working when other people were taking ski trips and partying."

"You're good at what you do. I can tell that."

"The better I do my job, the better I get paid."

"I never went to college myself. I never really wanted to be much more than my father. He was a longshoreman, on the docks in Red Hook, a part of Brooklyn."

"That's one of the rough parts, isn't it?"

"I guess, but it didn't seem so rough growing up there. Again, I think it was because of the family. My father, when he'd miss the shape-up, which was most of the time, he'd spend the day doing something else. Sometimes I'd see him on the way home from school, painting screens, washing cars. . . . I'd point him out to the other kids. Hey, there's my dad! I was proud. It didn't make no difference to me what he did. Funny, I'm still that way with people."

"Most people think differently."

"Would you believe, one day he had a shoeshine stand down on Hamilton Avenue? There wasn't any business, so he gave all us kids a free shoe shine."

"No money in that."

"It was Depression, so nobody had anything. It wasn't so important."

"Depends on your point of view."

"True. A lot of my friends' fathers had different ideas. They got into the rackets, got out of the neighborhood. Some did pretty well, I guess. A couple ended up at the bottom of the Hudson River. Some got free room and board at the expense of the state."

"What are you trying to say?"

"Everybody likes money, Ball, but it stands too high on some people's list of priorities. They'll do anything to get it. That's why the divorce rate is so high. The agency gets a certain amount of domestic work, so I see it up close. Money breaks up families more than anything else. And of course money is a cause of the high crime rate."

"Misplaced priorities?"

"Yeah, something like that."

I got up, yawned, and stretched. "I'm tired. I'm going home." The fact was, I wasn't that interested in listening to any more of Razzilli's musings.

"I'm tired too," Razzilli said. "My wife says she always knows when I'm ready for bed. I get philosophical."

12

Mrs. Stanley Hanks was an active woman, and it took me most of the following day to catch up with her. When I arrived at the Hanks's colonial-style mansion at eleven the next morning, I was told Mrs. Hanks was at a fund-raising meeting for one of the local charities. She still hadn't returned when I called back at two. On my third visit, at seven that evening, the maid took pity on me. She said that Mrs. Hanks had come and gone, but that if I still wanted to see her, I could catch her at the church. I asked which church, and she said St. Bartholemew's and asked if I knew where it was. I said I did, thanked her, and drove over to St. Bart's.

With its 100-foot-high steeple, massive stonework, and manicured lawns, St. Bartholemew's looked like what it was—the place where the city's moneyed and respectable families came to worship. I parked the Chevette in the big parking lot behind the church, and concluded that St. Bartholemew's was one of the few things in Murcer that had hardly changed since I was a child.

One of the attendants told me that the women's club was meeting downstairs in the clubroom. I found my way down a flight of narrow winding stairs into a cozily furnished and thickly carpeted basement anteroom. I pulled up a comfortable chair and waited for the women's club to wind up its evening's deliberations. At a few minutes after eight, a number of middle-aged women came drifting out of the meeting room. One of them pointed Mrs. Stanley Hanks out to me.

I waited while Mrs. Hanks went over a set of figures with two fellow club members. She was a trim, tall woman in her late fifties, with silvery blue hair and a self-confident, not quite regal bearing. She wore a medium-weight blue-gray suit, and a pink blouse added just the right amount of flair to the general impression of responsibility that her manner conveyed. She talked freely and naturally and, I noticed, was not reluctant to laugh when something struck her as amusing. I took her to be the woman in charge of the club, possessed of an outgoing personality and organizational abilities. Mrs. Stanley Hanks, I concluded, had found her niche.

When she had finished speaking with the other two women, I approached her and told her who I was.

"Of course. Maggie said you'd come by the house today. I'm sorry I wasn't home. How can I help you, Mr. Ball?"

I said it was a private matter, and that it had to do with her late husband. She went across the room and shut the door. She looked me straight in the eye and said, "I'm always glad of any opportunity to speak of Stanley. Sit down and tell me what's on your mind."

"Essentially, Mrs. Hanks, it relates to work your husband did as a member of the City Council Planning Board."

"What are you thinking of specifically, Mr. Ball?"

We were seated opposite one another, and I couldn't keep from noticing how Mrs. Hanks deftly crossed one leg over the other. She might have been well into her fifties, but she was still very attractive indeed. "I'm thinking specifically of certain decisions your husband made concerning the rezoning of property north of Murcer."

"Those lands were rezoned many years ago."

"About fifteen years ago, Mrs. Hanks. I realize it's a long time, but the decision to rezone those particular lands—"

"I know what you're going to say, Mr. Ball. The decision was unexpected and at the time not a very popular one."

"That's correct, Mrs. Hanks."

"And I suppose you're wondering why my husband decided the way he did."

"Yes. I was wondering whether there might have been some other considerations that might have influenced—"

She burst into a broad, friendly grin and shook her head. "Mr. Ball, the only considerations that ever influenced Stanley in such matters was the welfare of the city of Murcer and its citizens. I can assure you of that."

The response was, somehow, just a shade too firm and too practiced. I had the feeling she'd made the statement before, perhaps a number of times.

"The feeling at that time, Mrs. Hanks, was that it would have been more logical to encourage expansion in a southerly rather than a northerly direction."

"I'm familiar with all those arguments, Mr. Ball. That was all people could talk about for a year after the Board made its decision." She uncrossed her legs. "But with time the talk died down. Things have worked out well enough."

"No argument there, Mrs. Hanks, and I'm not trying to cast any aspersions on the memory of your husband."

"My husband's reputation is safe, Mr. Ball. He's remembered as one of the city's most dedicated and capable public servants."

"However, it's not inconceivable that other considerations or even outside pressure may have played a role in the decision he made."

Mrs. Stanley Hanks looked at me queerly. I was being just a bit too insistent. I was violating canons of good taste by talking about the dead in this way. When she spoke again, it was in the manner of the patient teacher addressing a slightly retarded pupil. "There are many persons in Murcer who are in a better position to evaulate Stanley's technical abilities than I am. He was an engineer, you know. But I'm the one best suited to talk about his character—his honesty, his dedication."

"And you feel—"

"I feel nothing could have influenced him except the good of the city of Murcer. What makes me admire my husband even more, Mr. Ball, is that things were not easy for us in those years. I had my problems, and of course they caused Stanley great concern."

"What kind of problems were those, Mrs. Hanks?"

"I was an alcoholic, Mr. Ball. I can say it now, and I can talk about it. But until I was able to recognize and confront the problem, it was a source of tremendous difficulty for my husband and my children."

"I know that's the hard part, confronting it."

"It was the accident that helped bring things to a head. Sometimes I almost think that the accident showed the hand of God, except that the little girl was . . . killed. But it was the accident that forced me to see myself as I really was."

I let Mrs. Stanley Hanks talk. Beneath that outgoing, plausible manner there was, I felt, an uncontainable egotism. Beyond repeating a certain number of pat phrases, she had no interest in speaking of her husband. What she really wanted to talk about was herself. I provided her the opportunity and she responded enthusiastically. It was interesting. I had the feeling she'd told it many times to meetings of A.A. As she talked, I wondered whether it wasn't this overpowering egotism that might have been responsible for her initially becoming dependent on alcohol.

The story Mrs. Stanley Hanks told was of a young woman who, when she married at twenty-five, was ill-prepared for the additional responsibilities that married life would bring with it. Of a woman who became more and more depressed by the extended absences from home caused by her husband's frequent business trips. Of a woman who gradually evolved from being a social drinker to a person with a marked alcohol dependency. Of a woman who, by the time she was in her early thirties, was showing all the signs of her habit—forgetfulness, blackouts, frequent loss of self-control.

Of a woman who, one rainy evening on a road outside Murcer, lost control of her car and ran down and killed a 16-year-old girl on a bicycle. . . .

"One thing I'll never forget, Mr. Ball, was the support shown me at that time by my husband and Pastor Williams here at the church. I don't know if I ever would have put my life together if it hadn't been for them. It was Pastor Williams who showed me the power of prayer. I remember praying to God and telling Him, if I was spared going to jail for what I had done I would never again take another drink and would devote the balance of my life to church work."

"And is that what happened, Mrs. Hanks?"

"The verdict of the hearing was accidental death. It was the official determination that I had not been guilty of causing the young girl's death."

Razzilli frowned. We were seated in his office just before noon the next day, and I had just finished repeating to him the story that Mrs. Hanks had told me the previous evening. "Did she say whether she had been drinking that night?"

"She didn't say and I didn't ask."

"Always the diplomat, eh, Ball?"

"Other people's feelings are sacred to me."

Razzilli winced. "If it was clear that she was drunk behind the wheel, there's no way she could have gotten off. Absolutely no way."

"What do you think?"

"I guess she hadn't been drinking that evening."

"Are there any other alternatives?" I asked.

"Sure, but they're so sordid I wouldn't want to even consider them."

I asked Razzilli what he had learned talking with the former Board members.

"I was able to talk with two, Ken Deutsch and Sy Raiter. They both confirmed what I thought. Hanks was the guy who turned the vote around. Deutsch even admitted he changed his vote at Hanks's urging. Raiter said Hanks visited him at home a couple of times to discuss the vote. He says he couldn't see going north then, and he voted against. But the vote to go north carried anyway, six to three."

I looked at my watch. "I'm supposed to speak with Mrs. van Beldin today at the hospital at two o'clock."

Razzilli nodded. "I'm gonna try and get a look at the testimony that was given at Mrs. Hanks's hearing."

"It was a closed hearing. That's not possible."

"Ball, when are you gonna learn that for me nothing's impossible in this city?"

"What do you expect to find?"

"Who knows? But if you're interested, I'm willing to fill you in."

"Of course I'm interested," I said.

"Meet me in Metzger's tonight at six. We'll talk about it. Now get outta here. I got work to do."

I took Razzilli's broad hint and left the office. I still had time before my appointment at the hospital, and I decided to stop by Sonia's office. Her secretary told me that Sonia had left shortly before noon and that she probably wouldn't be back for the rest of the day. I reminded her that Sonia had some papers she wanted me to sign.

After a short search of Sonia's office, she said, "I'm awfully sorry, Mr. Ball. I know she had them on her desk, but I can't find them now." I said that it was all right and that I'd make an effort to reach Sonia at home.

I knew that it was time to start talking to Gronski. He and Breyer deserved some kind of report concerning what I'd been able to learn in the last two days—first from Korban, then from Mrs. Hanks. I figured they might be able to make some sense out of it all. I certainly couldn't. If the police were able to connect Razzilli to it in any way, that would be fine. I would then be off the hook. I had taken things about as far as I could. I decided I would call Gronski later that evening, after I'd seen Mrs. van Beldin and talked again with Razzilli.

Then I drove across town to the hospital.

Van Beldin, dressed in a light gray suit and plain woolen tie, met me outside the door to his wife's room. He stuck out his hand. "Good to see you, Ball. Thanks for taking the trouble to come."

I asked him how his wife was.

He shrugged. "She's off the respirator, but she's still being fed intravenously. Heart and kidneys seem all right, so I guess you can say she's improving. I'll feel a lot better when she's home."

"Has she said why she wants to see me?"

"She says she'll only talk to you. I haven't pressed her."

I nodded and we went in.

I recognized Mrs. van Beldin as the worried-looking woman who had been at my aunt's funeral and who had left before I could speak with her. She was propped up in bed, dressed in an expensive-looking sleeping costume, a white sleeping coat with flecks of blue. At a point in the neighborhood of her heart there were three blue-black discs that were connected by wires to a machine on the wall, which I took to be the cardiac monitor. On another wall there was a large clock; over the bed, suspended from the ceiling, was a color television set.

Mrs. van Beldin smiled at me as her husband took care of the introductions. It was a reticent, bashful smile that gave her a kind of gentle, unwordly look, a look that might have made some men feel she was in need of their protection. But the steely blue of her eyes conveyed a fierce inner determination and the impression that Mrs. Peter van Beldin was perfectly capable of taking care of herself, thank you. She was, although not a beautiful woman, an attractive one. Her skin was clear and pale, her hair brunette and slightly gray, her features well formed.

A nurse looked in briefly, and when van Beldin said everything was fine, she went out again. Van Beldin and I sat down on chairs next to the bed.

"I'm very happy to see you again, Mr. Ball," Mrs. van Beldin said. Her voice was clear and surprisingly strong.

"We've all been under a great strain the past few weeks," Peter van Beldin said.

"What my husband is trying to do is offer some excuse for what I did. But there is no excuse. I'm very ashamed of myself." She paused. "Do you mind if I call you Clinton?"

"Clinton is fine," I said.

"My husband tells me that you're an engineer, that you work for a firm in New York, that you're successful."

I said that that was more or less true.

"And you're happy in what you do?"

"Yes, I am."

She sighed. "I've known you for a long time, Clinton, since you were so high." She put out her hand to show how high. "I knew your aunt. She was very pleased that you were so successful. I didn't see her often in the last few years."

"Don't excite yourself, Helen," van Beldin said. She ignored him. I got the impression she generally ignored him.

"The reason I asked you up here today is to tell you a story. Parts of it you already know. But what I tell you may clarify certain things for you, things that up until now have been puzzling." She moved slightly in the bed to make herself more comfortable. "Whether you tell anyone else the story is up to you."

"Helen, do you think you should—"

"My husband obviously doesn't think I should say any more than is necessary. However, I feel too much has been concealed for too long."

"I appreciate the confidence you're showing in me," I said.

She nodded. Her eyes took on a faraway look, the expression worn by people thinking about the distant past. "As you perhaps

know, Clinton, I'm a registered nurse. Shortly after receiving my
cap, I went to work in the private practice of Dr. Walter Lakeman. I'm sure you've heard of him."

"I suppose just about everyone in Murcer has heard of Dr.
Lakeman."

Mrs. van Beldin cleared her throat. "To understand what I'm
going to say, you have to know something about Dr. Lakeman,
what kind of man he was. He wasn't your typical small-town doctor. In his manner he was more like a . . . lumberjack. He was
big—about six-four—very direct. He had no patience for lying or
cruelty. He'd been in the Medical Corps in the Second War, and
I suppose some of those experiences carried over into his later
life. Above all, he was a fine doctor. I very much admired Dr.
Lakeman from the first moment I went to work for him. That
opinion has never changed."

Van Beldin nodded solemnly. This part he'd heard before.

Mrs. van Beldin looked at her husband. "Peter doesn't like it
when I talk this way about Dr. Lakeman." She put out her hand
and he reached over and took it. She withdrew it, and continued
with the story. "One other thing I should say about Dr. Lakeman: he was impulsive, so very impulsive." Her eyes reddened
slightly.

"Can I get you anything?" van Beldin asked.

She shook her head. "It was in Dr. Lakeman's office that I first
saw you, Clinton. I'll never forget it. You looked so . . . forlorn.
And with all those welts and bruises. One eye almost closed. Do
you remember it at all?"

"No ma'am, I don't. Not at all."

"How could you? You were five years old at the time. And I
suppose you wouldn't want to remember. I can't think you'd
want to remember." Mrs. van Beldin's voice trailed off. Then she
said, "Your father, do you remember him at all?"

"Not very well. He's only a vague memory."

She nodded. "It was raining that evening, and Dr. Lakeman
had already seen the last patient. It was after nine when I heard
the front doorbell. The doctor was in the inner office, so I went
out to see who it was. Your father was standing there, drenched,
holding you in his arms. He came stumbling into the waiting
room, and that was when I saw you—"

"Easy, Helen," van Beldin said.

"You were sighing softly, not crying. I remember how shocked

I was. Your face was covered with marks and bruises. One arm was hanging limp. There was a good deal of blood. I snatched you away from your father and immediately carried you into the doctor. Your father waited in the outer office."

Van Beldin twitched nervously but didn't say anything.

"When we got your clothing off, we saw your entire body was covered with similar bruises." Mrs. van Beldin produced a handkerchief and dabbed at her eyes. "While the doctor worked on you, I went out to ask your father what had happened. He said you'd been playing and had fallen down a flight of stairs. We spent a long time working on you. You were only half-conscious most of the time. When we were very nearly through, Dr. Lakeman asked me if your father was still in the outer office. When I said yes, he said 'Good,' because he was very interested in talking with him. I was still looking after you when Dr. Lakeman went out to talk with your father. Shortly thereafter, I went out myself but was surprised to find no one there—neither Dr. Lakeman nor your father—"

I looked at van Beldin. He frowned and said, "Where were they?"

Mrs. van Beldin went on as if there had been no interruption. "Then I heard sounds outside, unusual sounds. I went out the side door and at the back of the house I saw them. It was a chilling night. Two men, big men, standing in the rain, beating on one another like that. I screamed and called for them to stop, but they ignored me. Your father was down a number of times but always got up again. He succeeded in knocking Dr. Lakeman down once. Finally, Dr. Lakeman forced your father up against the house in such a way that he couldn't fall. He kept striking, hitting. His blows took on a kind of rhythm. I could see your father could no longer defend himself. I tried to hold his arms, but he pushed me aside like I was a child. He kept on and on, and as he did so, he kept saying over and over, 'Maybe you'll know better next time, now that you know what it's like yourself.' Finally, Clinton, your father slumped to the ground. Dr. Lakeman just stood over him, looking down, saying the same thing over and over."

Van Beldin stood up and walked to the window. He stood there for a long moment looking out. Neither he nor I said anything.

After a while Mrs. van Beldin said, "I don't actually think that

Dr. Lakeman was even aware I was standing there, the intensity of this hatred he felt for your father was so great. I asked him then whether we shouldn't go into the house. He bent over to carry your father with us; then he knelt down alongside him. After a moment he said, 'My God, I've killed the man.'"

I suppose the astonishment was written on my face.

"I'm sorry, Clinton," she said.

"That's how my father died?"

Mrs. van Beldin nodded.

"But that's not the story my aunt told me. It can't be. Everyone knows my father was—"

Mrs. van Beldin raised her hand. "I know."

Van Beldin turned from the window and moved back toward the bed. His face was set in a dark frown. "Helen, I think you should consider very carefully—"

She looked at him angrily. "I have considered carefully. This man is going to know the complete story. We'll worry about the consequences later."

I said, "My father's body was found in Bedford Street."

"After we realized your father was dead, we carried his body into the house. You were already sound asleep on the cot in the doctor's office. After we'd gotten your father inside, we saw what had killed him. He was bleeding profusely from the temple. He'd probably struck his head against the bench once when he fell. We did what we could but he was past saving."

Van Beldin poured himself a glass of water from the pitcher beside the bed. He didn't ask whether anyone else wanted any.

"Walter wanted to report the incident to the police. When he started dialing the number, I took the telephone away from him. I told him not to be a fool. The chances were no one knew of your father's visit, and no one had been in the waiting room when you arrived. All that was necessary, I said, was to dispose of the body. I told him it wouldn't be difficult. At this point the only one who could have said what had happened was you. I assumed you had no idea of where you were or of what had happened."

I nodded. I had absolutely no recollection of the incident.

"Walter was still unconvinced. I pointed out to him that all that could be gained by reporting the incident would be a man-slaughter conviction and very possibly a prison sentence. It almost certainly would mean the end of his career as a doctor. He finally agreed, reluctantly, and we decided on a course of action. "The first thing was to get you home without disturbing or waking you. We took the house keys from your father's pocket and drove you home. We undressed you and put you to bed. We reasoned that the next day you would have only the vaguest recollection of where you'd been, probably not enough to give anyone a coherent account. You would have thought it was your father who had brought you home and put you to bed."

Mrs. van Beldin looked toward her husband. He was now sitting with his face in his hands, staring at the floor.

"Then we returned to the office and drove with your father's body downtown. We decided that the most logical thing to do was bring it to Bedford Street."

Even in those years, Bedford Street was notorious, the place where derelicts congregated. It housed bars, brothels, and pornography shops.

"It was late when we got there, still raining. Walter drove your father's car, and I followed in his car. Since the streets were totally deserted, he merely parked the car, carried the corpse into an alley, and left it there. He parked your father's car a few blocks away. Then we drove home."

I said, "The assumption always was that my father had been mugged or else had gotten into some kind of brawl."

"We even took his wallet, emptied it, and then threw it beside the body in order to give the killing the appearance of some kind of robbery."

"It fooled the police," I said.

"We thought we were very clever, very clever," Mrs. van Beldin said. She sighed audibly. "But there's no such thing as the perfect crime. Isn't that what they say?"

"That's what they say," van Beldin mumbled. He appeared very angry.

"About ten days later a man came to the doctor's office, a coarse, unkempt man. His manner was very arrogant. He said he wanted to speak with the doctor and he wanted me in the room at the same time. Strange, even before he told us what he wanted, I had a sense of foreboding. Perhaps it was the way in which he spoke to us, as though he were laughing at us. He said that he'd seen us drag the body from the car and leave it in the alley. He'd been watching from the window of a men's room that looked out on the alley."

"Bad luck," van Beldin said. There was a heavy amount of irony in his tone.

"He'd followed us after we left the alley and got into the cars. He took down both license plate numbers. He assumed that we'd murdered your father. He was able to discover that Dr. Lakeman was in a financial position to pay for his silence."

"This was Joey Hauck," I said.

"Yes, yes it was. He wanted to blackmail Walter, Dr. Lakeman. He said he wanted one hundred and fifty dollars a week, rather a substantial sum in those years."

Van Beldin scowled at his wife. "And you went along with something like that?"

Mrs. van Beldin remained calm. "We didn't feel we had any other choice."

"Couldn't you have gone to the police?" van Beldin asked.

"We discussed that, but having disposed of the body, we thought we might very well have been convicted on a murder charge. We felt we'd become too involved to turn back at this point."

"I should say," van Beldin said.

"As bad as paying the money was the knowledge that this . . . monster held our lives in his hands. He had a kind of power over us. It was terrible the way these things affected Walter. He declined terribly. His entire personality altered. I saw it, of course, working with him on a daily basis. That was when I decided something had to be done."

"You were both very naïve," van Beldin said. "You should have made a clean breast of it to the police right away."

Mrs. van Beldin looked at me. "My husband has a way of making things seem very simple." She paused. "Some things, however, did work out well. Your Aunt Phyllis stepped in immediately to become your guardian. Dr. Lakeman advanced her the money to make the first payments on the house."

"You mean, my aunt received money from Dr. Lakeman?"

"Oh yes. He felt responsible for your welfare. The problem was, this Hauck creature had intruded himself into the situation in such a way that it became difficult for the doctor to maintain the payments. In the meantime, I had become somewhat close to your aunt. I saw that it would be possible to arrange for her to accept money on a regular basis only if she knew what had really happened. It took me some time to get up the courage to tell her the story of your father's death. When I finally did so, I was surprised by her reaction. She told me she had never liked your father anyway. And that he was guilty of physically abusing you didn't surprise her at all. She seemed to feel that everything had more or less worked out for the best. Of course, I had my own motive for telling her of the death of your father."

"What was that?"

"I had already decided it would be necessary to kill Joey Hauck. I wanted her to help me."

"She was willing."

"Oh yes, quite. The way I explained it, the lives of three people depended on eliminating the blackmailer. She made no protest. But I think she was primarily concerned about your welfare, the possibility that you would have a decent home, clothing, a college education. Her motives were unselfish."

"So that's how the two of you came to murder Joey Hauck."

"Was Lakeman involved?" van Beldin asked.

"No, not at all. I don't think he ever could have murdered anyone, not even someone like Joey Hauck. It was Phyllis and I, acting alone."

"Incredible," van Beldin said. "Absolutely incredible."

Mrs. van Beldin continued to speak in a flat, unemotional tone. "We did it very simply. Your aunt obtained the gun, from where I have no idea. We went to his home, an apartment he lived in not far from the freightyard. I rang the bell first and entered the apartment. A moment after I was in, Phyllis rang the bell. Just as he went to open the door, I shot him. I then opened the door for Phyllis, and as he lay on the floor in a pool of blood, she took the weapon and shot him again. So you see, we were both guilty of killing Joey Hauck."

Mrs. van Beldin lay herself back on the pillow, exhausted from the emotional effort of telling the story. Neither her husband nor I said anything, although I suppose each of us was thinking his own thoughts—van Beldin wondering whether the scandal would affect him or his family in any way, me wondering how this long-ago murder fit in with Dillerman and the murder of Sid Hockley. Mrs. van Beldin, I suppose, was wondering if she would one day have to stand trial for murder.

Finally van Beldin spoke. "There's still the question of how the story leaked out. Someone else knows."

"Until now, I never told anyone," Mrs. van Beldin said.

"From my aunt's letter, I would assume she never told any-one."

"Dammit!" van Beldin said. "Someone found out."

I looked at Mrs. van Beldin. She was sitting in bed with tears rolling down her cheeks. Van Beldin went to her and took her hand.

"I don't regret any of it," she said. "If I had it to do all over again, I would do it again, the same way."

The remark didn't surprise me. I'd known from the minute I'd first laid eyes on Mrs. van Beldin she was a determined woman. I left a few minutes later.

13

I walked out of the hospital and across the street. The name of the bar was Bedside Manor. I drank a vodka on the rocks and ordered another. I was vaguely aware of a group of nurses gathered alongside me at the bar, talking and giggling, but my mind was too absorbed with what Mrs. van Beldin had just told me to pay much attention. I finished the second vodka and debated ordering a third. I decided against it. At 4:30 I left the bar and walked back to the hospital parking lot. I drove across town to Metzger's, arriving there shortly before five. Razzilli wasn't due until six. I picked up a bottle of imported beer at the bar, carried it to one of the tables, and settled in. I spent the next hour watching the business crowd straggle in and thinking about what Mrs. van Beldin had said of the death of my father.

Helen van Beldin and Aunt Phyllis had guarded their guilty secret for a long, long time—almost twenty-eight years. Confession is good for the soul. Aunt Phyllis had made a clean breast of it in her letter to me written from the hospital; Mrs. van Beldin had felt the same urge to clear her conscience and had told me her story in person. Helen van Beldin had murdered Joey Hauck in order to protect Dr. Lakeman; Aunt Phyllis had murdered Joey Hauck in order to make possible a better life for me. The money she had received from the doctor over the years had made it possible for me to have a reasonably comfortable childhood, attend a university, and finally escape from the dreariness of Murcer. But it seemed that my success had been bought at a high price.

One way or another someone had found out about what had happened and had peddled the information to Korban, who had used it to blackmail Peter van Beldin. "Hello, Mr. van Beldin, I thought you might like to know. Your wife once killed a man. Do as I say, or I take the story to the police." Van Beldin, angry about being forced out of politics, had reacted by sending his bloodhounds, Hockley and Razzilli, around to find out who had sold the information to Korban. They'd come up with a prime suspect: me. At the same time someone, probably the same individual who had tipped off Korban, had sent around one of *his* goons, Jerry Dillerman, to beat up on me, with the object of either scaring me out of town or killing me. Either result would probably have been satisfactory. The murder of Sid Hockley was harder to figure, but it was possible he had tumbled onto something that might have revealed the identity of whoever was behind it all. The same person who discovered that Aunt Phyllis and Helen van Beldin had murdered Joey Hauck also seemed to be the individual who had turned up the information concerning the Special Improvement Districts almost a year in advance of the Planning Board's vote.

Razzilli was interested in discovering the murderer of his partner—or so he said. Van Beldin was interested in discovering whoever it was that knew his wife was guilty of murder—or so he said. I was interested in discovering who it was who had tried to frame me for murder. The way I figured it, all three were one and the same person. Or were they?

Of course I was also interested in Sylvia Cole, the little girl who had once lived around the corner from me, and who had matured into a most desirable woman. I won't deny that there was an emptiness in my life, and I had no doubt whatsoever that

Sylvia was the ideal person to fill that emptiness. The problem was, I could never hope to achieve a reconciliation with Sylvia before I had cleared myself of the murder charge.

By six o'clock they were two deep at the bar, and three bartenders were racing back and forth dispensing spirits with accomplished skill. At the far end of the bar I recognized Russell Kemner, who was in a lively conversation with two younger men who could have been newspaper reporters, and who gave me a cursory wave. I kept a weather-eye for Razzilli, but by 6:15 he still hadn't shown. At 6:30 I decided to give his office a call.

No answer.

Razzilli's secretary was named Pamela Porlock. I found her number in the book and dialed. She answered on the second ring. I asked her about Razzilli.

"Oh sure, Mr. Ball. I tried to reach you. Got no answer at your home. Mr. Razzilli got a call from someone, a man, about a quarter-to-six. He said he could speak only to Mr. Razzilli. A few minutes later Mr. Razzilli came rushing out of his office. He told me to tell you and Arnie Olson that he was staking out the Bide-a-While Motel out on the—"

"I know where it is, Pam."

"I got Arnie on the beeper, but I couldn't reach you."

"Did Razzilli say anything else?"

"Yes. He mentioned something about four, Cabin Number Four."

I hung up and then found the number of the Bide-a-While in the directory. I asked whether Mr. Dillerman was in Cabin Number Four.

She asked me how I spelled Dillerman. I told her. She checked and rechecked her file. Not only was Mr. Dillerman not registered in Cabin Number Four, no guest by that name was registered there or expected.

I hung up and raced out to the car.

It was now dark. The northwest wind that had been blowing all day had subsided, but there was a pronounced chill in the air. Rush hour traffic was easing off. Within ten minutes I was out of town and on the Murcer Pike. Ten minutes later I slowed down the car and eased it into the parking area of the Bide-a-While Motel.

The only light came from the motel office and from the windows of cabins situated in a long row at the far side of the big lot. I left the car under a tree not far from the entrance. I decided to reconnoiter.

Inside the lighted motel office a clerk was speaking to a small group of guests, but it was not the same clerk we had spoken with three days before. Cars were parked alongside the office and outside various cabins. I circled around behind the office, moving diagonally across the lot in the direction of the cabins. I was half-way there when I saw it—Razzilli's big Buick. It was parked in a far corner of the lot, completely in shadows. It was the perfect location from which to observe anything that happened at any point between the cabins and the office.

I walked toward the car but couldn't see anyone in it. I moved closer, close enough to see in the window, and that was when I saw someone. He was lying sideways on the front seat, his head down against the leather.

I opened the door on the driver's side and gave his body a shake. Richie Razzilli was dead, his body already growing cold. Behind his ear and in the back of his head were two bulletholes, probably from a .22. A neat, professional job. And very, very cold-blooded. Someone had obviously moved in from behind, from out of the woods behind the car. Razzilli very likely had had no more than a last second of awareness of what was happening. I felt beneath his jacket and removed his gun from its holster. Maybe, I thought, it would do me more good than it had done him.

It was a .45 automatic. I checked it out. Although the safety was on, he'd had a round in the chamber. Maybe he'd smelled serious trouble. Back at the motel office the guests I had seen inside were leaving and climbing into a car. A moment later they drove out of the lot. The only other signs of life were sounds of voices and some light coming from the nearby cabins.

I silently crossed the lot to the row of cabins. I decided to begin with Number One and make my way along. A man and a woman were in Number One, plainly visible in the lighted room from the rear window.

Number Two had no lights and no car. It appeared to be empty.

Number Three had lights on, but the drapes were drawn. Someone was there, but I couldn't see who.

I moved on to Number Four, where the lights were also on,

and the drapes drawn. At the side of the cabin was a car with Illinois plates. Seconds later the lights went out. I moved to a position alongside the door and waited. When he had the door open and was halfway through, I blindsided him, moving in quickly and jamming the automatic into his ribs with one violent motion. He stumbled back into the room. I shut the door, and found the light switch.

Standing in front of me and looking very frightened was Arnie Olson.

Lying prone on the floor of the cabin in a pool of blood was Jerry Dillerman.

"It's me, Mr. Ball, Arnie." His voice had a quake in it.

I shook my head and lowered the gun. "I thought you were someone else, Olson." I walked across the room and stared down at Dillerman.

"I had to do it. He killed Rich. I didn't want to. I got the drop. I couldn't control him. He came at me—"

"Give it to me from the beginning, Arnie. What happened?"

"I got a message to meet Rich out here, down the road. He knew Dillerman was here. He wanted to tail him, find out who he was working for. We drove into the lot in separate cars. Rich parked back by the woods out of sight. We knew Dillerman was in this cabin under another name—"

"Who told him?"

"He said the clerk called him. But Dillerman must've been tipped off 'cause while I was watching I saw this figure move out of the woods. I could see, but I was too far away to yell or do anything. There were flashes in the darkness. The guy snuck up from behind and shot Rich just like that. I couldn't believe it."

"What did you do?"

"I moved over here behind the cabin and waited. I got the drop on him outside, shoved him in. . . . That was when I saw him—"

"Dillerman?"

"His face, Mr. Ball. It was all messed up. It was horrible to look at. He stood there and pointed to it. He said that was why he wanted Razzilli."

I looked down at the body, and even in death the damage was obvious. His nose was bent and partially flattened. Below the left eye was a long, ugly slash.

"Razzilli hit him with the beer bottle," I said.

"Dillerman thought he was so good-looking. Always working out—"

"What then?"

"I wanted to call the cops. What else? I picked up the phone—and that was when he came at me. I don't think he cared whether he lived or died. The first slug didn't stop him, the second did."

"We'll have to move him," I said.

"Why? I was just gonna take off. Tell Pam—"

"No good. With Razzilli and Dillerman both dead, the cops'll figure one of us got Dillerman."

"I see what you mean."

Once we figured out what we wanted to do, the job itself didn't take that long—all in all, about two hours. We removed Dillerman's body and the small suitcase he had brought with him from the room. Then we drove ten miles further down the Pike and, using a shovel Olson had in his car, we buried the body in the woods. Then we returned to the motel for Dillerman's car, a nine-year-old Pontiac. We drove it into Murcer and, after taking off the plates and removing all personal items, we abandoned it on a sidestreet behind the freightyard. Due to its age and condition, it would appear to be a junker that the owner had not taken the trouble to drive to the scrapyard.

Then Olson drove me back to the motel where I picked up the rental Chevy.

"I hate to leave Rich, just lying there," Olson said.

I shook my head. "Nothing we can do for him now." I told him to drive home, call Pam, and establish with her that he'd never been able to locate Razzilli. "And, Arnie, an alibi wouldn't hurt."

He nodded. Then we climbed into our cars and drove out of there, leaving it to some unsuspecting individual to find the dead body of Richie Razzilli.

I got the call the next day shortly before noon. Could I report to police headquarters within the next hour? Yes, I could. Please do so. Click.

Before leaving, I decided to call Sylvia at the newspaper. "I thought you might be in the mood for some homecooked food this evening."

"I might be if I don't have to do the cooking."

"I'll pick up a couple of steaks. Come out to the house when you get off from work."

"Fine, but I can't say when that'll be. It could be late, like seven-thirty or eight."

"No problem."

Forty-five minutes later I ran into Olson on the steps of the Murcer Justice Building.

"It's a bad scene, Mr. Ball, real bad. They had me in there over an hour, telling the same story over and over."

"I'll give them the same version. Don't worry."

"Somebody found the body real early this morning. I dropped by the agency this morning, and the place was swarming with cops. Gronski was there. He wanted to know every case Razzilli worked on for the last couple of years. They questioned everybody."

"I don't think they'll make the connection between the abandoned car and Razzilli's murderer. There could be a thousand people with a grudge against Razzilli. As long as they don't tie Dillerman to it, we're safe."

"I'm wonderin' now if we should have done it. If we should have gotten rid of Dillerman like that."

"I think it was the right thing." I wasn't feeling as confident as I sounded.

"I coulda just said what happened—"

"You'd've taken a fall, Arnie. They'd've twisted it. You were getting back for your boss. Revenge."

Olson nodded. "I gotta get back to the agency. But the place'll never be the same without that big lug."

"Stay in touch," I said and made my way up the steps and into the headquarters building.

Gronski had Karl Breyer and another detective with him in his office. They all looked stern and mean. Even Breyer had lost the look of the benign college professor.

After some brief preliminaries Gronski said, "I suppose you know why we got you down here." His manner was impatient and very menacing. I knew they would be listening to my answers very carefully. The thought crossed my mind that maybe we had been wrong to get rid of the body. . . .

"I just met Arnie Olson outside. He told me about Razzilli."

"You hadn't known before he told you?"

"No."

"What did he tell you?"

"Only that Razzilli's body was found early this morning at the Bide-a-While Motel."

"When's the last time you saw Razzilli?"

I suppose I hesitated before answering. I was getting in deeper and deeper, but what was even worse, I would be completely on my own. I was getting into a jam more serious than I had been in at any time up until now. By helping Arnie dispose of Diller-man's body I had made myself an accomplice to an action the police would regard as murder. By lying and trying to cover it up I was giving up what was in all probability my last chance to extricate myself from the affair.

"Well?" Breyer said.

"Yesterday afternoon, in his office." I said the words slowly, deliberately. I've never thought of myself as a good liar.

Gronski smirked. "What time? Early afternoon? Late?"

"About one-thirty. I stopped by, then I left. We were supposed to meet for a drink around six, at Metzger's."

"And?"

"He never showed. I called his office, got no answer, so I called his secretary at home. She said he'd gone out to the Bide-a-While."

Breyer interrupted. "She also said Razzilli wanted you to know where he was going. Why was that?"

"No idea."

Gronski said, "What did you do then, Ball?"

"I had another beer, then I went home."

"What time was that?"

"Between six-thirty and seven."

Breyer said, "But you never went out to the motel. Is that right?"

I said I hadn't.

Gronski then asked me about my movements throughout the afternoon, after I had left Razzilli's office. I told him that I had visited Mrs. van Beldin at the hospital, that I had stopped at a bar across from the hospital for a drink, and that I had arrived at Metzger's at about five and stayed there until about seven. Gronski then asked if I had seen anyone there I knew and I mentioned Russell Kemner. He then nodded to the detective who immediately left the room, presumably to do some checking.

Then they asked what I had discussed with Razzilli and what I had discussed with Mrs. van Beldin. I remained suitably vague on both accounts. Then we took it from the top again. And again. They let me go sometime after three.

I took a walk around the city and tried to make my mind work. It was difficult. I was too shaken by events of the previous day—the revelations of Mrs. van Beldin and the death of Razzilli. No matter how I put together the pieces, they didn't fit. I felt frustrated.

I dropped into a luncheonette for a cup of coffee.

Then I did some more walking. And thinking.

Shortly after five I dropped into a tavern not far from the business district. I drank a beer standing at the bar and listened in on some conversations. One fellow had told off his boss; another had told off the IRS; another had told off his brother-in-law. I ordered another beer and moved to the far end of the bar, away from the blab. I seriously began having second thoughts about disposing of Dillerman's body. I wondered whether helping Arnie Olson had been the smart thing after all. It almost certainly meant the end of the possibility of ever being able to explain myself to Sylvia. It was this way, Sylvia. I helped dispose of a dead body because I imagined the police wouldn't believe Arnie killed Dillerman in self-defense and because they were looking for someone to hang the Hockley murder on and because . . . Oh sure, Clint, I understand. Perfectly.

When I thought about Razzilli I felt even worse. Razzilli had been on the level all along. When I'd told him that I hadn't killed Hockley he believed me. He'd shown confidence in me that I hadn't shown in him. That thought made the situation seem even more desperate. I was well into my second beer—or was it my third?—when I remembered a poem I'd studied as a kid in elementary school. All I could recall was a couple of lines—

> *Twilight and evening bell, and after that the dark,*
> *And let there be no sadness of farewell when I embark—*

and they somehow seemed to fit. I called the bartender over and told him I was buying for everyone in the house. He looked at me in astonishment.

"In honor of a friend of mine," I said. My expression was grave.

"Yes, sir," he said, and his expression turned grave.

For the next five minutes he worked, drawing beer, and pouring booze.

"And one for yourself."

"Yes, sir," he said and drew a beer.

With everyone served, I raised my glass and recited the poem. Everyone drank. No one smiled. I paid the bill.

"Thank you, gentlemen," I said, emptied my glass and walked out. It was the kind of gesture that I normally never would have made. It was the kind of thing only a person with an unusual outlook would do. In other words, a person like Razzilli.

I walked home.

14

On the way back to the house I stopped for groceries—potatoes for baking, steak for broiling, lettuce and tomatoes for tossing into a salad. Sylvia said between 7:30 and 8:00. I'd be ready.

I entered the house through the front door, hung up my coat in the front closet, opened the door to the living room, and flipped on the lamp.

"You're late, Ball. I expected you sooner."

He was seated on the sofa in the same place he'd sat when he'd been at the house the previous week. The only difference was that last week he'd been holding a can of beer in his hand; now he was holding a pistol, one with a short barrel. I'm no expert, but I thought it might be a .357 Magnum.

I worked to keep the surprise out of my voice. "I hope you're comfortable, Karl."

"Security in this house isn't all it should be. A piece of cake climbing in the rear window." He flashed a synthetic smile.

"I don't get it, Karl. Some kind of joke?"

The smile vanished from his face. He pointed with the gun. I put down the package and sat down.

"You had a nice run of luck, Ball. If you'd've been smart, you would've rode it right out of town. Back to New York or wherever."

I gestured with my hand. Karl brought the weapon up to where it wasn't more than four feet away and pointing directly at my heart.

"Any more sudden moves, you get it right here, right in your aunt's living room." He made the statement in a flat, unemotional voice. It was easy to believe he meant it.

"All right, Karl." I could tell there was something on his mind. He appeared tense, very close to the edge.

He was silent for a while, then he said, "You didn't give us the whole story down at the station. You were out there last night, is the way I figure it."

"Out where?"

He stood up from the couch, took two steps forward, and then with a motion so swift and sudden I never saw it coming, he swung the gun barrel. It caught me on the right cheek, below the eye. Within seconds, I was aware of blood.

"I am asking questions. I want answers. What happened out there?" He stepped back and looked down at me. "One of he cabins had blood all over the rug. Whose blood?"

I refrained from putting my hand to my face. I didn't want him to know it hurt. I didn't say anything.

"Answer me!" I was ready for it the second time, and I moved with it. The end of the barrel struck against my forehead, causing a mild ache but not doing as much damage as the first shot. "This isn't going to get you anywhere, Karl," I said. I didn't feel as confident as I sounded.

He stepped back. "Somebody got hurt out there. Hurt bad. I figure you were in on it."

"I told you I wasn't there."

"You and Razzilli been running around together the past couple of weeks like asshole buddies. He left a message for you and his other peeper to come out. His secretary told us that."

"So?"

"So you went out. Kemner saw you down at Metzger's. Says he saw you make a phone call, then come chasing out of the booth like your pants were on fire. Now I want it, the whole story."

You reach a point sometimes, a point where you get completely fed up with people bullying you and trying to force you to do things you don't want to do. Maybe I had already been close to that point. In any case, Karl's strong-arm tactics had succeeded in pushing me beyond it. Suddenly, I knew I wasn't going to tell him anything, not a blessed, goddamn thing. He could shoot me full of holes with his little pistol; it wasn't going to make any difference. I think he picked it up, because after staring down at me for a long minute, he exhaled, nodded, and eased his bulk down on the coffee table. Again he stuck the pistol in my face, this time not more than a foot away, and when he spoke his voice was without anger.

"I gotta give you guys credit. You were getting damned close. You found out about J.D.; that surprised me. And that's why I know you were out at the motel. J.D. always stayed there, was a friend of one of the clerks, even. Used to get himself some freebies that way. I know it was J.D. in that cabin. I checked with the clerk. J.D. was staying there under another name. So when you say you weren't out there, Ball, I know better."

Karl seemed to have a lot bottled up inside him. I let him talk.

"I didn't want him coming back to Murcer. And he wouldn't have if your friend hadn't messed him up like that. That's all J.D. came back for, to get even with Razzilli for what he did to him. I figure it this way. He got Razzilli, then you guys got him."

Karl's surmises were of course correct, and in that moment, sitting opposite him and staring into the barrel of his little snubnosed gun, I sensed the man's shrewdness and his insight into people, the qualities that had made him such an outstanding homicide cop. Working with the facts he had, he'd been able to piece it all together. I wondered how many guys over the years had gone up against Karl, clever, self-confident guys, only to find out he was way ahead of them. I could imagine the coldness at the pit of the stomach as they realized he had a knowledge of their minds and motives that they didn't quite have themselves. And then the creeping nausea as he slowly, systematically, peeled back the lies, chipped away at the armor of self-confidence. Until there was nothing left to do but to confess. Until they were actually happy to confess. . . .

"I can make you open up, Ball. You know that."

I knew it well enough. I didn't try to lie to Karl. It wouldn't have made any sense. But I wasn't going to give him the satisfaction of knowing he was right either. "Sure, Karl, if you think it's worth the time and effort."

I saw he didn't like that remark. He moved nervously, shifting his bulk along the edge of the low table. I thought of going for the gun. But he kept it at a point where it was just beyond where I could reach it safely, and there was no doubt in my mind that he would shoot if he felt himself endangered. The report might disturb the neighborhood stillness, but it was unlikely to attract much attention. I temporarily shelved the idea.

I watched the gun barrel nervously. "Your biggest mistake, Karl, was tying up with a flake like Dillerman."

"Don't call that boy a flake!" I was surprised by the vehemence of the reaction. "The one thing I want to know, is he still alive?"

"Search me, Karl."

He stood up and again I thought he was going to tag me with the pistol, but then he thought better of it, and stepped backwards.

The clock on the radio said 7:05. I was expecting Sylvia to arrive in twenty-five minutes, but she had been unsure when she could get off. If she were to come just a bit early and I were to get word out to her . . . The longer I could stall Breyer along, the better my chances would be of wiggling out of this situation.

"Anyway, I'm glad Razzilli got his," Karl said.

"Sure, Karl. You fixed Hockley. Dillerman fixed Razzilli." It was only a guess on my part, but it got a reaction.

Karl frowned, then shrugged. "Hockley. I had to do that. I didn't want to but I had to."

"You had to kill the guy?"

"When I saw you drive off that night I thought, 'What the hell, I might as well take a look.' I wasn't sure how much your aunt had told you. I got in through the back window. It was a mistake. . . ."

"You didn't know van Beldin had Hockley and Razzilli checking me out. Hockley'd been following me around all day—"

"Yeah, he saw me going in—I used the back window coming in, the front door going out—and he was waiting for me to leave. Right outside the front door. I said, 'Oh shit, Sid, come on in, I'll tell you what it's all about.'"

"He followed you in and then you shot him."

"Right away he started popping questions. Van Beldin had him and Razzilli trying to find out how it was that Korban knew about Mrs. van Beldin. I could see his mind working. . . . All of a sudden he got nasty."

"Still, you didn't have to frame me. Drop the gun under the bed—"

Breyer shook his head. "I wanted to see you try and talk your way out of that one. With those problems, I figured you wouldn't be spending a lot of time messing around with what happened twenty-eight years ago. Not with a murder rap hanging over your head. You should've left well enough alone, Ball."

"Wrong, Karl. It was you who couldn't leave well enough alone. Selling information to Korban wasn't bright."

"You got it all figured, eh, Ball?"

"That established a pattern."

As I continued to talk to Breyer, my mind kept returning to Dillerman. I thought about his jaw with the peculiar square shape, about the slight wave in the blond hair, about the shade of blue in the eyes that gave them their empty look. . . .

"I'm safe, Ball."

"You solved the Hauck murder, right, Karl?"

"I was a good cop. Buddy, you'll never know how good."

"Good at solving murders. Also good at concealing evidence."

"Christ, that one wasn't even difficult. One of Hauck's neighbors in that fleabag apartment comes to me with a story of seeing him with your aunt in the park. I talked to her once, I knew she was lying. But I gotta hand it to her. She didn't cave in right away like some people. I kept coming back at her. Finally, she gave it to me."

"Why did you let her off?"

"Would you believe, Ball, partly because of you? Like I told you, I knew what it's like growing up alone, without parents—"

"You knew me?"

"One time I came out here to the house to talk with your aunt, you were playing in the yard, building a house out of rocks and sticks of wood. While we talked on the porch I watched you playing. All alone."

"Didn't you have a job to do?"

"Come off it, Ball. Hauck was a lowlife. The world was better off without him. What was gonna be accomplished by charging your aunt?"

"She told you the whole story?"

"Everything. Beginning with how your old man beat you up and took you down to the doctor's office, how the doc killed him, how they tried to get rid of the body, how Hauck saw them."

"So you made a deal."

"Correct. Neither of us was to say anything."

"She never mentioned anything to Helen van Beldin."

"Of course not. Your aunt was as good as her word. No one knew I cracked it."

"But you took a piece of the money the doctor was sending my aunt."

"Like hell—"

"No?"

"No." Breyer's voice was calm again. "No, Ball, nothing like that. Not my style."

"Blackmail, Karl, what else? You took money from my aunt."

Breyer paused when he spoke, his tone was insistent. "I told you, Ball. I told you the reason."

"Because of me, Karl? Because you felt sorry for me?"

"Once your aunt told me the story, I could understand the situation. Maybe other people couldn't, I could. You alone, no parents, only your aunt. I grew up the same way, Ball. Where was the sense in charging her? Hauck was a nothing."

I was silent then. I watched as Breyer got to his feet. He kept the gun trained at a point between my heart and my stomach.

"I respected Phyllis, Ball. Things weren't easy in Murcer in those years. Not like today. No public assistance, no welfare programs. A woman alone, with a child, was really on her own. They're not making them like your aunt anymore, I can tell you that. She was one tough woman."

I could see what Breyer was getting at. Somehow Aunt Phyllis had been able to talk her way out of a murder charge, to get around one of the city's toughest, most dedicated policemen. It occurred to me how little I had ever understood my aunt, how slight was my understanding of the real woman behind the matronly facade.

"She really stuck her neck out for you. She knew just what to do about Hauck once she got the story from the nurse. She saved your bacon."

It was true. I'd never made an effort to understand my aunt. I couldn't wait to get away. Once I was away from Murcer I never wanted to come back.

"You wouldn't be a smarty-pants computer engineer today, my friend. You'd be down at the mill with the other people your age. Like your dad was and my dad—"

"All right, all right."

Breyer gazed at me without expression. Then he motioned for me to stand up. He moved around behind me. "I just thought you should know a few things, that's all." He gave me a shove forward.

"Is it necessary to kill me, Karl?"

"I'm afraid it is. I've done all I can for you." Karl pressed the gun into the small of my back and forced me forward toward the staircase.

I decided to keep talking, to try and keep the conversation going as long as possible. "Why did you warn me off Razzilli, Karl?" Breyer forced me to walk up the stairs. When we had reached the top he answered the question.

"The less you knew, Ball, the safer you were. I wanted you out of Murcer as quick as possible—"

"Except that Gronski—"

"Gronski wanted you inside almost from day one. He was absolutely convinced you were it. I kept going to bat for you, pointing out you'd never had trouble with the law. If you'd've followed my advice it never would have happened."

"Razzilli, you mean?"

"I mean J.D. What happened out there last night?"

"What's the big deal, Karl?" I couldn't figure Karl's obsession with Dillerman. No more than I could figure out why he had suddenly appeared this evening. With Razzilli and Dillerman dead, no one ever would have connected Karl with the Hockley murder. In another attempt to keep him talking, I asked him why he had come.

For an answer he gave me a hard shove, which sent me stumbling forward into the bedroom. "No more conversation. Little boy's gonna go nite-nite."

I switched subjects, trying my best to keep the tension out of my voice. "Two murders, Karl. What's the sense?"

"I had to fix Hockley. He could've figured it out. He was a wise-ass, a real pain. I spent thirty-five years building a reputation in this city. Nobody's gonna take it away from me." Karl paused. "You'd've stayed clear of Razzilli like I told you and never went to Chicago, Ball, and I wouldn't be here now."

Down in the street I heard an automobile engine start up and move away. The clock inched along another minute, maybe two.

I said, "It's still going to unravel, Karl, one way or the other."

"Why? Why should it? You're only gonna be an accident victim, my friend. A statistic. As for Hockley, Gronski has it figured that the same guy who shot Razzilli shot him. And for last night I got an alibi—the Friday poker game at the club. Gronski even stopped by. Besides, I'm the last person anyone would tie in with murder." Karl looked around the bedroom. "This where you sleep? On this bed?"

I nodded.

"Cozy, nice. Sorry you gotta go this way, Ball. Start taking off your shoes."

I did as I was told as slowly and clumsily as possible. I thought about Sylvia and the possibility she might be early, the possibility she might notice something wasn't quite right, the possibility she would be concerned enough to do something. . . . Sylvia, come. Ring the bell, fetch the neighbors, call the police.

When I had my shoes and socks off, he told me to remove my shirt and pants. I thought about my chances of trying to jump him but I realized he'd have three bullets in me before I was able to move off the bed. In the distance I could hear the sound of a neighbor's TV. Someone would say something, and now and again the conversation would be interrupted by snippets of laughter. A situation comedy. Ha ha.

When I had my shirt and pants off, he took them and told me to lie down on the bed.

"This is crazy, Karl. It's—"

Just then the doorbell rang. Sylvia! I couldn't see the time, but she was at least fifteen minutes early.

Karl walked to the window and drew the drapes.

"Shouldn't I answer the bell?"

"You gotta a terrific sense of humor, Ball." He came back and squatted by the bed. "This lamp's the only light in the house, and with the curtains drawn, no one can see it from outside. We sit tight, Ball, and we wait for whoever it is to go away."

The bell rang again, more insistently this time.

We waited silently, listening.

It rang again. Then there was the sound of footsteps, someone moving across the porch and down the steps. Sylvia, don't just go away. Do something. If we'd still been downstairs, I'd almost certainly have been able to attract her attention. . . .

Again, I tried stalling. "It must have been fun, Karl, playing God. Knowing everybody's little secrets, selling your silence. How many times were you able—"

"Shut up! Put both arms over your head."

I did as I was told.

Again I asked him what he was doing, but he only grunted. He wasn't interested in talking anymore. The bell had made him aware delay could be costly. I wondered where Sylvia might have gone. He stepped around the head of the bed, reached into his pocket, and with a practiced motion slipped a set of handcuffs around my right wrist. The other loop he made fast to the head-board of the bed. Then he did the same with my left wrist.

"Sorry, if you're uncomfortable, Ball, but it's only tempo-rary." He left the room then but came back a minute later with a glass of water. After setting the glass down on the small night-table beside the bed, he squatted down on his heels and looked at me with cold blue eyes. The hatred was unmistakable. "Tell me what happened to J.D., Ball." Karl was back to the subject of Dillerman again.

"Unfasten me, and I'll tell you what I know."

"You guys killed him, didn't you? You and the other guy, Olson."

"You figure it out."

"I did already." Karl looked thoughtful. "I did a lot for that boy."

Then it came to me, why Karl was so eager to find out what happened to Dillerman. "Not enough, Karl. Too little, too late. You got him out of a couple of jams, sent him some money. The kid needed more than that."

"Tell me about it."

"I don't have to. You know it yourself."

Breyer took a small bottle out of the pocket of his jacket and placed it next to the glass of water. I turned my head in an effort to see what it was but couldn't quite make it out.

"Just something to make you sleep, that's all."

"You're crazy, Karl."

"I'll tell you something else about your aunt that you may never have thought about, Ball. She may have been a spinster, but she liked men."

"That was part of the deal?"

"Part of the deal? No. Maybe she felt some gratitude. We were friendly, more than friendly."

"Aunt Phyllis didn't have many friends."

"She'd show up at my place once, maybe twice a week, we'd go at it hot and heavy. Get her going, she wanted more and more. And maybe she was forty years old, but she was a well-preserved forty."

"You're talking about my aunt—"

"I'm telling a story, Ball. Your aunt was a sideline, much older than me. I had the hots for another dame—Marie her name was—and she was supposed to be out of town visiting her brother somewhere, and what happens, she shows up unexpected. Key in the lock, comes right in. Phyllis and I are jaybird naked in bed. Marie goes storming out, wouldn't ever speak to me again. A real proud bitch, you know? What I didn't know she was a month or two pregnant already—"

"Marie Dillerman?"

"Marie Chavez. But in her fourth month she gets this guy Dillerman to marry her. A loser. He took off after a year or so. It was a while before I tumbled to the situation, but there wasn't much I could do." Breyer sighed. "She didn't want to have anything to do with me."

"Too bad."

Karl unscrewed the cap on the bottle and tossed some pills into the glass. "Open wide, sonny boy."

I turned my head as far to the side as I could. But I realized that, with the handcuffs constraining my freedom of movement, there was little I could do to keep him from pouring the liquid into my mouth. I kept my mouth tightly closed.

"You want to make it tough? Fine." He reached down and grasped my nose between two fingers. At the same time he rested his knee against my upper chest, and waited. A few moments later, I threw my mouth open in an attempt to gasp some air. But when he tilted the glass of water over my open mouth, I gave a ferocious heave with the upper portion of my body. The motion was just enough to deflect the liquid, causing it to spill down the side of my neck. Winded, I lay on the bed gasping.

Karl cursed, then stepped back from the bed. He took the bottle of pills from his pocket and showed them to me. "I got a whole bottle, Ball. I bought the large size." He turned around and left the room. When he returned he had another glass filled with water. "I'll be more careful this time."

I started talking again, working to keep all signs of panic out of my voice.

"How did it feel, Karl, knowing that Lakeman had killed a man? He was like royalty in this city, right? Lakeman this, Lakeman that. Must have been great, knowing anytime you could have taken him down off his pedestal."

Karl stood there holding the glass, shaking his head. I kept talking, my words pouring forth like a torrent. "I can see it from your point of view, Karl. No one was giving scholarships to medical school to kids from Oldtown, not to kids like you, not in those years. It must have made you feel good, all that power—"

"No, Ball. You've got it all wrong. I was a cop." Breyer said the words slowly, thoughtfully. "I had what I wanted. Other people had what they wanted. I wasn't jealous."

"But why, Karl? Why?" Something in the situation wasn't logical. I couldn't put my finger precisely on what it was. "Just answer me that one question."

"Why what?"

Then I had it. "The inquest, Karl."

"Which inquest?"

"For the dead girl. You gave evidence at the inquest, right? You kept the Hanks woman from going to trial. But not before you made a deal with Hanks. You had to know where the S.I.D.s would be located. That's right, isn't it, Karl?"

Again Karl shook his head. "Half right."

"Sure, Karl. You got the word to Hoglin, the lawyer up in Chicago. He was together with Korban. You got a payoff, a big one. They made millions moving on your information. Don't tell me you're an honest cop—"

"Ball, I'm a simple guy. You see how I live—a house, a garden. That's enough for me . . ."

I'd hit a sensitive point. He was talking again, and his expression had become sad, almost melancholy. "All right, you gave my aunt a break, I can buy that, Karl. I see your reasons. Maybe I should say thank you. I don't know. But you gave false testimony at the Hanks inquest. Why do that except for money? Maybe you had pride as a cop but in the end the money was more important."

Without saying anything, Karl sat down on a chair next to the bed, a dreamy faraway look in his eyes. When he started talking again, he spoke quietly but with a new intensity.

"I told you about my father, Ball. I told you how he was walking the picket line and how he got hit in the head by a strikebreaker when I was just a little kid."

"Sure, Karl."

"Nothing wrong with walking a picket line, is there? This is America, right?"

I shrugged.

"My old man, maybe he didn't speak such good English, but deep down he was more for America than most of the people born here. Couldn't say enough for the country, what it meant, the opportunities. . . . So management calls in its goons, and someone breaks open his head with a tire iron."

"You told me that, Karl."

"Sure. What I didn't tell you was how the owners of the factory treated my mother after their goons killed my father and made her into a widow. I never told you that my mom never got one lousy red cent from that company. I never told you how that crummy management never acknowledged any responsibility for what happened out there."

Karl paused. I was conscious of the ticking of the clock, but I had lost all track of the time.

"What did my mother know? She was too dumb to even hire herself a lawyer. Finally, there was some kind of hearing. Company paid everyone off, of course. Witnesses, cops. They even put up money for a lawyer to handle the guy's case."

"So what happened?"

"The verdict was accidental death. They hustled the guy out of Murcer." Breyer paused. "Do I have to tell you who owned the old paper box factory? Do I?"

I didn't say anything.

"Who else but the van Beldins, right? Marvelous people. They've done so much for Murcer, to hear everyone tell it. Sure. Plenty of money for fancy houses, big cars, snobby prep schools—but not one dime for my mom. Not one dime for a woman living out her life in a cold-water walk-up over in Old-town. For a woman who had to work twelve hours a day cleaning other people's houses and still could hardly make the rent money. I remember, Ball. I remember her hands so red and blistered she became ashamed to show them to other people. I remember the hopelessness in her eyes. I remember waking up nights and hearing her crying in bed—and yes, I remember the day she just keeled over and died from overwork. Yeah, van Beldins had a real live one there, a woman too dumb to know her rights, only smart enough to work herself to death."

"So you became a cop."

"And a good one."

"No, Karl, it doesn't explain the business with the Hanks woman—"

"I'm not finished with the story, Ball. One night late, a Saturday night it was, over seventeen years ago, raining buckets, I'm driving into the city when I pick up a call on the police frequency—an accident out on the Pike. I was less than a mile away, so I was there within minutes. It was a mess. The victim was a sixteen-year-old kid, a girl. There were a couple of rookie patrolmen on the scene, bent over the girl, tryin' to remember what they'd learned about CPR. A mangled bike on the side of the road. Couldn't really see that much, the only lights from the headlights and flashers. Ten yards up the road there's a big station wagon, smashed against the divider, and on the side of the road a woman so drunk she couldn't stand, down on all fours and spilling her guts in the mud—"

"Mrs. Hanks."

"That's right."

"You saw the possibilities—"

"No one ever said I was dumb, Ball. I took over. Started bossing people around, kept the rookies busy, made sure nobody got close enough to see what shape she was in. When I could, I got her out of there, took her into the station myself. Filled out some forms, took a blood sample. Finally, I took her home."

"What happened then?"

"Hanks answered the door himself. It took both of us just to get her into the house. I wanted him to see her, to get a good look. She still couldn't stand, kept slobberin', mumblin', laughin' to herself. Hair a mess, coat all covered with mud. I don't believe she knew as yet what she'd done. That she'd killed the little girl."

I thought of the elegant woman I had seen at the church. The contrast was stark, spine-chilling.

"Once we had her in bed, then we talked. Hanks was honest, completely straight—but the sight of his wife really shook him up. On top of it, the guy had a terrible guilt complex where his wife was concerned, almost as if he felt he was the one responsible for her drinking."

"So you made a deal—"

"He jumped at the chance." Breyer paused, recalling the story he was telling for the first time since it had happened seventeen years before. "I switched blood samples, rewrote my report to show she was completely coherent at the time of the accident. At the inquest I testified to how awful driving conditions were that night—"

"You got her off."

"The funny thing, nobody even questioned me. Nobody wanted to believe that such a fine, upstanding woman was drunk at the wheel."

"You got Hanks to rezone the land north of the city—"

"That's exactly what I did. Like everyone else, I knew the van Beldin family controlled everything to the south and west. I got Hanks to agree to go north, right, but you see that wasn't enough. Van Beldin, with all his clout, would have moved right in, bought up that land too. What I needed was someone just as smart and just as tough as van Beldin."

"Hoglin."

"I knew Jack. Not exactly a charmer, but a shrewd, tough cookie. He'd gone partners with Korban in Chicago. I got in touch with Jack, explained the situation. Once those guys had optioned the land, I knew there was no way van Beldin was going to get it. Murcer's a new city with Korban here. Maybe you notice the difference."

Karl stood up from the bed. He opened the small bottle and dropped some of the pills into the waterglass.

"So you were paying back the van Beldins—"

"Yes, Ball. And I really had to laugh when Lakeman's nurse upped and married Peter van Beldin. That added another skeleton to the family closet."

"And then you—"

But before I could finish the sentence Karl leaned his knee once again on my chest, and in such a manner that any movement on my part was all but impossible. With his fingers he squeezed my nose. He waited patiently until I threw my mouth open in a desperate effort to gasp some air, and in that moment he poured the contents of the glass into my mouth. I choked and sputtered but couldn't avoid swallowing most of it.

I thought about Sylvia and the possibility she might have suspected something was wrong when I didn't answer the door. "Look, Karl, maybe—"

"After you drop off, Ball, I'll remove the cuffs. Everyone knows you're a big smoker. People will assume you fell asleep with a butt in your hand and set the bed on fire. It happens all the time. I'll drop a lighted match here before I leave. This house'll go up like tinder."

I lay quietly, doing my best to keep my brain clear, but it was only a matter of minutes before I could feel the sleeping pills begin to take their effect. Breyer began talking again, but I found it harder to follow what he was saying. I heard him mention Dillerman. . . . His voice grew fainter, as though he was at the other end of a tunnel. . . . I thought I heard him mention something about money, $25,000. I knew I was falling asleep, and I fought against it. . . . But I really wanted to sleep. I made an effort to stay awake, but the thought occurred to me it might be better to fall asleep after all. . . . Why not?

15

I was back in Vietnam, at the controls of a helicopter, careening back and forth through the sky, an indeterminable distance above the earth. In the air all around me were enemy jets, darting specks of danger moving in all directions. On the ground I could see enemy anti-aircraft batteries spitting fire in my direction. The air was full of exploding shells, sudden eruptions of smoke and flames. I was aware of an enemy fighter closing in on me from overhead. I changed directions, increased my speed, but he continued to come at me. All at once I was aware of a sound close at hand, of smoke and flames. He'd hit me. . . . I wanted to eject, to bail out, but couldn't. I was trapped in the burning ship. . . .

"Clint! Clint!" Somewhere in the distance someone was calling my name. I wanted to answer but couldn't.

"Clint! Are you there?" The voice was louder now. "Clint! Answer if you're there. Clint! Clint!" It was a woman's voice, maybe Aunt Phyllis's voice. It couldn't be Aunt Phyllis's voice. She always called me Clinton. Never Clint. I wanted to answer, "Here, Aunt Phyllis," but no words came. I wanted very much to answer. . . .

"Clint! Clint!" It was a woman, but I was disappointed that it wasn't Aunt Phyllis. "Clint, my God, I almost didn't see you down there. Wake up! What's happened to you?"

I felt the heat against my body, and when I breathed I inhaled smoke.

"Clint, can you hold this over your mouth?" I felt something cool and wet against my face. I wanted to answer but couldn't. I wanted to say, "Turn off the heat," but no sound came. The smoke was so hot it burned my throat.

"Clint, I'll drag you. Do you hear me, Clint? I'll drag you." Someone was pulling me, tugging at me. I wanted to move my legs, but they were rubbery, with no feeling in them. Even the floor was hot. "Clint, can't you hold on to the handkerchief? You'll die of suffocation otherwise." I felt the wet cloth against my face again. It made it easier to breathe. I tried to hold it against my mouth, but it kept slipping.

The noise now was loud, a crackling, roaring noise, and seemed to be all around us. I wanted to tell the woman not to leave me. It wasn't Aunt Phyllis. I knew Aunt Phyllis wouldn't leave me. I hoped this woman wouldn't leave me.

"Clint, we have to go quicker. Can't you move at all? Oh, God!" I heard a sharp crack, almost like thunder, and I was struck by something hot. It burned my arm. I yelled but I don't know if any sound came. I heard the woman say, "The roof is going," but she continued to drag me.

"We're almost at the stairs, Clint," she said. "Just a few feet. I hope they hold us." My throat and lungs were burning now. Every breath brought pain. "I can't see anything, Clint, but we'll try the stairs." I felt myself being pulled down the stairs by my feet. I tried to open my eyes, but I couldn't see anything. Nothing but smoke and darkness. I rolled sideways down the last steps. Thump. Thump.

"We can't get out the front, Clint. We'll have to go out the back door." I could hear the woman coughing. "We won't make it, Clint, not like this. If only you could move, Clint. Can't you crawl? I can't pull you now. Can't you crawl?"

I tried to get on my knees, but it wasn't any use. I heard the woman telling me to crawl. I wanted to tell her I couldn't. I didn't care anymore. It was too hard to crawl. Better just to lie here.

"Clint, for God's sakes, move yourself!" It *was* Aunt Phyllis! She always used that expression when she wanted me to do something.

"Yes, Aunt Phyllis," I said. The words actually came. I heard them. But I didn't want to do what Aunt Phyllis said. Aunt Phyllis yelled and bossed all the time. From the time I was small until the day I moved away, Aunt Phyllis had something for me to do. I hated the way she bossed me and the way she always told me that if she hadn't looked after me no one else ever would have. That was why I disobeyed so often.

It was ferociously hot, my eyes were stinging, my chest was clogged with smoke. I didn't want to do what Aunt Phyllis was telling me to do. . . .

"All right, then, Clinton. You just stay there. Don't move. You just remain there."

That was when I decided I would try to crawl forward, after all. If Aunt Phyllis said stay there, then I would try to move forward. I placed one hand down, then the next on the hot floor.

"I'm leaving, Clinton. You remain here. Don't follow me."

Of course I wanted to follow if Aunt Phyllis said not to.

"You can't come, Clinton."

But I wanted to come. I continued to crawl forward. Someone placed a cloth in front of my face, which made it possible to breathe.

"You don't have to come with me, Clinton."

I kept moving. The crackling noise was louder now. It was the sound of things snapping and breaking. My skin felt as though it were on fire, but I continued to move.

"I'm going to go through the kitchen now," Aunt Phyllis said.

I knew with every movement I had to stop, but somehow I always found the strength to crawl another foot. If Aunt Phyllis didn't want me to do it, I would do it anyway. The smoke in the kitchen was much worse than it was in the other room. The floor was so hot I wanted to yell each time I placed my hand down. The pain seared my hands. And that was when I knew I couldn't go any further. . . . Aunt Phyllis called my name, she called me Clinton, but I couldn't go on. The heat was intense, the smoke suffocating, but I couldn't go any further. I couldn't crawl any further.

I felt myself being dragged again, but very slowly now. Aunt Phyllis was coughing loudly, constantly, but she kept dragging me, and when she couldn't drag me, she pushed me. I knew we would never come out of the kitchen.

With my last bit of strength I said, "You can leave me, Aunt Phyllis. You can go—"

But she kept dragging, pushing, pulling. . . .

I was breathing, breathing regularly, taking deep breaths of sweet, clean, cool air. I breathed deeply, inhaling as much into my lungs as I possibly could. There's nothing more satisfying than good clean air. Not anything. I breathed deeply and wanted to laugh. It was a wonderful feeling, just to be able to breathe.

I could hear voices all around me. People were speaking rapidly, excitedly. Someone in the distance yelled something about "giving them room."

I tried to open my eyes, but they stung so badly I immediately closed them again. I was lying on the ground, on a blanket. Portions of my skin were inflamed. I felt dirty.

All around me there was activity, the sound of cars and trucks and of people moving about. When I was finally able to open my eyes and keep them open, I saw I was lying on a lawn across the street from the burning house. A fire truck was parked down the block and a number of men were playing out a hose. There were at least fifty people scattered about, watching.

"He's breathing regularly again," someone said. "He'll be all right." I assumed he was talking about me.

"He inhaled a lot of smoke, that's all."

"That's bad enough. What about the woman?"

"She's on her way to the hospital, someone's driving her."

"How long was she inside that place?"

"Good lord, man! I saw her go in. The house was already blazing. . . . I couldn't believe it when I saw her coming out—"

"And dragging him—"

Sylvia! She hadn't left, after all.

"You talk about guts. I wouldn't have gone in there for nothin'."

"I still don't see how she did it."

I attempted to recall what had happened. I vaguely remembered a dream in which I felt myself trapped in a burning aircraft. Then I had heard someone calling me. A woman. In my dream I thought the woman was Aunt Phyllis. She had moved me, dragged me out of the burning building. The woman I thought was my aunt must have been Sylvia. . . .

A moment later I was aware of someone kneeling on the grass alongside me, peering down at me. "You awake, son?"

I recognized my aunt's neighbor, Gerald Hoffman. "I'm all right, Mr. Hoffman."

"You lie there. Ambulance should be here in a while."

All at once I pushed myself up into a sitting position. I made a mighty effort to clear my head of the grogginess. "I don't need an ambulance. I have to do something—"

Mr. Hoffman placed a restraining hand on my shoulder. "You need some attention. They'll have you fixed up—"

I pushed away his hand and looked around. By now the firemen had a steady stream of water pouring out of the hose, but it wasn't making much of an impression on the house, which was still ablaze. The people who had been standing near me on the lawn had gone forward to join the circle of onlookers. At the far end of the street another fire truck was backing in.

I stood up and covered myself with the blanket. People had forgotten about me, at least for the moment. "Can you take me over to your place, Mr. Hoffman?"

"You shouldn't be moving, son. Why don't you just—"

"I'm fine, Mr. Hoffman," I said. He looked at me with alarm but didn't attempt to stop me. We moved out of the circle of light and activity and down the far side of the street. No one noticed. Everyone's attention was directed toward the fire. Within minutes we were standing at the door of Mr. Hoffman's home.

Mr. Hoffman made one more attempt to dissuade me. "Are you sure you know what you're doing, son?"

"No ambulances, no hospitals," I said. "A little rest, then I have to make a phone call." He shook his head, then took out his key and opened the door.

After we'd gotten into the house, I told him to get the telephone book and to make some coffee. I searched the phone book and found four listings under either *Olson, A* or *Olson, Arnold*. I got Arnie on the second try.

"What's happening, Mr. Ball?" he asked. He sounded depressed, as though he didn't really care.

"Everything, Arnie," I said.

"You sound like—"

"Listen, Arnie. I got it figured out."

"You know who killed Rich?"

"And a lot more, Arnie. But we gotta move quick. You gotta get out right away."

"Hey, I just put on a TV dinner—"

I did my best to fight the grogginess. "Arnie, you don't get out of there right away, you might wind up with Rich."

All at once his voice perked up. "Whatever you say, Mr. Ball. I'm ready."

I tried to think. I knew I didn't want him coming over to where I was. "I have to meet you, Arnie. Where?"

"How about the office. Nobody's there this time of night."

"Fine. Arnie, give me a half-hour. But you leave now, right away. You got me?"

"Sure, Mr. Ball."

"And, Arnie, don't forget your gun."

By the time I'd hung up Mr. Hoffman had the coffee ready. He didn't say anything, just sat at the opposite end of the kitchen table shaking his head and watching me drink it. The coffee was hot and strong and I gulped it down. After I'd finished the cup, Mr. Hoffman got up and refilled it.

"You were lucky," he said at last.

I took another sip. "I know."

"The woman. It was the woman who dragged you out. You were in bad shape."

"You saw it?"

"Almost the whole thing. I was walking the dog."

"Sylvia," I said. "Sylvia dragged me out."

The old man peered across the table at me intently. He shook his head. "Not Sylvia. Not Sylvia Cole, the one who used to live around the corner, if that's who you mean."

I looked at him. "It wasn't Sylvia? Are you sure?"

"Look, young fella. I may be seventy-six-years-old, but I can still see, hear, and feel. When you're my age—"

"Sure, Mr. Hoffman, I didn't mean it like that."

"Sylvia was right there, of course. But she wasn't the woman run in. It was the other one."

"Which other one?"

"What happened was, I was coming back with the dog when I saw Sylvia coming down the walk from your place. She recognized me, said hello, and we stood right there in front of the house talking. I hadn't seen her in over ten years, not since she moved away."

"What happened then?"

"She said she'd made an appointment with you to stop by around seven-thirty or so, and she wondered why you hadn't answered. I said that it seemed a mite strange because when I first went out with the dog there was a light in there, downstairs. It was while we were talking that we saw the first signs of the fire—"

"Did you see anyone leave the house, Mr. Hoffman?"

"No, nothing like that. What we saw was flames coming out the upstairs bedroom window. We were just standing staring when the other woman come up. She asked if that wasn't your house, said she had some legal papers for you to sign—"

"Sonia!"

"Whatever her name is. Anyways, I told her that we'd seen the light in there earlier and that the fire had started in the bed-room. . . . Well, she just said 'Maybe he's in there,' and I said 'Maybe he is,' and she took off into the house, which by that time was really blazing. I went to call the engines. By the time I was back, she still wasn't out. Everybody thought she was a goner. I still can't understand how she made it, and carrying you the entire time."

"That's not the way I thought it happened," I said.

"Well, that's just how it happened. The last I saw Sylvia, the other one, she was talking to the firemen."

"She works for the *Telegram*," I said. "She was more inter-ested in getting the facts for a news story."

Mr. Hoffman shook his head. "You want some more coffee, son?"

I said I didn't. I told him I needed a shower and some clothes. He looked me over and nodded.

"You're about the same size as my son. Some of his stuff's still here." He pointed the way toward the bath. "And you'll find some lotion for your skin in the medicine cabinet."

I let the cold water run over me for a good five minutes. The burns weren't serious but they were uncomfortable, and the water took some of the edge off the stinging sensation. After I had put on the grease I felt considerably better—cleaner and cooler. By the time I had the clothes on, I was ready to rejoin the human race.

"I have one more favor to ask, Mr. Hoffman," I said.

"Name it."

"I need a ride downtown."

"Car's out on the tarmac. She's ready when you are."

We went outside again, and from the alley alongside the house we could see a small crowd of onlookers watching the firemen at work. Aunt Phyllis's old home was by this time a smouldering ruin, the source of the billows of smoke that clouded the air over the street.

In order to drive out of the street, we had to go around a police car that barricaded the road at the end of the block. As we approached the police vehicle, I did my best to make myself un-obtrusive by slumping to the floor of Mr. Hoffman's car. I knew that police and fire officials would soon be looking for me, but this wasn't the moment for lengthy conversations and explanations. Mr. Hoffman surprised me with the ease with which he maneuvered the old Buick onto the sidewalk and around a small tree. After that it was clear sailing into downtown Murcer.

16

The streets were mostly empty and a light fog had drifted in from the hills beyond the city when Mr. Hoffman pulled up in front of the building housing the detective agency. Saturday night in the Murcer business district. Wherever the action was, it wasn't here. I looked at my watch and was surprised to see it was only ten minutes before 10:00. I had packed a lot of activity into the last four hours. An evening to remember—or to forget. Before leaving the car, I thanked Mr. Hoffman for helping me out.

"No need. And I can see you don't want me asking any more questions."

"On the second floor of this building there's a private investigative agency. There's someone up there I want to see."

Mr. Hoffman shook his head in obvious disapproval but didn't say anything more. He put the car in gear and I climbed out. I stood on the sidewalk watching as he made a U-turn and drove off. After seeing his taillights vanish into the murk, I headed into the darkened building.

The interior lighting was adequate, but only barely. The darkened, empty second-floor corridor presented an eerie contrast to its hectic daytime appearance. When I reached the agency office, which was a good eighty feet down from the main staircase, I found the door ajar. There was no one in the outer office, but I could see a crack of light beneath the door leading to Razzilli's office. At least, I figured, Olson had made it. I called Arnie's name and pushed the door open.

The answering call—"Yo"—was muffled and indistinct, and while it could have been Arnie's voice, it could have been anyone else's just as easily.

But by the time the latter thought had crossed my mind I already had the door open and—for the second time that evening—I was staring into the barrel of Karl Breyer's snub-nosed Magnum.

He stepped around me and silently closed the door. Seated in the client's chair on the far side of the room with his head resting slackly on his chest was Arnie Olson.

"I had to give the peeper a tap on the head," Breyer said. "He'll be awake in a minute."

Breyer let his weight down slowly onto Razzilli's old desk. He sat there, half-leaning and half-standing, much as he had done three hours before in my aunt's living room. He shook his head, in the fashion of someone who had just heard some very bad news. "You're an amateur, Ball, you really are. And you can't keep from messing into things that don't concern you."

For a moment I felt dizzy. The recollection of escaping from the burning house and the realization that I had blundered right back into the same situation hit me with a sudden force. I did my best to clear my head. When I felt better, I walked over and gave Olson a gentle shake on the shoulder. He began to stir. I looked at his face. It was paler than usual. But I imagined mine was paler than usual too.

"How'd you get out?" Breyer asked.

"Someone carried me out."

Breyer nodded. "That was one of the problems. I couldn't stay around long enough to make sure. I'll say this much, Ball. You may be an amateur, but you're a lucky amateur."

"Nice of you to say so, Karl," I said.

"But the thing about luck is that it works both ways. And tonight I got lucky too. After leaving your place, I drove around for a while, then I decided maybe I should see what I could do about Mr. Peeper here, because the way I figure it he's the other guy who got J.D. So I ride over to his place, and I'm only sitting outside about ten minutes when he comes out, jumps into his car, and drives off. Naturally, I follow him down here. Lucky for me, unlucky for you."

I looked across at Arnie, who was now sitting with his head in his hands as though he was going to be sick. "You all right, Arnie?" I asked.

"He's fine," Breyer said.

"I'm sorry, Mr. Ball," Olson said. "If I'd've known he was it—"

"I should've told you, Arnie. I should've told you on the telephone."

"Sure you should've," Breyer said. "But it's too late now." He motioned us toward the door with his gun. Whatever he was planning, he wanted to get it over with quickly. I thought about making a dive for the weapon, but Breyer never permitted me to get close enough to where I might have had even a small chance of making it work. I supposed that what he had said about me being an amateur and him being a professional was essentially correct. That was the difference—between success and failure, life and death.

We moved out of the inner office into the outer office, both Arnie and I with our hands raised. Breyer was very deliberate. He shut off the lights in the inner office and closed the door behind him. Then he moved around us and, with his back to the outer door, opened it wide. Arnie and I, facing the door with our hands over our heads, were astounded to see my aunt's neighbor, Mr. Hoffman, standing outside the office in the darkened corridor. He'd obviously been trying to eavesdrop, and there was surprise and embarrassment written all over his face.

"You'll never get away with killing us," I said loudly. "Someone will stop you, Breyer."

Standing with his back to the open door, Breyer began backing out slowly, holding the door all the while. He still hadn't seen the old man.

"Someone will do something," I said. "Someone will—"

Breyer by this time had picked it up, and he made a sudden, quick turn to see what might be behind him, but within that fraction of a second old Mr. Hoffman did about the only thing he could do. He gave Breyer a hard shove from behind. It was enough to make Breyer come staggering forward back into the office and to momentarily lose control over the aim of his weapon. I swung at him from one side and Olson swung from the other. Then the three of us went down on the floor in a heap.

I grabbed Breyer's arm in an effort to keep him from aiming the gun at either one of us. Breyer squeezed off a round and the slug went off at an angle and into the far wall. I was able to get both hands around Breyer's wrist and kept banging it against the floor in an effort to make him drop the weapon. He squeezed off another round but then dropped the gun. As I was reaching out to grab the gun, though, Breyer was able to shove me away and simultaneously get free of Olson. He struggled to his knees and before I could get control of the gun on the floor he had another gun in his hand and was aiming it in my direction. Before he could fire, Olson hit him a mighty shot across the bridge of the nose.

Again Breyer fired wildly. I didn't have time to grab the gun on the floor, so I took another swing at Breyer, who again was scrambling, trying to regain the second gun, which was lying next to the desk. But Olson swooped in from the side and got to it first. Breyer tried to hit Olson, but I was able to restrain him from behind. Olson clambered to his feet and aimed the gun in our direction. Breyer was able to shake himself loose from me and made a move toward Olson. Olson fired, missing Breyer and narrowly missing me. Breyer made a headfirst lunge in Olson's direction but not before Olson was able to squeeze off a second round. The impact sent Breyer reeling backward against the desk. Then, slowly, with blood spurting from his chest in powerful gushes, he slumped to the floor, remained there briefly in a sitting position and then, finally, fell over.

Olson ran forward to grab Breyer but was unable to staunch the bleeding. The slug had severed an artery and Karl Breyer was dead within seconds after the impact.

"He's gone," Olson said. He looked at the gun in his hand. "My gun," he said weakly. "He took it from me."

I looked down at Karl Breyer lying in a pool of his own blood. He looked very small, almost shrunken. All of a sudden, he wasn't dangerous anymore, and I felt sorry it had to happen like this. But if it had to happen to someone—better to him than to me.

None of us said anything for at least two minutes. Finally, I turned to Mr. Hoffman, who had sat himself in one of the chairs along the wall and was staring at Breyer's bloody remains, and asked him if he was all right.

"I didn't expect anything like this when I came up," he said.

Olson walked over to Pam's desk and picked up the telephone.

"I think we better call the police," he said. Neither Mr. Hoffman nor I said anything.

I had a feeling it was going to be a long night.

I had, of course, seen them at work before. That was on the night I had found Sid Hockley's body draped over a chair in my aunt's dining room. And they arrived on this occasion in pretty much the same order they had arrived on that one—the uniformed men first, then the ambulance people, then a pair of detectives, then the coroner, then a team of technicians. And as on the other occasion, Lieutenant Gronski showed up last.

The first two policemen read us our rights. Gronski, when he arrived, ignored us completely, but the anger he felt was plainly visible. Now and then I caught him glancing in my direction. Each time I made it a point to look away. I was determined not to let myself be intimidated, dead policeman or no dead policeman. As I sat there on the hard wooden chair, I went over in my mind exactly what I intended to tell Gronski. Saying too much could be a mistake. A big mistake.

The Murcer Justice Building was only a short ride across town, and eventually Gronski had the three of us carted over there to make our statements. I made my statement to Gronski in the presence of another detective and an activated tape recorder. I began the account with the telephone call to Olson, saying nothing of what had happened earlier in the evening, and concluded it with the accidental shooting of Breyer.

Gronski interrupted when I described my arrival at the offices of the agency. "You say, Ball, you say Breyer held you at bay at the point of a gun."

"That's correct."

"Now, why would he do that?"

"He wanted our cooperation."

"Did he say where he intended to take you?"

"No."

"It wouldn't have been to police headquarters now, would it?"

"I'm sure it wasn't, Lieutenant."

Gronski flung down a pen he had been toying with onto his desk. After that, he let me tell the story without interruption.

When I emerged from Gronski's office it was sometime after

two in the morning, and I was surprised to see Mr. Hoffman seated on a bench in the corridor.

"I was thinking you might be wanting a place to sleep tonight," he said.

I said I would. We collected his car and drove most of the way home in silence.

"You're probably wondering what made me go back to that building," he said finally.

"Curiosity?" I said.

"It's an unhealthy habit of mine, being too curious."

"In this case it turned out to be a healthy habit."

"I'm glad you see it that way," he said.

The next day was Sunday, and I slept well into the morning on Mr. Hoffman's living room couch. When I finally got up, he had some of his son's clothing laid out for me. The shoes were on the tight side, but otherwise the clothing fit and looked well enough.

"What's going to happen?" Mr. Hoffman asked after we'd finished breakfast and were dawdling over coffee.

"Gronski, the homicide lieutenant, was a close friend of the dead man," I said. "He may want to hang a murder charge on someone."

"That'd be too bad."

"The dead man was a former policeman. He may try to build a case on the assumption that the dead man was in the process of taking us to the police."

"Was he?"

"No. Just the opposite."

"I described just what I saw," Mr. Hoffman said.

"You did exactly the right thing, Mr. Hoffman."

After finishing breakfast, I walked down the street to look at the ruins of my aunt's old home. There wasn't much to see. The wooden structure had been completely leveled and was now only a pile of ashes and rubble. I thought of the years I had spent living in the old place. My childhood now seemed to be so distant it was almost as if I had experienced it as a part of another incarnation. I wondered why I didn't feel more sadness. I supposed because things had never been right there—there had been too much hidden, too many secrets. For all her good qualities, my aunt had refused to look at life as it really was. And then the thought struck me that I was the one who had refused to look at life as it really was. One thing was sure: I had never had to face hardship, not the kind of hardship Aunt Phyllis had experienced. Even in Vietnam I had known that by keeping my nose clean and doing things right I was going to leave with a whole skin. When I thought of the burdens my aunt had carried around over the years I shuddered.

I thought about Karl Breyer and the terrible, awful irony of the chain of events that had led up to his death. I tried to imagine the chemistry of the relationship that had existed between Breyer, the totally honest homicide detective, and my Aunt Phyllis, a deep and complicated woman if ever there was one. And I thought of the role I played in the strange affair, beginning as a child and ending as a man. I could not be jubilant over Breyer's death. He had compiled a magnificent record, working to bring honesty and efficiency to a police department known at one time for its corruption. But the thought that his dedication to his work and his moral flaw, his determination to get back at the van Beldin family, seemed to stem from essentially the same source, was harrowing.

I walked around the charred remains, occasionally kicking at a piece of burnt wood or plaster that lay in my path. Here and there I recognized a piece of furniture, but beyond that, the damage of the fire had been complete. There was nothing to be salvaged. Perhaps it was for the best. I thought again of Aunt Phyllis's letter. "What I did I did for your sake," she had written. She had provided me with things I wouldn't have had otherwise, but I was now confronted with the question of whether I was actually better off because I had these things. . . .

In any case, you cannot go back and reclaim the past. Whatever I now was, whatever I had become as a result of what had occurred over the years, I had no choice but to make the best of things as they now were. I took one last look at the charred ruins, then returned to the sidewalk. I didn't look back.

I walked back to Mr. Hoffman's house and made a call to the hospital. I was told that Sonia Wegman had already been released. I borrowed a tie and jacket and told Mr. Hoffman I was going to visit a friend. On the way over to Sonia's place I picked up a bouquet of mixed flowers.

Sonia blushed when she saw me standing at the door.

"I was wondering how you were," I said.

"It's nice of you to think of me." She motioned me in and closed the door behind me.

I looked at Sonia, and I saw there wasn't the slightest hint of irony in her expression. She'd saved my life but somehow seemed flattered that I had taken the trouble to visit her and bring some flowers. It was a simplicity and modesty of the rarest kind. I watched as she took the flowers, filled a vase with water, and then placed them on a small table in the living room. The pleasure she felt was apparent all over her face.

It occurred to me that, in my rush to get my own life in order, I had made many hasty judgments of other people. Of Aunt Phyllis, for one. And Sonia, for another.

I wondered whether it was now too late to undo the damage done by these hasty judgments. On her left arm Sonia had a bandage. I asked her about it.

"When the roof began to fall, one of the burning beams struck me there. They fixed it last night at the emergency ward."

"But doesn't it hurt?" I asked. I knew that was a foolish question. Even if it had, she wouldn't have admitted it.

She asked me if I wanted coffee. At first I said no, but then I changed my mind. I begrudged the minutes she spent away from me preparing it. That was how much I now wanted Sonia.

When she returned, she took a seat next to me on the sofa.

"Are you feeling all right?" she asked.

"You got me out of that place just in time. I inhaled some smoke, that was all." I took a sip of the coffee. "I don't know how to thank you."

Again she blushed. "It wasn't anything anyone else wouldn't have done."

"Other people were outside. No one else did it. Why did you?"

"I've always been a kind of impulsive person. I act without thinking."

"Now it's my turn to do something impulsive." I took Sonia in my arms, held her, then kissed her. In some circumstances a kiss can convey feelings that are beyond description in words. For me this was one of those occasions. I hoped it was for Sonia.

Then I said, "Thank you for saving my life."

"You're welcome," she said with a smile after I'd succeeded in smearing her lipstick.

I kissed her again and succeeded in mussing up her hair.

"Is this the reason you came over?" she asked. "To muss me up?"

"Can you think of a better reason?"

"No," she said in a small voice.

As I looked at Sonia seated beside me on the sofa, I felt a surge of self-confidence, a feeling of renewal. It was a feeling in some ways similar to the feeling that had accompanied the recognition that my aunt's house was totally and completely destroyed, irrevocably gone, and that a part of me was gone with it. It wasn't in any way a depressing feeling, and it was accompanied by the thought that my life was on the verge of a new beginning. . . .

Later that evening, while I was lying on the bed in Sonia's apartment, holding her in my arms, Sonia said, "I'm waiting for something."

"I know you are, and I believe I know what it is."

"Until now I've had the feeling you haven't been completely open with me."

"No, I haven't." And even as I said the words I felt as though an enormous burden was about to be lifted from my shoulders. Growing up an only child without parents, I never developed the ability to communicate wholeheartedly with other people. My relationships with women, particularly, had always been cramped and inhibited. I now had the feeling that all kinds of disparate elements within my character were now clarifying themselves.

"Only tell me if you want to," Sonia said.

The funny thing was I wanted to. I wanted to very badly. I began with the events of the previous evening, everything that had happened before and after the fire, concluding with the death of Breyer in the office of the detective agency.

"That explains your behavior during the fire," Sonia said. "You were drugged. I could see something was wrong."

"I'm certainly glad you remembered that story I told you about my aunt," I said. "How she always called me 'Clinton.' She was the only one—"

"Everything seems to revolve in some way around your relationship with your aunt," Sonia said.

I thought of the account given to me two days before by Mrs. van Beldin in her hospital room. "That's true. I suppose I always knew I was involved, deeply involved. Or else Aunt Phyllis wouldn't have sent that letter to me. . . ." When I paused, I was aware that the only other sound in the darkened room was Sonia's quiet, regular breathing. "I recall now that at the time I hadn't even wanted to open it up."

When Sonia didn't say anything I continued with the story.

"The reason Aunt Phyllis so hated my father was always a mystery to me. Maybe that was one of the reasons I so resented her as a child. She knew how my father used to beat me—"

Sonia was about to interrupt with a question, but I held up my hand. I wiped some perspiration from my forehead. Talking about my father was difficult, but I wanted to tell things in my own way. "One evening, when I was five years old, he beat me so badly he became worried himself and took me to be treated by Dr. Lakeman."

"Did you have any recollection of what happened?"

"No." Then I thought of the dream, the recurring dream in which someone always seemed to be beating me. "Not a conscious recollection, anyway." Once again Sonia was silent and I went on with the story.

I described the circumstances surrounding my father's death as they had been told to me by Mrs. van Beldin—how Dr. Lakeman and Mrs. van Beldin had attempted to dispose of the body and how they were observed by Joey Hauck, the petty gangster.

"I suppose Hauck wanted money," Sonia said.

"Yes, and at first Lakeman paid. But when Mrs. van Beldin saw the awful strain the doctor was under, she decided to do something. She asked my Aunt Phyllis to help her kill Hauck."

Sonia sighed in the darkness but didn't say anything. She gently moved her fingers back and forth across my cheek.

"The two women successfully murdered Hauck, each of them firing a bullet into him so that each was guilty. Perhaps the chain of events would have had its conclusion at that point, except that Karl Breyer, who was then a homicide detective, solved the case. But he decided then not to turn over the evidence."

"Why not?"

"In some ways, that's the strangest part of the story. Breyer was a truly fine policeman, and completely honest. The last person to do something like that, at least under ordinary circumstances."

"What made this situation different?"

"Part of the answer lies in the way Breyer regarded my aunt."
I then told Sonia the story of Breyer's childhood, and how he attributed his father's death and the suffering of his mother to the manipulations of the van Beldin family.

"I think I see what you're getting at," Sonia said.

"He may have seen Aunt Phyllis as a woman similar to his mother, a woman with a child to support and victimized by circumstances. But there was a difference. Where Breyer's mother acquiesced, Aunt Phyllis fought back."

"He admired that."

"Definitely. Whatever reservations he may have had about people committing murder, Breyer was willing to overlook them in Aunt Phyllis's case. But I rather imagine Aunt Phyllis did her best to make him see things her way. Talked to him, felt him out, did whatever was necessary. Aunt Phyllis was determined she wasn't going to go to jail."

"I know my father had great admiration for your aunt. She must have been an extraordinary woman."

"I suppose I was the only one who failed to see how extraordinary she was." I paused, then went on. "Some kind of relationship developed between them over the years, between Aunt Phyllis and Breyer." I then told Sonia how a girlfriend of Breyer's had discovered them in bed together. "In a fit of anger she wrote an unsigned letter to my aunt that I found with the gun and the newspaper clippings. Later this woman had a child. Breyer's child actually, although she was at the time married to a man named Dillerman."

"That was the man who attacked you at the restaurant."

"Yes, that was Dillerman. Breyer had tried to help him over the years—getting him on the Murcer police force, and then buying him out of a jam after he had badly battered someone he had arrested."

"And this was why Breyer came to you last evening. To find out what had happened to his son."

"Breyer wasn't anything like himself last evening. He suspected that Dillerman had been killed at the motel, but he couldn't rest until he knew for sure. Of course the irony is, at that point Breyer was safe. With Razzilli dead, there was no one around at that point who could have connected him to the rest of it."

"Razzilli suspected Breyer?"

"Razzilli was going to pull some strings in order to find out who had testified at the inquest for the girl killed by Mrs. Hanks. Breyer's testimony would have made him suspicious."

"Still, it would have been impossible to prove."

"Yes. Breyer's record was too perfect. It still wouldn't have made sense. On the surface, it seemed that someone was selling information. I couldn't get it out of my mind that Razzilli was behind it all. As a private detective, he would have known all sorts of things other people didn't. On top of that, Breyer warned me to stay away from Razzilli."

"Why?"

"Breyer's feelings toward me were ambivalent. My meddling made him nervous. But he still felt some concern, perhaps because of his once having helped me, even if only indirectly. He only wanted Dillerman to throw a scare into me at Durango's, so that I would leave town. He tossed the gun under the bed believing that with a murder charge hanging over me, I would have to stop prying. He warned me off Razzilli because he felt that, working together, we might come up with something."

"I suppose he was wary of Razzilli."

"Just the fact that Razzilli and Hockley were working for van Beldin would have made him wary."

"But there are other questions."

"Actually, the key to everything was Breyer's hatred for the van Beldin family, a hatred he nursed over the years and kept entirely to himself."

"When Mrs. Hanks ran over the girl he saw his chance."

"At the time it was obvious that the Planning Board would have to take some kind of action, that they would have to make massive changes to permit the city to grow. Breyer made a secret deal with Stanley Hanks to make sure that the expansion would be in a northerly direction, away from the land owned by the van Beldin family. When the vote came, a year or so later, Breyer had already made contact with Hoglin and Korban. They'd quietly taken out options on the land north of Murcer. The funny thing was, Breyer didn't receive any kind of payment for the information."

"That he was preventing van Beldin from acquiring the property was enough."

"It was clever. By bringing in Korban, he broke the stranglehold the van Beldin family has had on the city for generations. It was an effective way of paying them back for what happened to his father."

We were both silent for a long moment, perhaps thinking of the many ways Murcer had changed in the last fifteen years. Then Sonia said, "And Breyer was once again hitting out at the van Beldins when he told Korban about the fact that Mrs. van Beldin had killed Hauck. Wasn't it strange that the woman who helped your aunt kill Hauck later married Peter van Beldin?"

"That was certainly ironic. If at that point Breyer had been able to forget his hatred of the van Beldins, none of these things would have happened."

"He'd already done a good deal of damage to the van Beldins."

"Yes, but I suppose the thought of van Beldin moving into the statehouse and perhaps again regaining the control he had lost was too much for him. That together with the fact that he had at his disposal information that would quickly put an end to van Beldin's political hopes."

"I can see where the temptation to act on that information must have been overwhelming." Sonia paused. "But at that point he seems to have sacrificed something else, his record for honesty. Korban paid him twenty-five thousand dollars."

I said, "I think I know why. In my last moments of consciousness, after being drugged, I could still hear Breyer talking. I have the vaguest recollection of him mentioning Dillerman and the money. He didn't want the money for himself. He needed the money to complete the payoff he'd made to get Dillerman out of trouble."

We lay quietly together in the darkened room for a long time. Finally Sonia said, "I can't help but think about Mrs. van Beldin and how much she's been through."

"She later married Dr. Lakeman. I wonder if she ever told him about the murder."

"I'm sure she never mentioned it," Sonia said. "She certainly moved up in the world."

"After the doctor died, I imagine she moved in better circles. Van Beldin told me he met her at a charity affair of some kind."

"How long have they been married?"

"Over eight years. But during this time Breyer was never able to use the knowledge of her involvement in the Hauck murder—"

"Because your aunt also knew."

"Yes. It would have been easy to see where such information came from. Between them the women could have figured it out. So Breyer waited."

"Until your aunt died."

"I suppose he could hardly wait to tell Korban since by this time van Beldin was actively seeking the nomination to be governor."

"And that was when you arrived back in Murcer."

"I walked right into it, didn't I?"

"Van Beldin assumed you had told Korban that his wife had murdered Hauck."

"Natural enough, I suppose. And then he turned his detectives loose on me to make sure."

Sonia and I lay silent for a long time. Finally Sonia said, "We have a big problem. Breyer was an important man and a good policeman—"

"We?"

"I've decided to once again act as your counsel, provided you want me to—"

"I'm not sure," I said, fighting to keep back a smile. "Murcer has so many good lawyers—"

As an answer, Sonia squeezed my little finger. I found myself laughing, really laughing, for the first time in many days. Even facing some kind of murder charge, I felt happier than I had ever been at any time in my life.

"How much of this do the police know?" Sonia said at last.

"Gronski knows a lot, primarily bits and pieces."

"What we have to do is put the pieces together in such a way that the story will be acceptable to the police and that it will absolve you and Olson of a murder charge—to get it changed to accidental death."

"Is that possible?"

"It might be," Sonia said. "Let me brew up some more coffee."

Before getting out of bed she kissed me and, at that moment, I felt a closeness to Sonia that I had never felt for any other woman.

17

The first thing I did Monday morning was ride into downtown Murcer and, using money I had borrowed from Sonia, I purchased some clothes and shoes. We had decided that for my appearance at police headquarters a decent image would be important.

On my way into the city I deliberately avoided buying a copy of the Murcer *Telegram,* which I assumed would be carrying Sylvia's account of the fire at the house. After leaving the clothing store, I took a short walk, finally ending up at the Mayfair luncheonette. The waitress with the thick eyebrows was in a rapt conversation with a burly customer in one of the booths, and when she finally got around to bringing my coffee she sloshed half of it over the counter before returning to resume her conversation. It was the kind of careless action that at one time might have irritated me. Now I only smiled.

Over the coffee, I went over in my mind the story Sonia and I had agreed upon. What we intended was to give Gronski a simplified account of the events as they had occurred, leaving out the role played by Dillerman and Korban, neither of whom had come to the attention of the police. By indicating Breyer was guilty of malfeasance, we hoped to suggest to Gronski that these actions might represent a pattern—that at the very least, there was a dimension to Karl Breyer, Gronski's mentor, that he himself had not understood.

Another factor was Gronski's own ambition. A new police scandal in Murcer would only lead people to recall the old days, when the city's department was racked by dishonesty and incompetence. A new scandal would unquestionably reflect unfavorably on Gronski and possibly jeopardize his chances for advancement. It would surely kill any plans he might have to seek a position beyond the boundaries of Murcer.

Lastly, but most important, was the question of Karl Breyer himself. We intended to offer Gronski a chance to preserve the memory of Breyer, who we hoped to picture as a man in danger of having the many fine things he had accomplished forgotten because of certain actions that were isolated and not necessarily characteristic. We knew we were taking a calculated gamble.

But we would have to give up a certain amount too, more than I wanted to reveal, and Sonia had spent a good portion of the evening persuading me of the necessity to tell the true story of the murder of Joey Hauck. I finally consented, knowing I would be jeopardizing the memory of Aunt Phyllis and perhaps making Mrs. van Beldin liable to a murder charge.

Sonia had been able to arrange an appointment with Gronski for eleven o'clock. When I met her on the steps leading up to the Justice Building, she appeared not only strikingly attractive but quite formidable, dressed in a two-piece salt-and-pepper suit and carrying an attaché case. I told the sergeant at the desk that we had an appointment and that I knew where Lieutenant Gronski's office was and he passed us through with a nod of the head.

Despite the fact that he was wearing a youthful sport jacket, Lieutenant Gronski appeared subdued, almost as if he had aged a couple of years since the occasion of our first meeting. Perhaps it was my imagination, but the gray flecks in the black hair seemed more numerous, the lines in the leathery face seemed deeper, the thin line of his mouth seemed grimmer. I had the feeling he thought of me as the cause of many of his troubles. I remembered his little story concerning the numerous people spending time in jail, people who in many cases weren't guilty of deeds any more serious than those I had committed. I looked at Sonia, who flashed me a brief but reassuring smile.

Gronski told us to sit down, then came around from behind his desk, and closed the door. "What's the problem?" he asked after he had once again seated himself.

"Our visit," Sonia said, "concerns the death of Karl Breyer the night before last—"

"The murder of Karl Breyer might be a more accurate way of describing what happened the other evening, Counselor. And your client, whether he pulled the trigger or not, is very likely going to go to trial for it."

"Would it be possible to speak to you on this matter off the record?" Sonia asked.

Gronski paused. He took out his pipe and tapped it on the palm of his hand, a mannerism that recalled Breyer himself. The action reminded me of the extent to which Gronski had been influenced by Breyer and underscored the delicacy of the task we had before us.

He stuck the pipe in his mouth, then bit down hard on the stem. "Why off the record? Do you think you have information I don't have?" Gronski sounded self-confident, almost smug.

"We're positive we do," Sonia said. "We think it may alter the way you view the events of the last two weeks."

"I'll listen to what you have to say, Miss Wegman, but I don't intend to be bound by any promises. If we later uncover information I learn from you here—"

"We'll let you use your own judgment, Lieutenant," Sonia said.

"In that case, fire away." Gronski got his pipe lit and leaned back in his chair. There was just the trace of a skeptical smile on his thin lips, the same knowing smirk that had sent shivers through me on the night of the murder of Sid Hockley. Sonia nodded in my direction, an indication that I should begin.

I started the account with a description of my father's visit to Dr. Lakeman's office when I was five years old. As I told the story, I saw Gronski's expression alter from one of skepticism to one of surprise. He peered at me intently through narrowed eyes, then interrupted me with a wave of his hand.

"Hold on now, Ball. You're saying that this Lakeman, one of Murcer's most respected physicians, was responsible for the death of your father?"

"That's right, Lieutenant, I am."

Gronski was silent for a moment, obviously thinking over what I had just said. "All right. So what if he was? What bearing does it have?"

"What happened subsequently, Lieutenant"—I spoke deliberately, choosing my words carefully—"was that Hauck, after seeing the doctor dispose of the body of my father, began to blackmail Dr. Lakeman. The doctor, who by this time was paying money to my aunt for my upkeep, revealed to her that he would have to discontinue the payments."

"Any proof of this, Ball?"

Sonia interrupted. "Real estate records will reveal that at this time Miss Hailley, Clint's aunt, began making payments on the house. She had no other source of income."

Gronski nodded, rubbed his hand up and down his cheek. "Go on," he said.

At this point I hesitated.

"I'm waiting," Gronski said.

Again Sonia nodded in my direction. I then told Gronski the story of the twenty-eight-year-old murder. I could feel my throat go dry as I did so. I hoped I was doing the right thing.

Gronski was plainly fascinated. "Interesting," he said at last. His eyes flashed. I wondered whether he was already considering the possibility of bringing charges against Mrs. van Beldin. Then he said, "Funny, I never even heard of this Hauck case."

"You can look it up, Lieutenant," Sonia said. "You'll find the file is still open."

"All right." Gronski smiled. "This is all very nice. And you people have done the city a great service by aiding the police. I just don't see—"

"You just don't see how it fits in with the death of Breyer two nights ago," Sonia said. "Is that right, Lieutenant?"

"That's it exactly."

"Breyer worked the Hauck case, Lieutenant."

"So?"

"In fact he solved it."

"You just told me the file was still open—"

"He solved it, but he never turned over the evidence."

Gronski scowled. "I don't believe that for one minute."

"But it's true," Sonia said firmly.

"On the basis of some old newspaper clippings I found in my aunt's home, I asked Breyer about the case. This worried him."

"Why?"

"Because he'd cracked the case, Lieutenant. He was afraid that Mr. Ball's aunt might have told him."

"Remember how I got roughed up out at Durango's, Lieutenant?"

"You're saying Breyer was behind that too?"

"Admittedly that's only speculation," Sonia said. "But it's a possibility. Subsequently, Breyer decided to do some poking around in Mr. Ball's home."

"Oh sure! Oh sure!" Gronski's voice was impatient, irritable. I was surprised he hadn't thrown us out of his office by this point. But the fact that he hadn't was probably a good sign.

Sonia ignored Gronski's interruption. "He was caught leaving the house by Sid Hockley, who was following Mr. Ball around the city—"

"And why was that, if I may ask?"

"Hockley and Razzilli were working for Peter van Beldin. Breyer shot Hockley."

"This gets funnier and funnier," Gronski said. There was, however, a hint of uncertainty in his voice. "Why did van Beldin have his operatives tailing your client, Miss Wegman?"

"That's easy to figure out, Lieutenant. Van Beldin was being blackmailed."

"Because of his wife, you mean?"

"Yes."

"And you're saying Karl Breyer was behind it?"

Neither Sonia nor I said anything. We let Gronski jump to his own conclusions. Finally, he said, "And I suppose you people are suggesting that Breyer killed Razzilli."

"None of us was there, Lieutenant," I said piously.

"That won't wash. Breyer was at the detectives' club that night."

"That was a great alibi, wasn't it, Lieutenant?" Sonia said. "But Breyer left the game at ten-thirty. Razzilli was shot between nine and midnight."

"You're saying that Breyer went out to the motel—"

"We're saying that it's a possibility that, under certain circumstances, would have to be investigated."

"And what circumstances would those be?"

"If Mr. Ball were to stand trial for Breyer's murder."

Gronski was silent for a moment. Then he shook his head. "No good, none of it. Karl Breyer, a former homicide policeman with a great record, is supposed to have committed two murders."

Again Sonia nodded in my direction. I then told Gronski how Breyer had drugged me and set fire to my aunt's home. I finished with an account of how Olson and I were held at bay in Razzilli's office.

"I'm supposed to believe all this?"

"Mr. Hoffman has already indicated what he saw and heard while listening at the keyhole."

"Karl Breyer was the finest policeman this city ever had,"

Gronski said at last. There was just the slightest quaver in his voice. I had the impression he was greatly shaken.

Sonia seized the opportunity quickly. "We agree completely. We'll even concede this was an isolated incident. It would be a shame if something like this were to mar his record." Sonia paused. "In the same way it would be a shame if Mrs. van Beldin were to go to trial for something that happened so long ago. Or if Mr. Ball and Mr. Olson were to be charged in Breyer's death."

"I still can't see the reason—"

"These things happen, Lieutenant," Sonia said. Her voice was full of sympathy.

Gronski tapped the desk nervously with his fingers. "And if I don't act on these suggestions, Counselor? What then?"

"In the event Mr. Ball and Mr. Olson should go to trial, you can expect there will be a lot of digging on the part of defense lawyers. The role Breyer played in this department even after he had retired will be scrutinized"—Gronski turned red—"very, very closely. Should even a portion of what we've told you today turn out to be true, I think there is an excellent chance Mr. Ball and Mr. Olson will go free. On top of that, the reputation of Murcer's law enforcement bodies will be badly tarnished. Perhaps irreparably."

Gronski frowned. He didn't like the thought that anything might put his career in jeopardy.

"We're asking that all charges against Mr. Ball and Mr. Olson be reduced to justifiable homicide or dropped. Also that none of the information discussed with you today go beyond this room. Particularly what we've told you concerning Mrs. van Beldin and Mr. Ball's aunt."

"And if I comply?"

"We see no reason why we should say anything further about Karl Breyer or the events of the last two weeks."

Gronski sat silently behind his desk for a long time. During that time I studied his expression closely in an attempt to get some indication of what he was thinking. He looked troubled but noncommittal. "I want you to leave now," he said at last.

I couldn't restrain myself. "Does that mean—"

"I'll give you my decision in a day or two." He showed us to the door and then closed it behind us.

When we were in the corridor, I turned nervously to Sonia. "What do you think?" I asked.

"It's going to be all right. He really has no other choice."

"Are you sure?"

Sonia smiled. "Law enforcement people make deals all the time. They have to."

"I guess I'm pretty innocent about a lot of things," I said.

"Stay that way. It's part of your charm."

I planted a kiss on Sonia's lips. She squeezed my arm.

"Let's find a quiet place to have lunch," she said.

Standing alongside me at the graveside were Arnie Olson and Sonia Wegman, and as I listened to the clergyman reciting the last rites for Rich Razzilli I couldn't keep from gazing out at the city of Murcer beyond the rolling hills in the near distance. It was still the same smoky industrial place it had been when I stood at almost the same spot on the occasion of the funeral of Aunt Phyllis. But it was somehow different. It no longer inspired in me the same feeling of dread and dislike I had felt earlier. The city hadn't changed. In some subtle way I had.

The service over, I approached the woman in black and introduced myself. Mrs. Razzilli was tall, as her husband had been, but the resemblance, at least outwardly, seemed to end there. Her hair was honey-colored, her skin smooth, her manner composed.

"It was awfully nice of you to come, Mr. Ball." She gave me her hand and introduced her two daughters, dark-eyed girls in their teens who strongly resembled their father. They looked at me inquiringly.

"I only knew your husband a short time, Mrs. Razzilli, but somehow it seemed I had known him for years."

She smiled. "I know. He had that effect on some people. A few, not many."

"He had . . ." I paused.

"Values, Mr. Ball?"

"Different values. A way of looking at life I had never encountered before."

"He spoke of you at home. He trusted you. He said he knew you hadn't killed Sid."

"I wonder how he knew."

Mrs. Razzilli smiled again. "I know he enjoyed your company. Could that be the reason?"

"We hit it off somehow."

"Do you think you'll be coming back to Murcer at all, Mr. Ball?" I felt the gentle pressure of Sonia's fingers on my arm. "If you do, I'd like you to come visit us."

"I definitely will be coming back," I said. "I definitely will be."